At the close of every autopsy report is the <u>Final Diagnosis</u>

It is followed by a list of the . . .

December 1998

Dr. Richard Brower

Incidental Findings

Incidental Findings

A Novel

by

Richard C. Powers, M.D.

DORRANCE PUBLISHING CO., INC.
PITTSBURGH, PENNSYLVANIA 15222

ISBN # 0-8059-4354-4
Printed in the United States of America

Second Printing

For information or to order additional books, please write:
Dorrance Publishing Co., Inc.
643 Smithfield Street
Pittsburgh, Pennsylvania 15222
U.S.A.

To my extended family

Prologue

Gannon glanced at the clock; midnight, two more hours until his shift was over. Picking up a calendar, the young surgical resident copied his work schedule for the next four weekends. Gannon checked his book, where he found Dwight Eisenhower's visit to the VA Hospital on September 12, 1952—the same day he was scheduled for his regular VA residency work. He was also scheduled for night call at the Gagliano Clinic.

Tonight Joe Sparacino was his partner at Gagliano. They had been busy with the usual cuts and bruises of small tool industries from the surrounding community's graveyard shifts. There were no nurses or clerks; the low-pay resident doctors from the enormous hospital a mile away cleaned up after themselves and kept the books. Both knew that the owner was making a lot of money off them by employing these well-trained moonlighters. But it was a job, and the income made it possible for the residents to support their families while completing a four-year training program. It also was illegal.

Sparacino and Gannon did not like each other. Each man was in his last year of training, and competition had forced them apart. Sharing the same shift at the industrial clinic was something over which they had no control. So when the alley doorbell rang, Gannon noticed Sparacino busying himself with debris from suturing a laceration, forcing Gannon to respond to the call.

As he swung open the door, Gannon was pushed aside by two swarthy men clad in tuxedos, supporting between them a third, who was not only disheveled, but was also wearing a shirt soiled with clotted blood and holding a towel against his belly wall.

"We don't want you, doc. Get the other guy—Sparacino. This guy's been cut bad!"

Gannon was not impressed. This type of event was not unusual on a Saturday night. The alley entrance was frequented by beaten-up club performers from Cicero, hookers from Oak Park, and wounded body guards from Bellwood, all anxious to get medical help without records or publicity. The wounded man looked vaguely familiar: Gannon thought he might have seen his face sometime in the newspaper.

Gannon motioned them down the hall to the suture room where Sparacino was just finishing. When the latter looked up, he did not seem surprised. He simply closed the door on the group, shutting Gannon out.

While wrapping plaster on his next patient's forearm fracture, Gannon could hear conversation and an occasional grunt of pain from the next room.

Then, suddenly, there were two explosions—*gun shots?* thought Gannon.

Without thinking, he flung open the door to the suture room. The patient was still on the table, with a clean dressing. On the floor lay one of the tuxedo-clad hoods, blood stains developing over his shirt front. Standing in the middle of the room was Sparacino, waving a smoking gun. Gannon looked him straight in the eye, then closed the door.

One week later, Sparacino and Gannon were seated before the desk of the Chief of Medicine at Westside VA, Hospital. The closed three-sided hearing was just finishing.

The tall, white-haired man who had conducted the hearing was standing with his back toward them, his fingers entwined over his buttocks, alternately twisting and untwisting his hands while he looked out a bay window from his fourth-floor office toward the green lawn outside.

"Young gentlemen," he addressed them, "I have listened to your stories and believe parts of them. Apparently the police believe all you told them, but I am sure there are other things. The problem I'm concerned with is the outside work.

"When you came here four years ago, you knew that you were to give your training program your undivided attention," he resumed. "This outside work is on a police blotter here in Maywood. We cannot deny it. We must lay a record of some sort of punishment."

The imposing figure caressed his mustache as he turned toward them and sat at his desk. Gannon's impression was that the doctor was genuinely sympathetic with them.

"Your department chief has authorized me to inform you that you may complete your training," he continued. "Further, he will sign the needed letters to apply to take the exams for the American Board of Surgery. However, neither of you has any future in academic medicine. That must be particularly galling to you, Gannon, for you have been under consideration to join the VA group downtown. Now, you are out."

He closed, sticking out his hand, with, "You are quite fortunate, really."

Unobtrusively breathing sighs of relief, the two young men confronted one another in the corridor outside.

"Thanks for lying on my behalf, Gannon. You saved my neck." They parted without shaking hands.

2

Chapter 1

Mouth—mouth—that is a part of something called a human being—was he a human being?—something was in the way, in his mouth. He felt he should spit it out but was not sure what "spit" meant. Air—he needed air—but what was air, and how could he get it?

"Look," whispered a masculine voice next to him, penetrating his consciousness like a shout into a rain barrel, reverberating in a progressively uncoiling tunnel of violet haze. "He's trying to spit out the endotrachael tube."

An answer came from the opposite side, this time softer, feminine, looping lightly around in the same barrel, but this time, in scarlet. "Well, that's the first helpful sign we've seen. Maybe he'll behave himself now. It will be nice to reason with him instead of locking him in restraints."

He could not breathe—he was suffocating—is this how it is to drown—what is drowning? Then he was swimming upward through a labyrinth of violet and scarlet lights, surrounded by a black void, lighted only from above. The light seemed to recede into the distance, and with it, the impenetrable surface that was the top. He waved his arms in the void but never moved; he was anchored in place, with the ever-receding light showing a way he could not follow.

Eyes—he knew he had eyes—but what were they?—parts of a human being. Could he but open his eyes, he could see, and he would know what he was. But his eyes would not open; he struggled in the black void to reach them with his hands, but his arms could not move. He could not breathe; waves of panic were becoming more violent, and he became nauseated as he struggled within an ocean of misunderstanding and mixed signals. Then suddenly, like a full moon slipping from behind a cloud, and outlining a landscape for the orientation of the lost, he remembered who he was. He was Chris Gannon—Dr. Gannon, a surgeon.

The sense of relief that came with identification was overwhelming. Suddenly, he was warm all over and able to catch his breath. He stopped struggling and fighting his way through the impenetrable blackness surrounding him.

A soft-spoken male voice addressed him again, this time in hushed and understandable tones, accompanied by a pair of warm hands grasping his fingers.

"Dr. Gannon, Dr. Gannon. If you will promise to behave, we will take the tapes off your eyelids. Then you can see where you are and remember what has happened to you. You must promise you won't get out of bed anymore or take a swing at me again."

Oh, if he could just swallow that thing in his mouth, or if he could just spit it out! But it was fixed and immovable. He would show them! He bit down hard.

"Now behave, Dr. Gannon. You have an endo tube in—don't you remember what that is? When you bite down, you only shut off your own air supply. Come on, now, let's get with the program!"

Gannon felt the sting of tape being pulled off his eyelids, and he tried to reach for the hand producing the pain on his face. But he could move nothing, neither hands nor feet. Only slowly did his eyelids part and then only minimally. The light was dim, but he could make out a human figure on each side. They were dressed in white, and he was lying in a bed of white, imprisoned within vertical bed-side rails, seen through the fog of his just uncovered eyes. He saw metal buckles and leather straps connecting both wrists and both ankles to the bad frame.

"Dr. Gannon, please be still," came the voice of a woman. "I am loosening the tape on your airway. If you show me that you can straighten up your act, I'll take it out. But you must behave."

Again he could not get his breath. Panic re-appeared, and he began thrashing about, biting down hard and arching his back, struggling to get free. Then, abruptly, a long device was withdrawn from his mouth. Not only could he breathe, but he could make a sound. It began as a squeak, rising to a high-pitched squeal, then dropping progressively in tone but increased in volume to "AWWRRRRR—"

"Maybe we let him up a little too fast," came the male voice, anxiously.

"No, I think he will be all right now," responded the woman. "Once he figures out where he is and that he can depend on us, he'll be all right."

Gannon closed his eyes. It was too much to absorb in such a short time. *That was my own EKG pattern I've just been watching,* he thought. He was covered with monitoring devices, his body crossed by wires and surrounded by lighted screens. *My gosh,* he thought. *I am in a place I helped design—the intensive care unit! I'm alive, but why am I here?*

Again came the gentle male voice. "I am David, one of your nurses. We are all glad to see you waking up, but we're going to put you back to sleep." He nodded to the female figure opposite. Gannon saw her manipulating one of the tubes in his arm, and then there was....oblivion....

Within that dimly lit world of serious illness and drugged stupor, Gannon's mind seemed to detach itself from his awareness and move off to a remote point like a spy satellite circling the earth. He passed through flashing lights, bands of colors he had never seen before, smelling exotic scents, and ever floating, floating, floating. Ultimately, his eye in the sky slowed and focused on a youthful figure of himself seated at a desk in an office, furnished in the style of the fifties. He was listening to a conversation on a telephone, replying to long paragraphs from the other end with only an occasional grunt or "yes" or "no."

"Say, Gannon, I think I have a case for you in your field. We both know that you have been waiting to show us what you can do!" He barely recognized the female voice at the other end of the line, but he had overheard her speaking frequently enough in the corridors of the hospital to know the deep and cultured voice was that of the surgeon who was so well established in the community that he, the younger, would soon clearly be regarded as a challenger. Penelope Bayard was a woman who had an unique idea in the forties and had successfully carried it out. Not only did she have the mental capacity and moral strength to gain a seat in a medical school, but she had pursued her way through three separate surgical residencies and had brought the product of her training to a small community hospital, where she had become the dominant surgical force. Against that background, Gannon guessed what was coming.

"Chris, my office girl's father is a retired barber. I've known that he had an abdominal aneurysm for several years. This afternoon he developed sudden abdominal pain. I have checked him out here in the emergency room, and I think the thing has sprung a leak. I have no background in blood vessel work. Do you have the instruments and an arterial graft to fix it? I think he'll die in an hour or so if we don't do something, and it's your chance to show the community what you can do. What can we lose?"

Gannon tried to make himself sound confident, but his mouth seemed filled with cotton in spite of unwanted sputum collecting in his voice box. "Yeah, we have enough to go ahead in an emergency. I bought a set of vascular instruments last year from a tool maker in Wheaton. They are special clamps with the patented teeth used by Willis Potts for the last ten years in blue baby surgery at Children's Memorial."

"But what can you do about a graft? Do you have any?"

"Yes, I am a member of a limited surgical group with access to the Chicago Tissue Bank. When I bring in a sterile human autopsy aorta to make a gift to the bank, I am allowed to take one out, frozen and preserved in a vacuum tube. I have had one set aside for the past six months for just such a case."

"Well, the patient is being moved to 309. He is not shocky yet. But if you would hurry right over, I'll start the arrangement for exploration."

As Gannon drove across town, he reviewed in his head what he would say to the next of kin. It would be a situation all physicians dreaded. The principals, including himself, would be total strangers, and there was no background of prior contact or acquaintance upon which to build confidence. Furthermore, Gannon was not yet very well known in the community. He still looked younger than his thirty-one years—no matter that he had served a couple of years in each of two wars and had been a father three times by the age of twenty-three. He still looked like a tall string-bean of a kid, whose black hair always needed to be brushed from his eyes.

Crossing the river, Gannon's train of thought ran a circuitous course. Why had he gotten himself into a profession which required so much preparation and still required proof of abilities almost daily for many years thereafter?—probably for purely selfish reasons. He had been raised in a family that was poor, in the depths of the Depression in the American dust-bowl. He had never wanted to be poor again.

At age six, his best friend, the baker's son, regularly took a dime from the shop's cash register and took them both to the drug store for an orange soda. He had observed then that the only man in the town who could plunk down a quarter for a mid-morning malted milk was Doc Olds. He also owned one of the two black Packards in town.

Perhaps the impetus was from another event in the same time. He had been invited by his father to attend the burial of an infant. Standing on a country hilltop in a March wind and looking at the swollen necks and dull eyes of the baby's siblings, he well understood why the undertaker whispered to his father, "Dying may be the best thing that will ever happen to this kid." Surely some physician could have dealt better with this family's problem?

Or, again, perhaps it was the cumulative result of years of sitting in the front pew at the foot of his father's pulpit and hearing the repetition of a New Testament theme which said, "To find yourself, you must lose yourself in others' needs." Surely, being a surgeon would be a way to express that idea.

Few of the doctors had been able to grasp the concepts of vascular surgery in the year he had been working, and, in point of fact, the entire discipline was only about six years old. Local physicians had yet to refer him anything but nonpaying accident cases. Gannon was in that first generation of surgeons to learn the field after its creation by the surgeons who had been taking care of arterial wounds in World War II.

The idea of informed consent was not yet much of a legal issue, but Gannon knew he was going to have to explain many things to the patient and family that were not even understood by his colleagues. He would be asking the family for their consent for surgery, with modest understanding of the problem on the part of the person about to put his life at risk.

Room 309 was actually a ward, a space that at one time had been a long, glassed-in sun porch in nursing students' quarters. Its privacy was maintained by curtains, and the charge was $9.50 per day, including all meals and all treatment. Patients who could not demonstrate a way to pay for their bills were usually admitted to the ward bed. Standing at the side of the first bed and holding the patient's hand was a very tiny woman, whom Gannon identified as Dr. Penelope Bayard. She was pretty enough, in a pinched sort of way, with a turned up nose and narrow lips. She wore her black hair short, cut squarer at ear level, with bangs cut possibly to hide an unusually broad forehead. Her manner was crisp as she moved quickly to the introduction: "Dr. Gannon, this is Mr. Fortescue. Mr. Fortescue, tell your story to Dr. Gannon here, just as you told it to me."

For someone who was thought to be suffering from a leaking aneurysm, the patient's voice was surprisingly strong and he looked remarkably comfortable. *So far, if this thing is leaking, it must be a slow leak* , thought Gannon. The history confirmed that Dr. Bayard had been aware of the aneurysm for several years, but that the patient himself had only noticed the pulsating mass in the last six months. Mr. Fortescue volunteered that he "thought the pulsing was from his own heart." Abruptly at noon, on this same day, he had experienced the onset of severe pain just behind the umbilicus. He had been a little nauseated but had not vomited. Several hours later the pain was now less and seemingly a little more spread out across the lower abdomen.

Gannon did a limited physical examination. He had expected the patient to evidence a rapid pulse rate, but the pulse was slow. He also had anticipated a low blood pressure, from hemorrhage, but that was not present. Mr. Fortescue was quite thin, and any observer could actually see what appeared to be a baseball-sized mass elevating the abdominal wall. Feeding it with the examining hand was not just confirmatory, but frightening. It was beating in exact rhythm with the heart. Gannon's mentors had always said that the diagnosis of abdominal aneurysm was made by physical exam, and this certainly was a fact tonight. Still, he felt he should make some effort at approaching the matter in a professional manner, so he asked the room at large, "Anything unusual in the count?"

Penelope Bayard answered. "The white count is fourteen thousand, with a few immature cells. If it's leaking, it must not be very rapid, because his hemoglobin is twelve and a half grams, and the red count just under five million cells."

"Let's step over here and put our minds together, Dr. Bayard," said Gannon.

He stood with his back to the patient as he spoke to the more experienced surgeon. "Since this would be the first case of its kind in the community, I think we should cover ourselves with a little more work-up. Let's get a couple of views of the abdomen, just for the record."

Dr. Bayard nodded her head, saying, "He can go directly to the OR from the x-ray department." By this time, Gannon's pulse had begun to race. He was the one who had the cold sweats, rather than the patient. In his efforts to play down the seriousness of this disease in discussion with potential referring physicians, he had mentioned little of the risk of surgery, and now his bluff was about to be called. He was going to have to produce, and preferably successfully. He would get other chances in the future, but it would certainly save a lot of trouble if the first aneurysmectomy were successful. He followed the patient's gurney down the elevator to the x-ray department and then waited for the wet film to come out of the rinse water.

"Hah! There it is!" said Gannon. He pointed to an arc of calcium flecks in front of spine and then placed his fingers on the film to make a rough assessment of the size of the aneurysm. "Well, it certainly is a big one, and most likely it is leaking. No one could criticize us for going in.

"I told the call people to go ahead and set up and we would come straight there as soon as the room was ready. Why don't you talk to the patient again," suggested Dr. Gannon, "and try to find his daughter and talk to her a little bit."

By this time Gannon was beginning to shake. *Of all the times to get nervous,* he thought, *this is the worst!* He returned to the x-ray room and made an effort to explain the problem to the patient. "Mr. Fortescue, our diagnosis is correct. Think of it as a large truck tire that is thinned out and about ready to blow. At the moment, the leak is slow, so we have some time to take it out before it blows." The patient understood nothing. Gannon was wasting his time.

The patient seemed to react about as much as an adult who was about have his appendix removed. "How do you propose to fix such a thing? I never heard of that."

"Well, we have to cut the vessel right here at the upper end," said Gannon, pointing at the narrow neck on the x-ray plate. "And then again down here in the pelvis. We'll put a similar strong vessel from a young person in its place. That is called a graft. Your daughter is just outside in the hall. Maybe you would like to talk it over with her."

Mr. Fortescue seemed to be getting the message. He drew the sheet up under his chin and stared at something far away, beyond the walls of this enclosed space. "How much risk is there, Doc?"

"I must be honest with you. Half of the patients who have this problem repaired on an emergency basis don't make it. No operation like this has ever been done in our town before, either. You would be the first. If we try to move you to downtown Chicago, I don't think you'll make it."

At this moment, the spiked heels of a determined woman could be heard clicking down the terrazzo floor. The patient's daughter swept into the room, impeccably dressed in a brown hound's tooth checked coat. She rushed to her father and embraced him then turned to face Gannon. "I just saw Dr. Bayard in the hall, and she explained the situation. You are young and obviously have not been in practice long enough to have done many of these, but Dr. Bayard says you are our best bet. We have to trust somebody."

She looked at her father and squeezed his hand. He still looked somewhat blank, but his mouth diligently formed the word "Yes."

Gannon was not elated at being offered the chance to prove himself. Instead, he had secretly hoped that they would decline his recommendation. He was just in his second year in private practice and was about to roll the dice, with some likelihood that the result would be bad for all concerned. A major failure at this point would create much gossip and probably set his career back five years. But a significant success could make his future certain. As he climbed the back stairs to the surgeons' locker room he felt more than the usual tightness in his chest. Then he stopped short. *Shame on you, Gannon,* he thought. *It is the patient who is taking the chance, not you.*

At the scrub sink Gannon's performance was comedic. He forgot to note the time and scrubbed fifteen minutes instead of the required ten, and twice he had to replace the brush because he dropped it in the sink.

There was time to reflect on the past year. Surgically, it had not been a fruitful experience. He had done only four majors, two of which were very difficult injury cases; the other two were referred by older physicians because the patients were poor and had no insurance. Of the four, only one had been able to pay his surgical fee. He did life insurance examinations at night in neighboring communities in order to support his wife and three young children. Their apartment was filled with cockroaches. His wife, Helene, struggled to hold a family of five together on a low income.

These were the days when the referring doctor was the first assistant at surgery, so the tiny female surgeon, with a five-year head start in terms of reputation, was scrubbing next to him at the sink. She seemed excited, but not dismayed. They spoke of issues unrelated to the surgery, referring to his own lack of progress in private practice, the number of children he had had at an early age, and her unmarried state. Meanwhile Gannon could hear much scurrying about in the operating room. It was night, and the crew would be limited. Even though the use of frozen and dried human arterial grafts had been discussed, neither the circulating nurse nor the scrub nurse had ever seen such unique packaging (a glass vacuum tube) and were scared stiff about dropping the graft on the floor! There was no way to re-sterilize the graft, and there was only the one.

Gannon had anticipated that, with all the hurrying around in preparation, something would go wrong and he was not disappointed. The scrub nurse contaminated herself during the draping and had to redo the whole thing. He watched as the circulating nurse dressed his first assistant, disappointed as her comely figure disappeared into the ballooning gown. Finally, it was with some pride that he picked up the scalpel and made the classical full length abdominal incision from rib cage to pubis for removal of aneurysm. Even his first assistant, who was used to radical tumor surgery in women's pelvises, sucked in her breath.

It was difficult for Gannon to describe the almost spiritual experience that accompanied entering the human body. The viscera warmed the examining hands, and the sinuous nature of the gut as it slid among the gloved fingers created an erotic sensation. "Exploration of the abdomen" implied examining directly all of the normal parts also, displacing and palpating the large solid organs, such as the spleen and liver, and peering into those most private cavities of the human being was a ritual experienced millions of times since surgery began its modem sequence about 1880. He was convinced that all other surgeons felt the same sensations when entering the abdomen; he had observed that his teachers all seemed to linger over this part of surgery.

Gannon observed that there was no tell-tale red blush over the wall of the aneurysm either to the right or the left in the pelvic area. "It doesn't look to me like this thing is leaking."

"Damn!" said his first assistant. "I thought surely it had ruptured. Why did he have so much pain?"

"It was stretching," Gannon replied. "I'm sure there's a crack inside between two of the layers, so that as it was stretching, we were just hours away from a frank rupture.'"

Gannon was not confounding his assistant or lying to her to justify why they were in the belly; he was speaking the truth. The "stretching" aneurysm was usually a short time away from rapid hemorrhage and sudden death. Furthermore, the absence of hemorrhage gave the operators a better chance, as the kidneys could usually be protected by continuing circulation throughout the operation. So Gannon ran his hand around the upper end of the bulging, white, pulsating mass in front of him. This is the real thing, all right. By any standard it was a large aneurysm, but at least there was time now to gain control at the upper end of the vessel. "Gaining control" meant having pin-point control of the flow through the upper end of the vessel, so that it could be opened or closed at will and any blood loss virtually kept at a minimum by the application of the appropriate clamping device. Still, to apply the forceps meant that one had to gain some operating space between the spine and the back wall of the vessel in order to get the clamp across. This was the key to a successful aneurysmectomy.

Once the clamp was on the upper end of the vessel, the rest of the surgery could almost be done with impunity, except for keeping the occlusion time at something under an hour. So Gannon began the tedious finger dissection in the plane between the back wall of the aorta and the front wall of the spine. This required blunt work, pushing and pressing and wiping behind the vessel and in front of the bone in order to develop the potential space into actual space. The trick was to break through the fibers and complete the open space behind the vessel without putting one's index finger right through the back wall of the aneurysm, which was already thin and frayed. Gannon swallowed hard, because now he knew he had a real chance and that he had better deliver. The neck of the aneurysm was long enough to maintain circulation to the kidneys. Suddenly, to his great relief, one index finger popped through the correct plane, allowing him to apply the Southwick clamp. This was an ingenious device, invented in the early fifties, L-shaped, and divided into two parts so that one could be passed behind the aorta first and then the second attached by a screw mechanism and then brought down gradually so that the vessel was not suddenly shut off. He screwed the clamp down so that approximately 50 percent of the vessel was occluded, still allowing for half of the blood supply to the lower extremities to continue. A similar type of dissection was necessary over the pelvic brim, for the control of the two major vessels to the legs.

Finally, he closed all of the clamps to their fullest extent and incised the front wall of the aneurysm the length of four inches. He was certain that his inexperienced help fully expected a gush of blood to the abdomen, but his own prior experience, modest though it was, told him that most of the vessel was filled with solid clot in the interior leathery wall of the aneurysm, and so it was. The thick, grumous organized clot was literally scooped out by handsful then the walls, front, and sides of the aneurysm were removed by rapid scissor dissection in just a matter of seconds. To his own surprise, the only bleeding was from the small vessels in the back wall, each requiring just an x-suture of silk. Rapidly, he fashioned the frozen and dried graft from the human donor and tailored the upper and lower ends to fit the receiving vessels, following with locking suture lines at both ends of the graft. As a last movement he loosened the clamps slightly, to flush all air and clots from the graft and then tied the sutures in place. Anticoagulant catheters, previously placed in the leg vessels, were removed at this time also. Gannon slowly let out his breath, trying not to show his sense of triumph to his first assistant. The presence of an expansile pulse within the vessels running to the legs confirmed that the system was open, and the final flush of success came with the fact that there was not a single leak at the suture line. Gannon was sure that Dr. Bayard fully expected the whole system to clot off and for the patient then to lose both of his legs, if not his life, in a few days. But she was wrong.

During the closure of the long abdominal wound, Gannon introduced a method in human behavior with anesthesia personnel, scrub nurses, which he was to use for the next thirty-five years. He focused the thoughts of the operating crew on other issues. He asked his first assistant her opinions regarding the administration of the government by General Eisenhower, he being in his second term. Together, they reviewed the elements of this being a golden era in the time of the United States, a time when it seemed that the country was first realizing its true place in world history. Some discussion centered on music and the Art Institute of Chicago. Healing was taking place, not only in the wound closure, but in the psyches of the operating room team. They were "cooling off".

In spite of the discussion of these nonprofessional elements, Gannon sensed a change in attitude on the part of his first assistant. The fact was that he, Gannon, had brought it off. Gannon's perception was that Penelope Bayard's feeling were those of disappointment rather than elation. The more Gannon thought about it, the more reserved he became, as was the case with Dr. Bayard. Both realized now that the other was a strong competitor in the community, and it was unlikely that they would be able to work on the same team in the future. Each was beginning to perceive the other in a different perspective, perhaps that of a potential enemy.

Mr. Fortescue's daughter was the only surviving member of the family, and the discussion with her was relatively perfunctory, considering what the participants had just been through. Everyone was drained of emotion. Gannon was certain that the daughter had only the vaguest idea about what had taken place. Her boss, Dr. Penelope Bayard, would have to flesh it out at another time.

Gannon did not perceive that this episode would affect the entire balance of his life and that this night was the start of a lifetime of competition between the two surgeons. The senior was not content, apparently, with being able to do all the other kinds of surgery except blood vessel work and was probably unwilling to give over the field to Gannon. In retrospect Gannon would observe that on that night, Dr. Bayard began a search for a solution to what she now regarded as a future major problem and that either she had to return to an additional training program or simply employ someone else trained in the field.

Gannon did not recognize that while this was a limited problem for the senior surgeon, it was going to be much more of a problem for the junior surgeon.

Penelope Bayard had left for the ladies' locker room. As the team pushed the patient's gurney toward the recovery ward, the anesthesiologist whispered, "Look out, Chris! Did you feel her beady eyes on the back of your neck? You might have been better off in the long run if the patient had not made it!"

Chapter 2

Gannon slowly opened his eyes to a narrow slit, just enough to see the outlines of the room. It was night, and the lights were dimmed. He had been awake for some time, listening to the comings and goings about his bed. He was certain that each time he was observed to be waking the nursing staff was knocking him out again with intravenous drugs. He was alert to who he was and where he was, but he was still disoriented as to time. How long had he been here? He was having trouble stringing words together, his mind stupefied by the inability to recall the names of objects.

Desperately he wanted to tell them how much his shoulders were hurting. They were throbbing, throbbing constantly, particularly when he pulled against the leather restraints on his wrists. If only he could verbalize his complaint and ask someone to investigate it, maybe they would x-ray them. So he reached up with his right hand, as far as the leather cuff would allow, grabbing the bed rail and rattling it loudly. The face that appeared immediately between the curtains was that of the male nurse, whom he remembered from the earlier encounter. "Take it easy, Dr. Gannon. I intend to let you up tonight on the evening shift and keep a close eye on you so that you do not hurt yourself. Do you need something now?"

At first Gannon was only able to grunt. Then he formed words, expressing an idea: "My shoulders, especially the left one. It is killing me. Maybe it is out of the joint again, as it was before."

The nurse stepped into the room and picked up his right hand, to comfort him. "What do you mean? Have you had trouble there in the past?"

"Yeah," Gannon was straining for words, "I dislocated it before, maybe a year ago, on a mountain, in a ski fall. Why am I in here now? I cannot remember anything in recent time."

"I'm sorry, Dr. Gannon. You haven't been conscious enough for your doctors to talk with you. We have not been allowed to let you up for two days now. You had a stroke while doing a radio program, with a major seizure that lasted five minutes. We keep putting you down with IV drugs because you have been very difficult to handle physically. Maybe you threw that shoulder out during the course of the seizure." The nurse gently put his fingers over the apex of the shoulder on the left side and ran his fingers around over the ball that was sticking out there. "My heavens! I don't think any of us have noticed this before. Do you have a lot of pain right there? I think that the head of the humerus is out of the socket."

"Don't knock me out again, please! I know it is night, but why don't we bring someone up here and take an x-ray? Ask the doctors. What is your name? You have been very kind."

"David."

But try as he would, Gannon found himself slipping into the black void again. Whirling colors and lights focused themselves into a scene in his bedroom thirty-five years before.

Gannon sat on the edge of his bed, running his hands through his hair. He had just put the telephone down. The caller had been the night supervisor at Waterford Hospital asking him to come in and see a patient. *Why did all these calls come just after falling deeply asleep?* he wondered. In fact, the emergency room had kept him busy during this first year of work, although there was not much money involved. As he pulled on his socks and stood up to button his shirt, he muttered to himself about "night calls." His caller had advised him to "be careful—it has been raining very heavily and the roads are slippery." As he lifted the garage door and looked out into the night, he could see that the rain was pouring down: "Pitchforks and hammer handles," his father used to say. Emergency room work at this time in a surgical career was the traditional way for the young surgeon to develop a practice. He had to demonstrate his wares to the institutional nursing staff in order to get their endorsement, and that latter element was necessary before being sent any referrals from private practitioners in the community. The emergency room was an opportunity because the older, more settled surgeons were reluctant to come in at night.

There was always mental conflict when driving to the emergency room. A decade before, in a training program, a cardiologist had suggested to him to "walk slowly, the Lord will answer most problems one way or the other by the time you get there." Such, he felt, was the situation now. If the injured man survived his safe and slow driving to the station, most likely he would be salvageable. At the south door of the hospital, he rang the bell next to the locked door and stood impatiently in the rain, waiting for the supervisor to round the corner from the emergency room and let him in.

According to the ambulance driver, the patient had been comatose from the beginning. In the fifties, funeral directors were the ambulance drivers and rotated emergency pickups on a nightly basis. On this call the driver had been a fortyish, very spindly, balding man with an overly large set of teeth and a great sense of humor. They had met before, under similar circumstances.

"Hi, Doc," said the driver, patting him on his back. "I don't think you're going to be able to do much here."

"I did not see any cops outside, Bill," said Gannon. "Are you able to give me any help? Did anybody out there see what happened?"

"Yeah, there was a witness. Some guy was just getting into his car in the parking lot, when he saw it happen. The accident was in front of the Old Farm Restaurant, about 10:00 P.M., a couple of hours ago."

Gannon began his examination of the patient. He lifted the eyelids and noted that the eyeballs did not move and that the pupils were fixed at the size of one millimeter. He brushed the eyelashes, but there was no reflexive effort to close the lids. Quickly he ran his hands over the facial bones and cranium, feeling for a soft spot or some evidence of bleeding, finding nothing.

Meanwhile, the driver was still talking. "Well, ya know, doc, this was something really strange. The guy in the lot saw a hen pheasant crossing the highway in front of the restaurant, with a half-dozen chicks walking behind her. The rain was coming down, when suddenly he heard a screech of brakes and lights from a car flashed on the pheasant. The car on the road stopped soon enough to not hurt the birds, but the poor guy was rear-ended by a semi right after that. By the time I got there, the cops had been there for a while, and they said he hadn't moved a bit. He was slumped over the steering wheel."

Gannon continued his examination. He elicited no pain response when he ran his finger down the back of the patient's neck and then down over the shoulders and arms and onto the upper extremities. There was no flail or loose movement to his arms or legs either as the examination progressed. There were no open wounds anywhere on the body; there were no abrasions on the abdomen or the chest wall. The patient was breathing a little rapidly, but otherwise showing no respiratory distress. After a quick check on the wrist, he estimated the pulse at about eighty and said to the nurse, "Check his blood pressure and have the lab tech come down and get some blood."

"Looks bad, Doc, doesn't it?" said the driver.

"Yeah, Billy Boy. I think this was a wasted trip for both of us. Drive carefully going home. Don't be the next statistic." Gannon waved goodnight, knowing that they would meet again on future nights.

"Miss Mellen, I'm not going to wake up a Chicago neurosurgeon at this hour. Isn't there some new guy practicing anesthesia as an M.D. who just started here?"

The supervisor looked puzzled, "Why, I guess there is. He's a pink-cheeked kid named Finney. How can he help you?"

Gannon could see doubt developing in the mind of the supervisor. He tried to sound confident by saying firmly, "The small pupils suggest two-sided intracranial pressure. I don't find anything else except the coma. If I'm right, this is going to get worse over the next hour or so, and the patient will simply stop breathing. Maybe Finney has some idea about how we can support the respiration and keep him alive. I don't find anything else. If we manage his breathing apparatus, maybe his head will improve and he will wake right up!"

The nurse looked doubtful but went to the phone dutifully, apparently conceding that Gannon had a valid point. Gannon returned to his examination and repeated everything, finding nothing additional. Within ten minutes, a short, stout, young man appeared and said in a breezy voice, "What's up? Whatcha' got? What makes you think I can help?"

"I can't find anything except neurological signs that suggest a major head injury. Maybe it's just generalized brain swelling. It's been three hours since the injury, and the only signs are coma plus constricted pupils. I thought maybe you could do something to help support his ventilation until he wakes up. That's all"

"Well, yeah, I think I do have an idea. I was poking around last week on the fourth floor and came across a Drinker respirator parked out there in the hallway. Once in a while they must have had a bulbar polio and finished using it just a few months ago. We could put him in that.

Gannon, relieved that there was going to be some disposition of this problem, said, "That's a great idea! Let's bring the respirator right down here to the ER, Miss Mellen, and we can load him in. I'll see if I can find some member of the family in Chicago to talk to and see what help the police can give us."

14

The Drinker respirator was a seven-foot-long cylindrical metal casing, set on wheels for mobility, painted an ugly olive-green, with an opening at one end through which protruded the patient's head and with several portholes on each side for nurses' hands to provide care. It was useful for the patient whose breathing muscles were paralyzed, cycling compression and vacuum alternately by means of a large, electric-powered bellows suspended from its underside: hence the name "iron lung."

The two physicians wrestled the dead weight of the patient onto the table that fit into the cylinder, drawing the latter slowly down over the body. When the switch was thrown, the bellows went into action, and the patient's chest began to rise and fall about sixteen times per minute.

Gannon and Finney completed all these preparations by three o'clock and then, looking at one another, turned their hands up. Finney said, "I can't think of anything else to do. He does need an in-lying catheter. We can keep his IV's open and maintain his acid base balance and urinary output and maybe put him on a feeding tube in a couple of days. Meanwhile, the Drinker here will do whatever we need. There is a neurosurgeon at Augustana Hospital in Chicago. I have his phone number at home. We can call him in the morning. He might even take him on a transfer. "

"I bet not. I'm sure he has all he can do with salvageable cases," said Gannon. "Come on, let's go home. We've done what we could do."

So Gannon and Finney brought all their knowledge and little experience to bear on the poor wretch in the Drinker respirator. Days went by. The feeding tube worked, but it gave the patient diarrhea and made management difficult through the portholes of the respirator. The nurses, at first impressed by the vigorous treatment being administered by the two new doctors at the hospital, then became annoyed because the nursing care problems were so intensive. After five days, the pupils which they were watching almost hour by hour began to dilate, and having done so, then became fixed in one position and would not react to light anymore. The two young doctors looked at one another—"What to do now?"

If there was a family, none had appeared. No one had been able to make contact with any survivors. The two of them were left with a patient who, for all intents and purposes, was apparently dead. Repeated neurological examinations failed to show evidence of survival. In their discussions together, there were times when each took on an accusatory note when asking the question, "How long do we keep this up?" Meanwhile, the respirator was going *whoosh, thump; whoosh, thump* around the clock, and both sensed administrative questioning of the two young doctors who had gone to such heroic circumstances in the care of the man who now was known as "the man who loved pheasants."

At one week each was looking guiltily at the other. One Saturday morning they agreed that they should throw the switch and whatever would happen, would happen. So each, at the same time, put his thumb on the switch and pushed downward. The *whoosh, thump; whoosh, thump* stopped, and they looked inside the ports to see if there was any respiratory effort. There was none. They waited fifteen minutes and then applied a stethoscope to the chest and heard nothing. Although the staff was looking the other way, they surreptitiously slid the patient's chart beneath Gannon's elbow for him to make a progress note, including the date and time of death.

"Say, Finney, what shall I write? Do we know when he died?"

"Put down right now. We don't have any idea when he checked out. He may have been dead two days ago. By the way, this was a trauma case, and I am sure the coroner will ask for an autopsy. I sure would like to know what is inside that skull."

"Okay, girls," said Gannon. "'Let the coroner know that our man is dead and tell him that we want an autopsy also. I feel a little nervous about this. We don't have any family, and we really don't know the date and time of death."

Toward lunch time, both Finney and Gannon heard a page from the autopsy room. *Why are post-mortems always done in a basement room*, thought Gannon as they padded down the stairs. Inside were stacked a dozen metal doors, opening into the sterile room with the cradling refrigerator trays along one entire wall. Occupying the middle of the room was a porcelain fluted, eight-foot table, with appropriately spaced faucets and running water. The pathologist was already at work on their patient. *White!* thought Gannon, *everything is white—the wall tile, the glaring ceiling lights, the body strained of its blood. Is white related to purity and sterility and being clean? There is nothing clean about death.*

They stood aside as the diener incised the scalp and rolled it down over the dead man's face. There was no getting around it; the whir of the electric saw being used to cut the full thickness through the cranium in a circular fashion was unsettling. While each had paid his dues in the autopsy room, in his respective training program, this was a new experience. An instrument with prying handles was inserted through the saw marks, and the skull divided in half. A "hinge" of fibrous dura mater was left at the back of the cranium, and the skull then bent downwards. No brain was visible. In horror, all observed a thick, pink fluid leaking from inside the skull. The brain had liquefied! How long? Two days? A week? *This is like a Faulkerian novel*, Gannon thought.

The two young men looked at one another. "Well, that does it. His brain has liquefied. I'll bet he's been dead three days. At least we have no doubt as to the diagnosis and can sign out the chart accordingly."

Gannon slowly turned toward the door. Waves of nausea were passing through him and he fought showing any weakness to either Finney or the pathologist. *What a frustration*, he thought. *We went through all this agony for the past week, and for nothing. No wonder the nursing staff has been looking askance at us.*

Said Finney, "It could be worse, Chris. Suppose he had a wife and ten kinds standing out there in the hall. We would have the job of explaining to them just why his reflexes put on the brakes for a mother pheasant and her chicks. What a waste—both him and us. How stupid!"

Driving to his office an hour later, Gannon reflected one more time on his choice of profession. Why had he not followed his father into the ministry? One of the strongest reasons was that the family was poor. His mother was always taking in boarders. His father began formal education late, so was often "away at school" during Gannon's childhood. His family needed money, so Gannon had begun income-producing work at the age of twelve and had never stopped. To have become a pastor would have meant more poverty and more importantly would have been a challenge to his father's history. No, better to be a rich doctor than a poor preacher.

Chapter 3

Once again Gannon experienced that frightening sensation of swimming upward through deep and dark waters, his body crushed by the weight of the waves crashing over his head, the surface receding from him and producing the panic that goes with suffocation as he fought against unseen restraints. Bursting into the daylight, he found himself yet one more time in bed in the intensive care unit. He decided that if he struggled too much and made too much of a fuss, he would be drugged again and returned to the depths. So he chose just to fidget a bit with the tag end of his hand restraints and to flex his knees a little in order to determine whether or not he was still strapped down.

At that moment he was seized with an overwhelming urge to pass urine. Desperately he tried to put his knees together for relief, but the shackles on his ankles held him fast and the desire to void relented only slowly.

"I think he's having bladder spasms again," came a female voice. He recognized his nurses, man and a woman, leaning across the bed rails.

The deep male voice that had come previously from the bearded face murmured softy, "Look, why are they torturing him with that Foley catheter? It's driving him nuts! One of his doctors said he could have an external catheter if it looked like it was bothering him again."

"I tried that style on the night shift last night, but his penis was too small; it just leaked all over the bedclothes. I had to change his bedding twice, so I put the Foley back in."

Gannon was in agony. The bearing down feeling was relentless and there was a constant desire to run to the bathroom compromised by an inability to escape because of the shackles and bed rails. *If they would only let me up*, he thought. *If they would just take the damn Foley out and let me wake up, I could take care of myself. What's wrong with them? Every time I start to wake up, they knock me down.*

The soft female voice came again, "I'll give him another fifty of Valium. Then you take the Foley out and slip the condom on again while he's not so restless."

Shortly thereafter, Gannon could feel the catheter sliding out under the bedclothes, followed by the manipulations of his tormentors. *Oh God*, he thought, *won't this ever end?* Then it came again, that blessed blitz of darkness.

After a short period of seeing whirling, multicolored fights, his mind's eye focused on a memory of the main operating room at the Veterans' Hospital. He and the team were doing a morning case. But today was not routine. In addition to the presence of a senior resident, Ben Matejus, and a senior consultant, Sam Mizzou, the room was also occupied by a chromium-plated machine standing six feet tall and about four feet in width on each of its two sides, standing off to the side of the patient on the operating table. Next to it was a technician in cap and gown and laboratory coat, vigorously swabbing the interior of what appeared to be a ten-inch open aluminum canister. Gannon saw himself standing next to his favorite senior consultant, Sam Mizzou.

The figure he had identified as himself stepped to the side to be gowned and gloved, and as he did so, he leaned toward Dr. Mizzou and asked, "What the hell is he doing? He's been at that for thirty minutes now. "

His mentor spoke with a soft southern drawl. "He and Dr. James have been working on this pump for five years. The oxygenation of the blood occurs as the gas bubbles up through the liquid, filling a series of concentric cans, then flowing up and over the wall of each and passing into the next larger canister. But we learned early on that the blood would clot on the wall of the chromium surface before we gave intravenous heparin in the middle of the operation, so he is heparinizing the lining of the chromium.

"How many times have you used this pump on humans?" Gannon asked.

"This will be the fourth case. We did the first three at Lincoln University Hospital downtown. There are still some wrinkles in the system The unidirectional flow of the blood is controlled by a tricky valve because we have to return blood to the body at the same rate as we remove it. The pump is primed with five units of bank blood in the reservoir."

A short while later that soft southern voice said with some tension behind it, "Go, man, go!"

So Gannon put the knife on the chest and made a long sweeping incision over the rib cage that would permit entrance into the left chest. This was a patient on whom, a year before, Gannon, as a senior resident, had done a finger fracture of the patient's mitral valve. That had been a so-called "closed commissurotomy" in which he had passed his index finger through the wall of the upper chamber of the heart, with a heavy suture around it to prevent leakage, and slipped that finger through the valve in a transverse fashion, pressing and using a wiping motion in order to break down the adhesions at the opposite ends of the two-sided valve. It had been his first mitral-commissurotomy, and the patient had recovered uneventfully. Unfortunately, the patient's rheumatic disease was relentless, and the valve leaflets had become adherent again, necessitating more specific surgery, under direct view, using scissors and suture for reconstruction. Hence the operation on this day was an "open operation," using a pump and oxygenator for the blood, and opening the left major heart chamber for repair of the valve under direct vision.

At this time, 1959, heart-lung machines were under development all over the country, but no one had succeeded in producing an apparatus that did not have some problems. This machine, developed in Chicago, was based on the oxygenating principle described by Mizzou, while a pumping mechanism using a series of fingerlike rollers moved the blood along in a pulsatile fashion, much like the thrusting action of the human heart. A key element was that the patient's circulation had to be short-circuited using tubing placed directly into the heart chambers in such a fashion as to bypass the heart itself, running the blood through the pump and returning it to the patient at a reasonably equitable rate without going through the heart. Hence the term "heart-lung" machine—a mechanical pump to replace the heart and an oxygenator to replace the lungs.

After the chest field was set up, Dr. Mizzou took over. The scrub nurse produced several large, long plastic tubings which were inserted sequentially into the heart chambers, first being filled with blood, and then being connected to the machine, after which the pump was started. Mizzou heaved a sigh of relief when the blood was seen coursing through the various plastic tubings, being returned to the patient's body via a vessel in the groin. The heart was absolutely still. Then, to the consternation of all others at the table, he rapidly made an incision in the major chamber on the left side of the heart, exposing the valve that had been finger-fractured the year before. The team, watching, was amazed at the interior of the chamber and the opportunity to look directly at the valve and the cords that attached it to the walls of the interior. They could see how narrow the inflow tract had become because of scarring, and the point for incision of the scar was obvious. Three snips of scissors freed the valve, and it was demonstrated that it would flap in the flow of blood as soon as this was established. Mizzou picked up a heavy suture and needle and rapidly began to close the heart wall. Only three minutes had elapsed since the heart had been opened.

Suddenly, the anesthesiologist leaned over the screen. "Hey, guys, I got no blood pressure. What did you do down there?"

Mizzou hissed, "Nothing. Don't bother me. Everything on our end is okay." He continued to pass the needle through the wall of the ventricle.

"The hell it is! My God," exclaimed the anesthesiologist. "My God! The inflow tubing has no blood in it! Where is all the blood?"

"Damn," cursed the pump technician. "The return tube has collapsed! That can only mean that all the blood's in the reservoir in the pump! Is there any blood in the aorta at all!"

"No," hissed Gannon. "It's absolutely flat. My gosh, we've exsanguinated the patient! All the blood is in the pump! How could we do that?"

"Very easily," shouted the technician "By just turning the intake valve the wrong way, that's how!—and that's exactly what's happened!"

Gannon could not see the technician's hand, but he saw a twisting motion, and abruptly the pulsating, throbbing flow of blood reappeared in the return tube to the thigh, followed shortly thereafter by dilatation of the large vessel under his finger in the chest, and then the return of the pumping action to the outflow tube, filling the system and establishing the circulation again.

"God damn, what a mess! Gannon, put your finger over that last stitch. We'll let the last bit of air out of the chamber before I tie the stitch down! We may get by yet!"

By this time, the chest was one third full of anti-coagulated blood. The final knots were tied by Mizzou beneath the surface of the blood within the chest.

Mizzou hissed again, "This blood is not clotting. Did you forget to give the protamine for the heparin?"

The anesthesiologist was flailing about among his myriad of bottles and IV tubes, shouting at Mizzou, "I just gave it. If the ventricle wall is still oozing, it should stop within thirty seconds." Gannon sucked the unclotted blood up out of the chest and heaved a sigh of relief as, true to the prediction of the anesthesiologist, the blood stopped spurting between the sutures, and the ventricle wall expanded. More importantly the chamber itself began to pulsate at a rate of about ninety times per minute, and soon the anesthesiologist shouted, "I've got a blood pressure of 160/90." Meanwhile, Mizzou had rapidly removed the tubes from the vessels adjacent to the heart, tying down the sutures as he did so, and allowing the air to escape from each chamber.

"Gannon," he raid, "we just might get away with this! What a butch-up! It just shows you what the human body can take! We made every mistake in the book, but still we're going to get a live patient out of this! If he has no problems neurologically it will be one hell of a miracle."

Mizzou scrubbed out at this point, leaving the resident team to close up the chest and set the chest suction catheters. The most relieved man in the room was Gannon. He would be able to talk to the patient in four or five days with confidence. More importantly he would now be able to walk down the hall to the family waiting room and tell them how smoothly everything had gone and how the patient had made it through one of the first heart pump operations in the United States. Having done so, he returned to the scrub sink and crooked his finger at the second assistant.

"Come on, Ben, let's get a cup of coffee in the cafeteria. I just talked to the family, and I'm really wrung out."

A trip to the cafeteria in this hospital was a long one. If the fire doors separating the six buildings had been left open, one could have seen the full length of the corridor from the south to the north end of the building, a full one-half mile. It was a thirty-year-old structure but had served the veterans of the Midwest very well during that time and had the best set of patient records, including four-by-four glass photographic slides, that Gannon would ever see. Unfortunately, he, along with the hundreds of other residents, had no idea how good they had it at the time. So the two friends, one finishing his residency and the other in the early years of serving as a consultant, walked side by side in surgical greens and white clinical coats. The surgical resident was differentiated from the medical resident by their two variant uniforms. Those on the medical side were in white shirts and ties and carried their stethoscopes suspended by the ear pieces around the necks, while the surgical side wore wrinkled surgical greens, sleeveless, and carried their stethoscopes in the pockets of the clinical coats. This was a very carefully drawn line and separated the two divisions of the hospital rigidly, albeit not officially.

This was afternoon, the time of day when junior residents caught up on dictations of histories and physical exams of patients, while the senior residents compiled the surgical schedule for the balance of the week. It was to the advantage of the seniors to see and schedule as many possible cases as could be accommodated because the summation of their experience was going to be no more than a collection of operative reports covering four years, transcribed on tissue-thin paper. They would leave with very little else except a letter of recommendation from the Chief of Service.

The cafeteria was shared by the entire hospital population. Patients, either ambulatory or in wheelchairs, spent a good deal of their time at the tables, sipping cups of coffee while playing various card games and smoking cigarettes at an incredible rate. This was common ground for the hospital employees, from orderly through chief surgical resident, with mingling of a variety of cultures and societal levels. Visitors to patients used this as the meeting place to deal with news for their relatives from their doctors, so there were often sets of glum faces alternating with those with pleased expression, as this huge institution wound through its daily routine.

Gannon and Matejus found a comer table and set their cups down next to a couple of doughnuts. "Boy, what a mess," said Gannon. "It's a good thing you were there. We bled the patient out right into the machine. I didn't think it was possible for that to happen. I don't think Mizzou did either. But it was only the fourth time the pump had been used, and apparently it was put together right every other time. I would not want to know what the Chief is going to say when he hears about this one."

Gannon and Matejus had been working together now for about six months. Of the two senior residents, one had a bad habit of sucking around the consultants, while Matejus, the quiet one, always stayed in the background, taking notes and doing his work efficiently and quietly. When Gannon asked him about why he was a chain smoker, he explained that he had picked up the habit in a concentration camp near Vienna in the months after the end of World War II. He was shorter than Gannon by five or six inches. His body was thin and underweight, another effect of time spent in a camp for displaced persons, thought Gannon. His cheekbones were high and prominent, and his hair was already graying. He was older than Gannon, by some five years or so, and certainly much more worldly. The camp had been in the American zone, the purpose of all refugees from central Europe having been to flee to the West to escape the advancing Russians. Several times, when the allowable terms for Ben Matejus and his friends to stay in an American camp were at an end, the American major in command gave them careful and specific instructions about how and when to jump the train in order to be returned to the American camp and be awarded another term. By successfully doing this several times, Ben and his friends escaped being returned to their home country in Russian occupied Albania. For ten years, Matejus had been winding his way along a path similar to that of many other displaced persons, through Canada to the United States, serving under a sponsor while satisfying citizenship requirements and even spending a couple of years in the military.

"Let's get off that, Chris," replied his table partner, in the fractured Americanese that would restrain his communication skills all his life. "I want to talk about something else. You'll be done as a consultant in June, right?"

"Yup."

"Well, Chris, would you keep me in mind? After I finish the vascular service, I still have my fifth year of general surgery do to. We have worked well together here, and I think we would make a good team. At home, you have only two other competitors in general surgery and no competition in vascular surgery. You ought to be in a position to take on a partner about a year from now. You will be getting referrals by then, and I can take the burden of the night work in the emergency room."

Gannon looked at him with raised eyebrows. "Well, you certainly are optimistic about my future. I've done very little but free work for years. I'm still doing insurance exams at night in order to feed my group. I'm still not certain whether I will make it or not."

"Look, I'll cover my rear end by applying for a full time job in the VA somewhere else in the U.S. But, for now, I want you to think this over and keep thinking about it as you go through the second year. Two heads are better than one. Also, I think each would give courage to the other. You have a facility with English that I shall never have. But, also, I have been out in the world a little longer than you have, and I think that gives me an advantage in personal relationships, and, frankly, in just plain surgical experience. Don't forget that I spent a couple of years at Ravenswood before I got in the VA."

"Want another cup? I'll buy," offered Gannon as he stood and moved toward the cafeteria line. Standing in that line, Gannon reviewed this revolutionary proposal In his chosen community, there were no practitioners with a foreign accent. He wondered how the town would react to such a circumstance. Would they hold it against him, Gannon, because Matejus struggled with the English language, or would they write them both off as intruders and regard them as social pariahs because of a language problem? It had looked to Gannon as though this was an established medical community, one for which he would have to battle for recognition. He wondered if Matejus came with him would that increase the hardship of cross-referral? On the other hand, he had heard that there were several displaced European physicians in the rural parts around Waterford, particularly in the small communities ten to fifteen miles to the west. Perhaps these physicians would actually be attracted to the practice if he chose to partner up with a man with an accent. Certainly there were many young residents now who were graduates of foreign medical schools, and they would be coming out of training programs over succeeding years. As the white establishment in Waterford sought for young men to take over parts of practices on a partnership basis, they would find that the reservoir of residents was dominated now by graduates of foreign medical schools. So even if they gave the two of them trouble initially, they would find that before long there would be an influx of such young men and women. Not only would there be a supply, this movement would be encouraged by federal immigration policies, acceding to the demand by eastern hospitals for a resident staff working for a low salary.

As Gannon returned to the table, he observed that Matejus was presenting himself in that habit of folding his hands in front of his chin and letting the smoke from his cigarette drift slowly upward. This forced him either to narrow the slits of his eyes or to have an excuse to narrow them, producing an intimidating look. Gannon had always guessed that this was a practiced matter. He had to concede that it worked.

With all of these thoughts rumbling through his mind, he shifted to the immediate. "Well, this ought to carry us through to supper. Do you have the call?"

"Yes, I do. I'm covering A-4 also," responded Matejus. "Scott is having a birthday party for his kid tonight and asked me to cover. He said there was nothing going on anyhow."

"Well, let's shake hands on it for the time being. Not only will I keep you in mind, but I shall put you in the forefront. I do think we would make a good team. For the moment, let's finish up all the dictations and get ahead of the game."

Chapter 4

Gannon could just make out those same two voices talking together outside his room. The male nurse spoke first, "Yes, I know that he has been less restless since the left shoulder was put back in the joint. But still he seems to complain about the right side, even with the left side in a sling. He has had so much sedation over the last twenty-four hours he can barely speak."

"Could be. I noticed the same thing. When moving him up in bed, I avoided the left shoulder, but when I squeezed the right shoulder, he groaned. Do you suppose he has something going on there also?"

Through narrowed lids Gannon saw the two nurses part the curtains and enter his space. David's beard was still his dominant feature, but Gannon had come to recognize the beautiful brunette as someone with the same name as his own, Chris.

Moments later, Gannon was aware of being pulled around in his bed and having a square, cold, flat plate placed behind his right shoulder. What he could not see was the x-ray technician setting up the tube at an angle to get a straight shot of the right shoulder, although he certainly felt the plate being removed when the shot was over.

The voices of his two nurses returned, their conversation more animated than it had been. "Good gosh," said the voice now known as David. "The right shoulder is broken, with a loose fragment."

Chris whispered loudly, "Sure enough. He has been lying there for two days with bilateral shoulder injuries! And each time he was upset, we hit him with more Valium!"

Toward noon, a couple of young orthopedic surgeons whom Gannon had only known a short time came in, x-rays in hand. The shorter looked at Gannon and said, "You have a butterfly fragment loose over the head of the humorous on the right side. Both shoulder injuries resulted from the seizure you had in the emergency room. Did you know that bilateral shoulder injuries are associated with severe shoulder contractions at the time of convulsions associated with electrocution? That's my joke for the day." He chuckled a bit as he turned away toward the curtain, saying, "Just put another sling on him. I also will leave an order to take the shackles off his ankles."

Gannon watched, this time with relief, as nurse Chris returned with a syringe and shoved the needle into the hub of the IV. Once again, blessed blackness.

The figure opposite Gannon was a curly headed man probably in his late thirties. He was of short build, somewhat husky rather than slight, and had a smiling and affable manner. "Hello, and welcome aboard. I'm Sam McKee. My appointment book says that you're a young surgeon who wants to practice here. Is that right?" The man stuck out his hand and gripped Gannon in a two-handed, slightly sweaty grip. "I'm the administrator here."

"Yes," replied Gannon hesitantly, "I'm a new applicant. I think you know that one of your surgeons is in the latter days of a lethal illness. Based on this, one of the preachers in town thought I might come here and open a practice, as there would be work for me."

"So that's why you selected Waterford! We're kind of a poor town, and I think we're going to lose our major industry in a few years. It may be a tough go here."

"Honestly, I wanted to stay around Chicago. I think Chicago has many of the big city promises that my family would enjoy. I have three kids, and I like Illinois. I came to Rockford as a child, and I have never seen a crop failure in this region."

"Well, your reasoning is fundamentally correct. This is really a farming community, with a hundred-year agricultural history. You're right. There never has been a crop failure. This is the bread basket of the Midwest, and there's always plenty of rain. Where was your residency?"

"At the westside VA in Chicago. I finished a tour of duty in Korea in June of '52 and went straight there. It was a great experience. It was run by a dean's committee, you know. There were committees from Northwestern, the University of Illinois, and Michael Reese Hospital that ran the residency program. Cook County Hospital and the VA system have been the two most sought after residencies since the war."

"Well right now we're having an influx of new doctors, about a dozen, I believe. But you're the only general surgeon among them. Do you have a hook? That is, do you have some kind of subspecialty?"

Gannon leaned over and opened a large, thick briefcase. "I made a mistake a couple of years ago and had all my diplomas and documents framed. So I brought them in today, still in their frames. I thought it would be better for the credentials committee to have the originals in their own hands. That committee meets in a few minutes, right?"

"Yes, but we'll have a cup of coffee first. In your letter, you mentioned 'vascular surgery'. I'm not sure I know what that is. Is that a new field?"

"Yes, just since World War II. Prior to that time, surgery of the blood vessels was limited to the tying off of veins in the lower extremities, for varicose veins. But, with all the arterial injuries in World War II, systematic approaches to blood vessel repair of arteries came into being, and now there's a whole generation of surgeons doing arterial work everywhere. Actually, I'm in the second generation of such surgeons, the first group having started around 1949."

The administrator did seem genuinely interested. Gannon's information had been that hospital administrators were preoccupied with income and expenses and not in outcome of patient care. Perhaps his informants had been wrong, he thought.

The senior administrator pressed on. "Do you need anything special for diagnostic equipment? The chief of the X-ray Department thought you might be doing some special studies on the arteries and would need some diagnostic x-ray equipment. Was he right?"

"Well he's talking about x-ray studies called angiograms. This involves inserting large caliber needles in the blood vessels and injecting dye and taking x-ray pictures. No, at this time I wont need anything special for that. We have always used spinal needles for injecting the dye and just hand pressure on the syringe, and timing by counting on ordinary x-ray plates linked together. I would need a few instruments. They're made here in the Chicago area for most of the rest of the United States oddly enough, right over here in Wheaton. I don't think the cost would be more than two hundred and fifty dollars in order to do most blood vessel procedures."

"Well, that's a relief. But most likely there'll be improvement and advances in the technology, and I'm sure we will be looking at some big bucks down the line."

"I certainly hope so. I expect to be moving right along as the field progresses elsewhere. There is a cliché about the road of progress always being under construction. And I see evidence of construction around here; it looks like you're preparing to put up a new wing."

"Bricks and mortar," he said. "That's what I understand. I can get the building up and the beds in, but you fellows have to bring in the new ideas. You are introducing a whole new field of surgery to this community. But, remember that this town is very conservative, patients and physicians alike. You will have to get out there and sell this aggressive approach to arterial reconstruction. You'll have to show them some examples of what you can do, and nobody is going to send you any work that is not far gone or inevitably fatal under present circumstances."

Gannon stared at the ceiling and folded his fingers together on his chest. "I've been through that already at the VA. The medical residents, who control the patients with hardening of the arteries and diabetes, were very reluctant to have anything done about limb loss before the extremity turned black. My predecessors had to educate the residents to the idea of surgery for correction of hardening of the arteries. So I suppose I will have to do the same here."

"Now, before we go to the credentials committee meeting, I want to offer you a couple of suggestions. Remember, you come as a new doctor and that makes you a threat to the livelihood of the doctors who do the same kind of work. You may have expected to be welcomed with open arms, but that will not be the case. Don't be upset or nervous if the interviewers are cold or begin to pry into your life. They will most likely want to know whether you're going to take money out of their pockets or not. Try to get them to see that you can not only help the patients but help them too, and that you will be an economic help rather than an economic threat. That is, you will bring new patients to this institution. Does that make sense?"

Gannon stood up and began to button his jacket. "Thanks for the advice, Mr. McKee. I have had some coaching in this area of discussion and talked to some other young men in LaGrange on the west side of Chicago. They had an awful time when the new hospital opened, and the LaGrange establishment was challenged by quite a large group of doctors. I'll try and play myself down." In spite of trying to show a confident mien, Gannon recognized that he was approaching the hand-shaking ceremony with damp palms. He could not control his nervousness in situations like this.

"Two of the people on the committee are surgeons. One is a straightforward general surgeon who's been here about five years and is just now getting established. However, it's my impression that he is a kind fellow. I don't think you need to worry about him. The other is a woman surgeon with a lot of training in the east. In addition, she has family connections in the local community and has been highly successful since her beginning here seven years ago. Look out for her. She may be a little tough, because she thinks everybody should have the same kind of training she has or not work at all. Good luck. I'll take you across the hall to the library, where I'm sure they're already waiting." He took Gannon by the elbow and urged him toward the door.

McKee pushed him gently out into the hall saying, "Yes, the committee is there. That's about the only private place we have. From my point of view, your credentials look excellent, but our constitution provides that a credentials committee from your department must pass on them. Just stand on your own training and experience and don't let them buffalo you."

Gannon had heard about credentials committee hearings from other residents who had finished ahead of him and knew that they were very serious matters. Each new applicant was looked upon negatively. So if there was an excuse to delay his application or to refuse it completely, someone would certainly grab that possibility.

The library was dark and lined with musty old books. Gannon suspected that fresh air was not admitted into this room on many occasions, perhaps not more than once or twice a month. He noted immediately that the books were dust-covered and suspected that most of them had not been off the shelves since they had been put there. As he walked around the room to take his seat, he noticed that the editions of the textbooks were older than his own. Maybe this would give him a leg up.

McKee spoke first. "Dr. Gannon, this is the president of the staff, Dr. Browner. He does family practice and lots of obstetrics. Most of the committee are your peers from your prospective department. This is Dr. Penelope Bayard, and even in the VA forty miles away, I suspect you have heard of her, because of her extensive training. Next is Dr. Peterson, whose training was at the Mayo Clinic. Both are general surgeons. Dr. Adams practices urology and is a graduate of the Northwestern Medical school. I notice that you are also. Perhaps you can find some common ground. Obstetrics and gynecology are combined with the surgical department, so there is one gynecologist represented, Dr. Whiteside. The fifth member, Dr. Caesar, never attends meetings. But I have never seen him cast a 'no' vote against a new young man."

McKee shook hands cordially enough and closed the door behind him as he left. Browner spoke first. "Well, Dr. Gannon, we're having an influx of new physicians this month, about a dozen, I believe. I think this reflects the finishing of training programs for young men who were in the Korean War. Do you think so?"

"Yes, sir. That's exactly what this is. I looked at the list of new applicants myself. I see that there are a couple of internists beginning a practice, a gynecologist who is going it solo, another obstetrician who is going to Dr. Whiteside here, and a half-dozen others. So our class will be a large group, I gather."

Browner seemed cordial enough. "Yep. You have to slug it out together. As with most of us, you will develop a cross-referral among the young people in your age group, and the age of your patients will increase as you age yourself. As you can see, what little hair I have left is white. Your three decades on the stage will be over before you know it."

Gannon sensed hostility from only one person, this being the highly trained lady surgeon. She was not relaxed. Peterson was reserved, but the others seemed affable enough. Perhaps that was because he would not be in direct competition with any of the balance of this committee. He wondered about the fifth member, who apparently was so powerful that he could afford not to come to committee meetings and not be punished for his neglect.

Dr. Bayard spoke first. "We note that you have tissue flimsies of all your operative reports for your entire four years. That is very unusual. Why do you bring these?"

'"Well, I want to do a general surgeon's work. Surely today you will question my competency. And I think the only reasonable answer is to give you copies of my operative reports. In addition, I am trained in blood vessel surgery. Anything I say without supporting documentation could be regarded as suspect."

The committee members looked at one another without speaking. Finally Dr. Bayard spoke again. "Well, it's still unusual. I don't think we've ever had that before. We just got our first set of new Joint Commission Guidelines recently, and they hinted that such documentation would probably be asked for within a matter of years. I see by your record that you spent the last six months in vascular surgery at the VA. Can you tell us about that?"

Gannon smiled to himself. When he had selected that service for his final seniorship, he had felt singularly fortunate. He knew that his teachers would be a three-man partnership that was on the front end of the entire field, so he felt confident now in discussing procedures that were not even yet recorded by the insurance carriers as being valid and as being something for which they should pay. When he mentioned having done four mitral commissurotomies and having done the first abdominal aneurysm by a resident in the Chicago area, Bayard stirred in her seat for the first time. Whiteside leaned forward, obviously interested. He said, "So you're going to take our surgical department into a new arena? That will be very interesting. We have no one that does that kind of work. So, really, you have no competition in that area. You should be able to develop it without resistance."

This was a new idea for Gannon. Sam McKee was apparently right. The room was silent for awhile as the doctors passed his photo around. Whiteside spoke again, "You say you have all your diplomas and documents under glass, in that briefcase, right?"

"Yes, I stupidly put everything in frames, not realizing that anyone would ever want to see them again! But I can pass the documents around the group here, so that you can see they represent a real person! " He smiled as he said that, although his gorge was rising.

As the papers and pictures were being shuffled and passed from one to the other, there was that kind of silence in the room designed to inform the applicant that he was absolutely at their disposition and that a majority negative vote would mean he would have to fight to gain a position on the staff. This was an "open staff" hospital, not affiliated with any university, and therefore not controlled by the need for a faculty appointment. Gannon knew that, in general, a physician who was credentialed to work in the community hospital really could not be turned down by a hospital staff. However, they could try, and then he would have to go through the courts to gain his position. All of these things were going through his mind in this silent room.

The staff president then turned to him as he pushed on the last item of credentialing. "Now, Dr. Gannon, I'm sure you realize that you will be in a probationary period here for a year or two. The first year will be very restrictive, in the same sense that you will have to keep Dr. Peterson here informed of all major cases that you are doing or going to do. He may or may not choose to observe what you are doing, or to actually scrub in, for direct observation. Dr. Peterson is your sponsor, and will write a letter to the audit committee on a quarterly basis keeping that committee informed of your goings and comings." He looked meaningfully at Penelope Bayard and asked, "Any other questions or comments?"

Gannon was greatly relieved that the lady surgeon was not going to be approving his cases. The room was silent. A couple of members obviously were anxious to leave and get on with other things and rose to shake his hand. It was notable to Gannon that the two general surgeons just turned and left, no handshake. Browner made one last comment. "Now watch it. Don't be apprehensive about asking your two peers here in consultation. It will be reassuring to your patients and to them that you are a straight man. And don't wait until you're in trouble to call them in consultation. One piece of advice is, when you think of asking for help, go get it. It will stand you in good stead throughout your career. I hope it is a long one and a good one." He stuck out his hand for a final shake, and they left the room together.

Chapter 5

Dreams, dreams, and more dreams. Flashing lights, then black oblivion. Gannon peered through narrowed lids. He must be careful not to move or to let the nurses know he was awake, or they would put him down again.

Slowly his vision came into focus. No nurse was present. Instead, his bed rails were surrounded by at least ten people. The older woman was—?—Helene, his wife. Short and overweight, but still pretty enough. He had not screwed her in years, because he could not get it up anymore. How had that happened? The rest of these people were his six kids, plus three daughters-in-law, all grown. Big family—but why were they all here?

"I caught him standing by the bedside yesterday," came a voice. *Son David, not nurse David*, thought Gannon. "Said he had to make a phone call, that he was late for some lunch. He repeated the first three numbers over again and again—882-882—but couldn't seem to get the last four digits. He was weaving around. We hauled him back into bed, then the nurse hit him with Valium."

Gannon opened his eyes fully and spoke. "Thanks for coming, everybody. But why am I here? What happened to me?"

As a group, all ten leaned in to touch his body—a connection.

As Gannon stretched and brushed his hand through his hair to wake himself he looked at the bedside clock. After squinting, he could make out 3:30 A.M. *Good gosh*, he thought, *why would any dumb cluck be out on the road at this hour in this weather and crack himself up?* He quickly splashed some water on his face and soaped his hands, pulling on his shirt and pants. He was not going to wear a tie at this hour. He could hear the wind whistling beneath the front door, a sign that usually indicated very heavy weather. This was confirmed when he lifted the garage door and saw at least eight inches of fresh snow on the ground; his drive was plugged with wind-blown drifts.

Relying on a learned technique for getting out of his own unplowed driveway, he revved the engine and backed rapidly out of the garage into the street, busting drifts so that he could get onto the pavement. He grinned at his own success as he put the car into motion toward the highway, a half mile away. *It could be worse*, he thought.

The hospital parking lot was also heavily drifted, so he parked off on the side not far from the emergency room door and slogged up to the entrance, pressing the button that would call the night supervisor. She was quite close, hovering near because of the nature of the patient's injuries. Having been let in and after brushing off the accumulated snow, Gannon quickly examined the patient, a man with dried and caked blood distributed over his face and scalp whom he guessed could be about forty-five years old. He was unconscious. In addition to the obvious partially avulsed scalp, the patient was in marked respiratory distress. His body was heaving with every rasping breath, his abdomen lurching up and down in a rocking boat fashion as the examination proceeded.

The night supervisor spoke up. "His respirations are about fifty-eight per minute, with a pulse of 132 and a blood pressure of 86. The best we know is that he was driving a medium-sized truck when he was hit broadside by a passenger car. There were a man and woman in the other car, but they were taken to St. Benedict's hospital We drew this poor devil"

Poor is right, thought Gannon. *I'll bet he has no insurance and no job.* His clothes, which were bloodied and covered with gravel and dirt marks, had been cut off and pushed off on the side, but they showed very little evidence of prosperity on the part of their owner. As Gannon surveyed and examined the patient, several things became readily apparent. The scalp laceration was full thickness, went from ear to ear, and the scalp had actually been detached from the underlying calvarium. He found no defect in the spine of the neck, but the patient groaned as he palpated the bony part of that structure. *I wonder what's going on there?* he asked himself. He followed that thought with another, wondering what the extent of the obvious chest injury would be. They would have to have some x-ray studies, but he was certain that that process would be a risk in itself. While the abdomen was rocking back and forth, there were a few bowel sounds present, suggesting an intact intestine. There was some questionable tenderness in the left upper quadrant, but the patient was not distended. There was no active bleeding from the external wounds, which was consistent with the low level of blood pressure. A knee had a gaping wound in it, from which protruded a couple of spicules of bone.

"Well, has the x-ray tech come in yet? Or does she live way over in Wauconda somewhere?"

An overly sweet voice replied, "I'm right behind you, doctor. I was here ahead of you. What do you want me to take and how shall I go about it?"

Gannon flushed, "Well, whatever's going on is pretty obvious. Let's stick with portable films right here in the ER and see what we can learn. Do the neck first, so I know how freely we can manipulate the spine during the other studies."

Gannon held the first x-ray against the side of the neck and then said, "The lateral view may be enough for the neck. If it's broken, then we'll know we have to put in the sugar tongs before doing any more manipulation."

The night supervisor began to flutter about. Gannon knew she was upset about his doing so much in the emergency room. So he looked straight at her and said, "If it's broken, we'll do as I said for the reason I said. It doesn't matter what else is wrong with him. We can't correct anything else until we solve the neck. Meantime, why don't you go up to the OR and find a local set for me, plus the tongs, so I can set them in the skull if we have to."

Waterford did not yet have a neurosurgeon. Gannon knew that he was on thin ice, applying traction for a cervical spine fracture, but for two years now, he and the other general surgeons had been handling neurosurgical problems by telephone to Chicago, so no new ground was being broken. Just then the technician returned with the dripping wet film, which Gannon turned toward the ceiling light for viewing. Sure enough, the fourth cervical vertebra had slid forward on the fifth, and the curvature of correct amount was distorted by that amount. He muttered to himself, "Damn!" The night nurse returned with a local anesthesia set, scalpel, suture material, and a caliperlike device about the size of an adult's head, bearing two pointed arms and looking like a set of small ice tongs.

"I don't think we have to worry much. This must be a pretty stable fracture. He's been handled by the two guys from the ambulance and hasn't been paralyzed yet! That's sure the acid test for the stable spine fracture!

"We can forget the scalp laceration for the time being and probably fix that when everything else is done. I'm sure he has something going on in the chest." Rapidly he injected local anesthesia into the scalp adjacent to and behind the ear lobes. This was followed by a short incision in each anesthesia area. He picked up the tongs and, having estimated the width of the skull inserted the points directly into the bone, turning the hand ratchet down in order to get a good bite into the skull. Meantime, the x-ray technician reappeared with a thin line of rope about six feet long, along with a weight holder and three pounds of metal weights to attach. Quickly Gannon fashioned a traction system out of these parts, tying the rope to the end of the sugar tongs and passing it over a pulley attached to the table in order to stabilize and hold the neck while other manipulations were done.

"Do you think we can get him up to forty-five degrees for a good semi-upright chest x-ray?" he asked the technician.

"We'll need a couple more people in order to lift his chest to get the film behind him. Can you handle that, Miss Conway?" she asked.

The night supervisor disappeared up the elevator and soon returned with an orderly and another nurse. Then awkwardly but carefully they simultaneously lifted a space through which the x-ray plate could be passed.

The findings on the wet film were worse than Gannon anticipated. The stomach gas bubble was above the diaphragm and in the chest, establishing the diagnosis of a rupture of the diaphragm with migration of abdominal organs into the left chest. Several associated rib fractures were not relevant. It also occurred to him that not only was this going to be a difficult surgical problem because of positioning and the already immobilized broken neck, but that the greatest risk was going to be taken by the anesthesiologist as new in town as he was. "Call Finney right now so I can explain to him what the problem is, and he can think about it as he comes across town."

He resumed. "We'll just wrap the leg in some sterile gauze for the time being. Since we've got a good crew here, let's take him up to the operating room just as he is. We'll do the surgery on the gurney without any more movement than necessary." With plenty of help, the trip to the elevator and up to the operating room was not difficult. While the other procedures had been going on, the laboratory technicians had drawn samples and returned with two bottles of cross-matched blood, and the night supervisor had started a large caliber needle in the forearm. As expected, the red blood count was about half normal so transfusion was begun as soon as they were in the operating room.

Just then the anesthesiologist, Finney, appeared still wearing the upper half of his nightshirt. Somehow, at night, he always looked blowzy and unkempt. "Well,

Chuck, we have to do a combined chest and abdomen incision in order to fix what looks like a ruptured diaphragm. Do you think you can induce him safely with the Crutchfield tongs in place? I didn't know what else to do."

"Looks good to me. I don't see that we have a lot of choice. You going to drag somebody in to take care of the leg?"

"How about Lee? He's been here about as long as we have. He's not afraid. We can bring him in when we're closing the chest and he can take care of the leg without having to come in and stand around waiting for us."

Gannon's assessment of the anesthesia problem and the chest injury was correct. But the anesthesiologist possessed great skill and manipulated the endotracheal tube into position with hardly a flutter or a movement of the tongs and neck.

His own incision was L-shaped, being well down in the left armpit, on top of the ninth rib, and then carried directly vertically onto the abdominal wall for a distance of about six inches. Upon entering the chest the first organ encountered was the spleen and behind that lay the stomach and a couple of loops of small intestine. He could not hide his elation that the diagnosis was correct. The trick now was to put the abdominal organs below the diaphragm and to keep them there without further injury, particularly to the spleen, which would have to be removed were it lacerated. So he extended the wound into the abdomen and then carefully applied hand traction to the abdominal organs and brought them below the diaphragm. As the collapsed lung expanded, the patient's general condition immediately improved. At the head of the table, Finney heaved a sigh of relief. "We've got him now. I can bag him easily. That will bring his pulse down and drive his blood pressure up as we get control and get some blood in him."

The repair of the diaphragm was not difficult, accomplished by using a heavy silk suture and running it over and over, back and forth, to close the defect. Said Gannon, "We'll set a chest tube on this side to keep the lung expanded. I'll drain the abdomen. Miss Conway, could you put a call in to Dr. Lee and tell him about his leg so that he can come in and do whatever is necessary?"

The team finished in silence, each secretly feeling very good about what had been accomplished during the night in this small community hospital. For the first time, Gannon noticed that the left hand of the patient had only three fingers.

"Did someone say that this guy was a piano player and that he was driving home from work in the snow when he got hurt? I wonder how a guy can play piano when he only has three fingers on his bass hand? If he makes it maybe he can show us sometime."

When Gannon stepped out into the parking lot, a bright orange sun was just coming up. The snow had stopped, and the drifts were glistening and sparkling in the early light. *Hope the damn car starts,* he thought. *Even if it doesn't, I think we can chalk this one up. Wonder if he has any family? Certainly hope somebody has turned up a relative or two.* He turned the collar of his coat up around his ears and tromped on the starter. After a little grinding, it kicked off, and he heaved a sigh of relief. He hoped the old bucket would make it through the winter. Truly, the three-fingered musician was not going to help with any new car payments.

Driving home through the unplowed streets, he reflected on his performance this night. It had been stellar, both diagnostically and therapeutically. His mother would have been happy, as she had always enjoyed seeing him perform. A distant memory was tap dancing before a group of kindergarten mothers. She had entered him in a "declamatory contest" when he was six. At age seven, when there was barely enough food in the house, she had bought him a fiddle. When he was ten, she persuaded his father to put him in his pulpit as a guest preacher. At age fourteen, she had placed him in a private speech school at a time when they were only a little more prosperous. All this was a long time ago.

Chapter 6

"Do you want to shave yourself this morning?" asked nurse David, opening the mirror on Gannon's bedside table. "Maybe you should take a look first."

Gannon grunted softly at what he saw: a sixty-five year old man with a deeply wrinkled face and white hair. "I've had white hair for twenty-five years, but it is thinner now." An iron-gray stubble of several days growth covered his cheeks and chin, the latter receding in profile and thought by him since childhood as evidence of some deep-seated weakness. He had thick lips, with everted vermilion borders, an inherited characteristic exhibited by all his sons. His ears were a little too prominent. Thick eyebrows frequently needed trimming.

Skinny and bony legs protruded beyond his sheets. His left forearm was scarred by an ugly ten-year-old skin graft. He had been holding his weight below 200 pounds, suspended on a six-foot frame. Altogether not too bad, he thought.

"David, why am I in ICU? Nobody tells me anything. I am always being sedated." Gingerly, he drew his sheeting up to his chin, wincing at the shoulder movement.

"I think it's time someone brought you up to date, Doctor. Do you remember that you do a weekly radio show? Do you remember anything about the last one?"

Gannon thought a little and strained for memory. "I remember my show, but honestly, no, I can't recall the last one. I remember sitting down with three guests. Two were guys who had open heart surgery several years ago and belonged to a heart club, and the third guest was an RN who runs the rehabilitation unit at the hospital. But I don't remember the program at all. Did it ever take place?"

David's voice came again. "It sure did. Just at the end of the program, you put your head down on the desk and slid off onto the floor. For the next hour or so, it was touch and go. The nurse did CPR right there on the floor, and then the paramedics came. They took you to the emergency department, where you were intubated. Sometime during that interval you had a major seizure lasting five minutes. Most likely, that's when you injured your shoulders. "

"I'm going to trust you to do the shaving, David," said Gannon. "It simply hurts too much to move my shoulders."

When his nurse had finished this menial but difficult job, Gannon drifted off into a natural sleep, and once more his mind's eye focused on an element of history.

The surgeons' lounge was empty, except for himself. Gannon was waiting to do an afternoon case, it being traditionally the lot of the junior staff surgeons to be placed at the end of the surgical schedule. The more choice morning times were left for senior surgeons. He already had been waiting an hour for the nurses to say, "You may scrub."

Use of the word *"lounge"* was certainly an overstatement, he thought. The lamp tables were littered with half-empty coffee cups, partially consumed cigarettes floating in the beverages. The furniture was stained with years of usage, the brown upholstery frayed at the corners, in a style that would have been described as "modern" in the forties. The smell of surgeons' shoes oozed out of the locker room and tempered the acrid tobacco scent ground into the carpet. Altogether depressing, he thought.

"Dr. Gannon?" came a nurse's voice from the door. "Would you come into room four please? Dr. Caesar is doing a case and would like your help."

Caesar? Help him? he thought. This was the guy so self-assured that he need not attend required meetings! Why would he say he needed help in an orthopedic case? Gannon stuck his head through the door into operating room four anyhow. Caesar was waiting for him, hands folded on the field.

"Come on in and get your feet wet," he said. "Scrub up and put some gloves on. Be thinking about how to remove a tumor from the groin, with the major vessels wrapped around it."

Gannon tied his mask, tucked his OR shirt into his pants, and picked up a scrub brush. His thoughts began to organize themselves. *Get control of the vessels above the groin, on the pelvis side,* he thought. *Put control tapes below the tumor on the thigh side, then simply remove the tumor. This was the kind of problem that was difficult for others, but a cinch for himself. He knew how to dissect major arteries—it was that simple.*

The reality of the circumstances turned out to be more than he had anticipated. The tumor was malignant, low grade, but as large as a California navel orange. The major artery and vein, side by side, were embedded in the wall of the tumor mass, pushed forward by the growth and lying parallel to the femoral nerve, which supplied all the muscles of the thigh.

These structures of greatest concern were bent upward over the mass. His problem was to separate the vessels from the tumor, without major hemorrhage from the vessels or damage to that huge nerve accompanying them and without destroying the blood supply to the rest of the leg. Slowly and tediously he worked, teasing the vessels away from the tumor, placing shoestring tapes at strategic locations above and below the mass, then finally applying the vascular clamps to the vessels directly and shutting off all the blood flow. Then, with a bloodless field, it was but a matter of cutting the tumor away.

Throughout the entire time, Caesar made no comments. He had been described to Gannon by others as a "crusty" man, abrasive and arrogant, but brilliant and creative. He was Waterford's only claim to international recognition. He grunted a couple of times during the two hour dissection but served very capably in his adopted role of first assistant; he kept good exposure and a clean field.

During wound closure, Caesar described the circumstances. The patient, about sixty, had been an employee at the hospital for many years. She had several daughters. The youngest daughter was her principal companion and seemed to have an extraordinary relationship with the mother. "There probably will be a lot of hand wringing and teeth-gnashing by this collection of daughters. They are first generation 'old world' people and hold doctors in both veneration and suspicion," said Caesar, as they went toward the doctors' lounge. "Don't let them upset you. After all, we were in there all afternoon, and they have been waiting!"·

At that, Caesar underestimated the reaction of the family. There was much weeping and fawning over the two surgeons, even though Gannon was a stranger. Returning to the locker room, Caesar looked at Gannon quizzically. "You know," he said, "I have been told by others that you are not a very good surgeon. But you did fine today! That was a university type case, and we took care of it right here. You did a good job, kid. You will bear watching."

No doubt it is a good thing to have the approval of Dr. Caesar, thought Gannon. He could use the endorsement. Gannon's practice was not growing by leaps and bounds.

Damn! thought Gannon, not another night case from the emergency room! Fumbling around in the dark, he knocked the telephone off the nightstand with a single, loud clang. A voice could then be heard coming from the earpiece, "Hello? Hello? Is Dr. Gannon there? Dr. Gannon?"

"Answer it for God's sake, Chris. I'm trying to sleep," came a drowsy voice from next to him in bed. "They never pay you anyhow."

Gannon swung his feet over the bedside and collected the speaking end of the telephone, "Yes? Dr. Gannon."

"This is Maggie DeLaney, from the hospital. Dr. Freudin is in the middle of a case involving a child. He says the artery to the forearm is damaged. It's a fracture case, open. Can you come in and help him?"

Dr. Freudin was Caesar's partner in orthopedics. This was definitely a command performance. He flicked on the table light and glanced at the clock: 2:00 A.M. he noted. The usual time—his bed partner rolled over, groaning, and brushing her hair from her face. "Do you have to go? I'll make some fresh coffee while you dress. Just don't wake the kids." She slid out of bed and padded toward the kitchen. *Ever loyal Helene*, he thought. How much could a woman be expected to give? She had borne him three children by the age of twenty-four, living in an attic on the north side of Chicago. He had been one of the first students to graduate with children from Northwestern Medical School.

He gulped down the coffee and kissed his wife, throwing on a topcoat. He never wore a hat; it was a kind of symbol with him. There was a ring visible around a full moon as he found his way through the drifts to the hospital lot, not yet plowed.

"What's the deal?" he asked DeLaney while at the scrub sink.

"The youngster is about ten," answered Maggie. "A little girl. She fell while skating on a pond tonight. She broke the long bone just above the elbow. He has the joint open. There is no pulse in the arm, and the hand is cold and blue. He thinks the artery is damaged. I already have the vascular instruments out."

Marvelous Maggie, he thought. Always thinking ahead. *Not only was she right, she was prepared.* "Maggie, can you call someone else in to circulate in the room? I want you to help me. We've done several cases together now, and you're good— really, the best! Please scrub in!"

"I'll ask the switchboard operator to find someone to circulate." Clearly she was pleased. They were striking a positive note together.

Dr. Freudin already had a wide exposure of the elbow joint, and the problem was obvious. The major artery to the forearm, with its accompanying vein, was stretched across the hypotenuse of the triangle formed by the upper arm bone and its large, loose fragment making up the joint. Dr. Freudin was a much taller man than his partner, Caesar, and was working with the table elevated to his own chest height.

"Dr. Gannon," he said, speaking as Gannon was being gowned and gloved, "the pulse in the artery stops right here, at this blue spot. It was stuck against a bony spicule from the lower fragment; stretched right over it. Maybe the arterial lining was knocked loose and clotted off the vessel"

Gannon felt the vessel, only three millimeters wide in this child. "Maggie," he said. "Get up a needle and tubing with some dye. I'II do an angiogram for the record. If we don't fix this, she has a good chance of losing the arm. Dr. Freudin, why don't you stabilize the fracture first, with a plate or something, then I'll graft the artery as a final move, so we don't mess everything up fixing the bone."

The two men gazed at one another over their masks. "Sure," said Dr. Freudin. Both were aware that command of the operation was changing, from the older to the younger surgeon and that there was a great deal of liability being shifted around. Limb loss was a glaring deficiency in a court room. Dr. Freudin picked up a hand drill and began to make holes for screws to hold a metal plate in place.

Plating the fracture site took only a few moments. Then Gannon inserted a needle above the obstruction site in the vessel and injected a radio-opaque dye while an x-ray was taken. A neat picture of the obstruction was visualized.

With some doubt in his voice, Dr. Freudin asked, "How do you propose to fix this? Looks kind of tough to me!

Gannon isolated the arterial segment between tiny arterial clamps then opened the vessel. Dr. Freudin was correct; the spicule of bone from the fracture had cracked off and inverted the very thin lining of the vessel with total obstruction. "The intima of the vessel is too ragged to tack down," Gannon said. "We'll simply remove the piece. I'll take a similar piece from the vein next to it and use it as a graft between the arterial ends. It should work like a charm."

And he was right. Having run the two tiny suture lines, he released the clamps, and a pulsating flow was reestablished. Tying off the vein ends was a negligible offense. When the wound was closed and a plaster cast applied, Dr. Freudin turned to him and said, "My partner, Caesar, said you would bear watching. He was right." He dropped his mask and stuck out his hand.

As he turned his car onto Liberty Street heading toward home, he became aware of the first stirrings of an erection. He had noticed before that completion of a really good case created that kind of response. His sex education had begun when he was five, when he and her brother peered at Marian through a knothole in an outdoor toilet. Then, the same girl, somewhat older, stripped him down and lay on him in her parents' bedroom. When Verna treated him similarly on a rubber crib sheet in the family doghouse, a couple of years later, he then knew how he was expected to perform. At his new job as church janitor, firing up the boiler at 3:00 A.M. one winter's night, he found himself with a deep inner urge to manipulate himself and the resultant first ejaculation sent him flying into the chancel to kneel and beg forgiveness for his sin.

His first serious kiss had come in the back of a Model A Ford from a girl four years his senior. But the resultant lightning bolt was nothing along side the thunder clap he experienced when he first put his hand inside Helene's brassiere at Wilmette Harbor. Relief came when Helene learned that only a little aggressive handwork inside his trousers would result in orgasm. Thusly did they, and most others of the same generation, preserve their virginity. Neither could remember the events of their wedding night.

It was just after first light when Gannon turned onto his house lane. The plows had been through. Helene was frying bacon and eggs when he opened the kitchen door. She turned to him and asked, "How'd it go?"

"Terrific—it was terrific—I did a really good job." Swiftly he put his hands beneath her pajama top and began to caress both nipples. "How about it? We've been talking about a second group of kids. Shall we begin? Right now?"

She smiled and unzipped his pants. "Sure, why not? You're certainly ready. A good case will do it every time!" She took him by the hand and led him to their bedroom.

"I know exactly why you are having trouble getting started," said Mr. Olson. "You are a young stuffed shirt who is too proud to write enough prescriptions!"

The man sitting opposite Gannon at his desk was clad in the classic short white laboratory jacket of the pharmacist. His name was Henry Olson, and he and Gannon had struck up an acquaintance through the church which they both attended. "If you wrote more prescriptions, then the word would get out among the pharmacists in the drugstores in town, and they would send you patients. That is how it works. A few refills from pharmacists, a few from hospital nurses; all these things help. And I hear that you're not very sociable either." The druggist leaned back in his chair and folded his arms across his chest, looking at Gannon through narrowed lids.

"I see what you mean, Henry. I am a 'therapeutic nihilist.' I don't use much medicine, even when there seems to be a reason for it. Eighty percent of patients will get well whether treated or not!"

"I'm just interested in your future. I'm at the end of my career, and I see what you are suggesting. It is not cheating to order medicines that are not of a particular help to the patient. They spend millions on useless over-the-counter-nostrums. It's just good business, for both you and me."

Gannon flushed pink and fidgeted in his chair, embarrassed. "But we're not in the business of medicine; we're in the profession of medicine. I don't really feel that I should take advantage of people just because I have knowledge and can play on their fears."

"So you are another of those idealists, huh? Why don't guys like you wake up before it is too late? There's a little black magic and smoke and mirrors in medicine. Some people refer to that as an 'art' of medicine. And whether you want to or not, you have to get out there and sell yourself. A man shaking a gourd can make a living in medicine! If you are invited to join a bridge group, you have to go. The women will lap it up. You are not playing the game!"

Gannon stood and walked around the tiny room. He had been pleased to know Mr. Olson because he ran what some would call a "legitimate" pharmacy. He only filled prescriptions. All other drug stores sold toothpaste, hair products, and the like, or anything related to the care of the body. But Olson seemed "pure." Gannon liked that. Olson leaned forward with his elbows on his desk, jabbing the air. "I know what you should do, and you should do it today! Dr. Wameke has his office just upstairs. He is quite successful mostly because he was ineligible for World War II. But he knows how to sell himself and writes a lot of prescriptions! You should go upstairs this afternoon, just about closing time, and introduce yourself. I have not heard him mention you at all. And you have been here three years! He is sixty years old, and the only surgery he ever learned he did by observing and helping here in town. He had no specialty training at all. Probably he sends a lot of surgery into Chicago."

Gannon thought a little. "Well—I suppose I could. Do you think that is ethical? All I ever did was put the usual one-inch announcement in the paper for seven days. I understood that that was all one could do when opening an office."

"Look! You have a very special training in a very limited and new field. You have to get out there and sell it! Has anyone at the hospital asked you to present any papers before meetings? Do you have any slides or things like that from your residency that you could show?" He reached for his telephone. "I'm going to call Dr. Wameke right now. Then you just run upstairs and introduce yourself. I'll grease the skids."

Gannon shook hands with his new friend and said, "Thanks for the advice. It seems too simple. Maybe I'll make myself known to the general public by doing civic work, such as in our church and with the Boy Scouts. I was never any good at bridge, believe me."

Olson added, "Remember, now—write more prescriptions. It won't hurt you a bit."

The stairs to Wameke's office were steep and narrow. As he entered the physician's waiting room the nurse and secretary were slipping their coats on, ready to leave. One of them said, "Don't sit down, Dr. Gannon. Dr. Wameke said to send you right in. His office is around the corner to the left." Both of the women waved goodbye as the door clicked behind them

Gannon edged down the short corridor hesitantly, uncertain as to what to expect after Olson's phone call. When he stepped into the doctor's office, the latter was seated at a large roll-top desk, writing. The setting was that of a classic Norman Rockwell magazine cover. The physician looked his age, with sparse gray hair, and wore a light gray laboratory coat. His uniform was completed with a white shirt, blue serge pants, and a tie. On the wall were framed diplomas, a picture of a graduating class, and a narcotic license. A white, enameled, glassed-in instrument case sprawled its four legs in one corner of the room The space smelled of alcohol and was painted stark white. Dr. Wameke looked up from his desk, "Mr. Olson just called me. I guess you were visiting him. Were you feeling sorry for yourself, because you have not been getting any work?"

"Yes, I really thought I had paid my dues after all that time and specialty training, but unless I get some work pretty soon, I will forget everything I ever knew." He said this as he smiled and stuck out his hand to shake that of the older physician.

"Well, honestly, Gannon, none of us can figure out why you came to this town anyway. We don't need specialists. We all do our own surgery. Anything big, we send to Chicago. Truly, whatever the surgeon in Chicago charges, I get half in the mail a few days later. Under those circumstances why should I send work to you?"

Gannon was surprised at such candor. This was frank fee-splitting, anathema to the American College of Surgeons, and the doctor did not appear to be embarrassed about it at all. It seemed to be the way things were done.

"I suppose you are one of these guys who won't send any money to the referring doctor, am I right about that? Penelope Bayard had that idea, at first, too. So all she ever got were chest surgery cases sent by the tuberculosis sanitarium. Personally, I don't see any sense in your staying here and continuing to bang your head against a wall. You should leave town, and you will be way ahead, in the long run."

At first Gannon was surprised by the frankness, then stunned by being told to "leave town." Apparently he had been stupid to have assumed that he would be welcomed to the community cordially. Just as he had recognized at his credential interview that he was somewhat of an economic threat to the two other surgeons, now he realized that the family practitioners were not too happy about his coming, either. He had never expected to be told so in such a frontal fashion.

He tried another tack. "But Dr. Wameke, I have something special to offer. I operate on people's blood vessels, specifically their arteries. There have to be all kinds of problems like that in this community. Probably most of them never diagnosed until late in the disease."

"Well, you are an upstart all right. You think we cannot diagnose circulatory problems in the legs? I've been operating on varicose veins for years."

"That's exactly my point, Dr. Wameke," said Gannon. "Many circulatory disturbances are on the arterial side, not on the venous side. I can help you, both diagnostically and therapeutically. I'm not going to steal any of your patients; nobody else does this work! I think I have something to offer to the community, including the doctors."

"Well, young fella, this conversation is over. I will tell you today that I am not going to ever refer you any patients and that most of the other guys won't either. Why don't we just shake hands and call it a day."

In disbelief, Gannon stood and grasped the offered hand. *What a contradiction! This old guy tells me that he won't send me any work and then expects his hand to be shaken at the end of the interview.* As he let himself out the door, he thought how merciful it was that Dr. Wameke was not on the credentials committee. He would never have been allowed out of the starting block.

Turning east on Chicago Street, Gannon 's mind turned again to his decision to become a surgeon. There was no doubt at all that he was greatly influenced by two events occurring in the summer of his tenth year.

Wilma was twelve, short and chunky, structured like her parents and usually dressed in white socks and black patent leather shoes beneath a blue, flowered dress with a high belt-line and a high neckline. Her father was a station agent and owner of the local Chevrolet franchise. Wilma was allowed to roller skate and play marbles or pick up kittenball but was strictly forbidden to participate in vigorous, competitive games.

No one explained to Gannon why these restrictions were in place. But one summer's night she simply died in bed. At the funeral in the crowded family living room Gannon was seated in the front row, his face a few inches from the small, white casket. He overheard the adults whispering about "a hole in her heart. " The only thing more devastating was the ride to the cemetery in the care of his friend, the undertaker, when he was seated alone in the huge rear seat next to floral arrangements, his arm dangling through a soft, velvet hand-hold. Wilma, *Wilma, Wilma, where are you now?* Why could nobody fix a hole? It should have been simple. He wept unendingly.

Dickey was also twelve, but possessed the stature of an eight-year old. His tiny figure was further marred by a protruding breast bone which no buttoned, white shirt could disguise, hence the term "pigeonbreast." What other defects were covered by that deformed sternum was a frequent subject of on by gossips in this population of 400. His slateblue facial color was exaggerated each time he tried to keep up with his friends. One sunny, August afternoon, he simply lay down and died.

He was laid out in a tiny, white casket, placed in front of the family fireplace. Again, Chris Gannon's father was charged with explaining to the community why this death was really not unfair in the eyes of the Lord. Unfair or not, Gannon, riding a second time in the flower car, was certain that it was unnecessary, that there should be a solution. Had he known then that one day he really could help in developing answers to these problems, his decision to become a surgeon would have come more easily.

Chapter 7

"They won't take my side rails down, Helene. Am I really so far out of it?"

Gannon felt his wife's fingers tighten around his. "Chris, you cannot dwell so much on this. You're out of the shackles; the slings are holding your shoulders all right. They are talking about transferring you out of ICU tomorrow."

Gannon opened his eyes, and tears welled up as he sobbed, uncontrollably "H-H-Helene, how could this happen? I'm only sixty-five. T-Thank G-God this happened a week after my birthday! Medicare should pay for most of the bill. M-my h-heavens, it's $2,000 per day in here! And everything hurts—all the time!"

Helene leaned forward, her body scent mixed with a faint cologne. He wanted to embrace her but could only wipe his tears in frustration.

"Hush, Chris. The kids have taken this beautifully. You know--no, you probably don't know—that at noon the first day we were told you were not going to make it; then an hour later we were told that you would survive. We were on a roller coaster. We are grateful that you were rejected; not even God wanted you!"

He smiled at her little joke and blew his nose.

"Go to sleep," whispered his wife.

By Easter of 1960 Gannon and his family were fitting right into the community. Their little group of five were marching almost in lock step through Cub Scouts, YMCA swim teams, skating contests, and Little League. Gannon himself took over the Cub Pack in their local grade school, quadrupling the membership, becoming a Scouting fanatic, and being selected to the Scout board. He was so self-righteous that he began to teach Church School to adults, becoming more and more conforming and more and more rigid.

On this beautiful warm, sunny Sunday, Gannon was driving his pregnant wife and three children home from church, packed into a little English TR-3, the first purchase hinting at success. The Golden Age of the Eisenhower years was closing out, and the approaching youthful rebellion was just a faint distant rumble on college campuses. Gannon was feeling good about himself; he had become a citizen of the community. He felt like Galsworthy's "Man of Property."

A blue and white sedan, identified by a painted seal on the door as being "Fox County Sheriffs Police," was parked in front of their home. A burly, middle-aged man in a light blue uniform was nailing an envelope to their back door.

Gannon shouted from the street, "Hey, what's up? Who are you? Do you have the right address?"

The visitor was fiddling with the envelope, pulling out its contents. "You by any chance Doc Gannon? I have a summons for Doctor Gannon."

Gannon jumped out of the little car. "Is this a traffic matter, or what? I can't think of anything I've done wrong. I have no tickets."

"No, Doc. This is more serious than that. I wouldn't be here on Easter Sunday if it weren't that this was a good day to catch people coming home from church. You remember a family named Dobnik? They're madder than hell at you." He handed Gannon the envelope. "Sign here! I've got a dozen of these to serve today yet!"

Agitated and shaking, Gannon turned to his wife. "Do you remember my telling you about a difficult case a year or so ago, the lady with the groin tumor that Dr. Caesar asked me to help him with? Name was Dobnik. She was the one with the extremely dependent daughter. They showered me with flattery, called me a "savior." I lost track of her a year ago; Caesar was seeing her, I suppose. Let's see what's up; give the envelope back. Go on inside, kids," he said, a little too brusquely. The chin of his twelve-year-old daughter began to quiver, as though she was going to cry.

Gannon read the process, as Helene busied herself with the Easter ham and the kids dutifully set the table. The phrase "did neglectfully and carelessly" leaped off each page as he flipped through the accusations, line by line, repetition by repetition. He was becoming nauseated, alternately feeling hot and cold, dry then sweaty. He could not defend himself to his family, because he did not want them to know of the accusations.

Why? Why? Why? What a terrible blow, just as he was getting started professionally. He had been careless in a couple of ways. The patient and her large collection of daughters, whose office visits had been memorable for their crowding together into the examining room, had stopped quarterly follow-up checks at one year; he had not seen them for a long time. His carelessness was not in patient care but in failing to send a certified letter, requesting that she return for a cancer checkup. He deduced from the subpoena that she had a recurrence of cancer and that the lawsuit was filed because she was dying. Who was caring for her? Was that doctor the reason for the lawsuit? He looked to see if Caesar was listed as a defendant: he was not.

He carried these thoughts to Easter dinner, picking his way through a salad, mashed potatoes, and sliced ham. But he could not enjoy it. Something was deep in his mind, some recent memory, that wanted to surface. There was a key in there somewhere, but he said nothing to the other four at the table.

His youngsters, as was usual on Sunday at 1:00 P.M., were preoccupied with "Bugs Bunny" on the television. They tittered and giggled and played with their food, bending around the table to see the antics more clearly.

Then, he remembered a recent incident. His office and that of Penelope Bayard were on opposite sides of the same parking lot. One evening, turning the key in his auto lock, he heard a gaggle of women's voices. He turned toward the sound and saw Mrs. Dobnik and her daughters standing in the doorway to Dr. Bayard's office, all crying and gesturing toward Gannon. Therein lay the answer to this latest problem; the trigger had been pulled that day, and he was getting all the blame.

The realization stung him sharply. The children at the dinner table were all laughing at the same time.

"Damn it! It's the rabbit or me!" He flung down his napkin, strode into the adjacent room, and flicked off the TV switch. The three youngsters were stunned.

Gannon was sure they had never heard him swear before. Embarrassed, he threw on a jacket.

"Okay, you can have the rabbit. Personally, I'm going for a walk." Helene's reproving glance made him feel no better.

He turned east toward the park and its beautiful lagoons. Although it was sunny, there was a chill breeze blowing, so he turned his collar up against the wind. It was probably a good time for him to take a walk and shake out his thoughts. Not only was he now faced with his first lawsuit, but one of his minor ventures into civic leadership was creating far more problems than he could have anticipated. He had been an excellent Cubmaster for two years, and out of that had been selected for election to the Board of Trustees of the Boy Scout Council. But what had looked like a perfectly reasonable and rational civic undertaking had been coming apart at the seams in recent weeks.

Factionalism among the board members had resulted from an effort on the part of the professional Scouters to free themselves from a long-standing entanglement in the local community. Gannon's personal research in these matters had confirmed that, somehow in the late twenties, a fund-raising campaign had taken place on a community-wide basis, led by a house-to-house solicitation by Boy Scouts to raise money for the purchase of a two-hundred-acre farm divided by a beautiful creek and occupied in strategic areas by small groves of oaks, maples, and ash trees. The land had been under control of a private board of trustees for the years since and was used for outdoor camping by the Boy Scouts themselves in the summertime, with seasonal meetings and entertainment the rest of the year. It was certainly an up and going operation, as Gannon had interpreted the history.

For many years these same men served also on another private board which was responsible for an Indian pageant, a highly successful outdoor theatrical performance given for two weeks each summer for many years. The survival of the pageant was dependent upon one central figure, whose goal in life had been the recognition of the plight of the American Indian, and hundreds of volunteers who gave of their time and effort in order to produce the show. The commercial and artistic segments of the community had long supported this enterprise.

Striding along in the sun and the wind, Gannon reviewed a long evening meeting earlier in the week, a meeting at which he had revealed himself as supporting the professional Scouters, in opposition to the two sets of private board members. Gannon was upset at himself, first, for having revealed his position on the issues, and then for observing that almost certainly he had adopted a position with the wrong group, the carpet-baggers from outside Waterford.

The president of all three boards was the same man, and Gannon suspected almost immediately that somewhere in all of this there was a distinct conflict of interest. For months at Boy Scout Council meetings, the president of the council spent more time representing the needs of the pageant people and of the real estate trustees than he did programming for the Boy Scouts of America. Gannon doubted that there was much money involved from the pageant, this running for about ten days each summer and with only about five thousand seats for sale at each performance. Probably most of the earnings went for the production, which by any standard was certainly lavish and highly entertaining. He wondered if there was any accounting of the income and expenses of the project. Then there was the matter of the land, which was becoming incrementally more valuable with the passage of each year. It was prime real estate, ready for development at any time, and still controlled by the private board of trustees, although the money had been raised by public subscription.

It was issues such as these to which Gannon had been addressing his interest on that given Wednesday evening in the week preceding, when the meeting got out of hand over what seemed to be a minor issue: horses. A half-dozen swaybacked equine actors were used for one month out of the year, including rehearsal and performance times. For the rest of the year, they were allowed to run loose and graze on the 200 acres. All users of the campground had looked upon them as friends and seemingly harmless. But the Scout executive had become exorcised over the matter of consumption of the hay by the horses. He had begun complaining about their huge feet and shoes stomping out the grass in certain areas of the fields, placing monetary value on the consumed hay, and finally simply presenting a bill to the pageant board of trustees for "animal feed." On the night of the reading of the bill, Gannon was certain that the shouting and swearing could be heard all over the local community.

"Damn you! Who ever heard of such a thing?" "You must be nuts! We've been grazing horses here for many years, and this is the first time we ever got a bill!"

And, of course, one accusation led to another. The professional Scouters, believing that the annual rental paid by the pageant group was small in amount, then asked for an increase in the rental rate. This further wounded the old guard, who had been steadfastly defending the consumption of hay by the six horses. From that, the argument shifted to "whose land is this, anyhow?"

"Well, the Scouts are allowed here through the permission of the land-holding corporation! If the corp wants to kick the Scouts out, they can certainly do it!"

"You pageant people are making thousands of dollars and dividing it up among you! Do you report all that income to the Internal Revenue Service?"

Efforts by the president to gavel the audience into submission were a failure. His efforts to adjourn the meeting led nowhere. Gannon observed apprehension, almost panic, in the watery blue eyes of the president of all three boards. It occurred to Gannon that perhaps there was some truth in the complaints and that somewhere there was some skullduggery. So he had let himself into the argument at the ethical level of the issue of conflict of interest, finding himself allied with a weak minority group, all of a younger age group in terms of community service and essentially powerless within the town because they were employees, rather than employers.

The debate was carried outside the meeting room and into the parking lot, with accusations and threats mixed into the shouting. As he passed one small group, getting into his own car to go home, he overheard one older man, speaking in a stage whisper, say, "You two fellas are dog meat; you are only school teachers and we can fix it so you're fired out of here! You had better back off."

In the intervening days, Gannon had been able to confirm that exactly that kind of threat was underway, characterized by midnight phone calls being placed by members of the community establishment. If school teachers are that vulnerable, Gannon thought, we have to do something about that. And so, on the day before being served the subpoena, he had made his decision and commitment to take out petitions and run for membership on the Board of Education.

Now, walking through the park, he wondered if he wasn't making a series of mistakes that would lead to later trouble. He had obviously made enemies of some portions of the legal community, through the Scouting affair, and was about to produce more vulnerability for himself by running in an election. Still, he had always felt that public service was a place for the more intelligent and better educated, for theirs was the responsibility for community leadership. No, he would continue to carry his petitions around. As a matter of fact this Sunday would be a good day to get signatures.

So he went up the steps in front of his house, two at a time and thrust his head in the door, shouting, "Helene, let's get in the little red car and go get signatures for my run for the School Board! In spite of everything, let's make something out of this day!"

Chapter 8

Late in the evening of his third night in the intensive care unit, Gannon was simply unable to rest. His wife's visit had stirred so many thoughts of their forty years together that his memories were chasing one another through his brain like a group of runners in the four-forty. His shackles were off, but every roll and turn rattled the bed rails and agitated him. The cold, February half-moon was visible through his one window, low in the sky, crawling slowly across the carpet floor. The dim figure seated in the visitor's chair was wrapped in a military-style tan raincoat, the long, blond hair bent over a novel, reading. On occasion, when he leaned against the painful shoulders, she stood up and crossed to his bedside and held his hand, answering his expletive with, "Hush, Dad, get some rest." It was Diane, his daughter, strong and beautiful, now over forty, mother of her own two high school students.

She, too, had been conceived in the attic bedroom of their medical school apartment, probably on a Sunday afternoon. She had always been in a hurry as a child, head down, knowing exactly where she was going, striding directly into the winds of life. Determined and well organized, she was the only child who refused to accept his recommendation for college, her defiance justified by a high grade point at graduation.

She had come home from the university with no lover, most probably having made her decision independently about whom she accepted for defloration. She had married a local man, a creative genius, a giant with little education and even less discipline, who had promptly proceeded to drink himself into the grave. Gannon had thought, many times, what a waste! But Jim's immortality was in his two offspring, both, like him, very intelligent.

Since she was his only daughter, Gannon did not have to explain to her brothers why he loved her so much. One bitterly cold day early in her widowhood, he had seen her unloading children and groceries from an ancient Volkswagen, her coat tattered, boot heels worn down, with the determined look still present, but oh, so excruciatingly poor.

"Diane," he had called to her, "I have enough money to make a down payment. Let's go buy you a house!" She had leaned into his shoulder and sobbed uncontrollably.

Perhaps she, too, was sharing this memory as she brushed her fingers through his hair.

"Hush, Dad."

Ben Matejus and Chris Gannon had been working as partners for about two years, when at the end of a busy day, Matejus came into Gannon's office and closed the door. They sat in chairs opposite one another at the same desk, as they would do for many years into the future.

"I have some tough news, Chris," said Ben. "I got a letter from the Boards today. The letter says that I won't be allowed to take the written part of the exam."

Gannon straightened up in his chair, jutting his chin out. "Well for heaven's sake. Why not? Is any explanation offered?"

Ben hesitated, then said, "They specifically indicated that they would give me no reason in writing, but that if I was determined to know why, then I could come to Philadelphia and they would explain verbally in an unwitnessed conversation."

Gannon was fuming. "In the application, was there a place for you to tell them that you were admitted to the American College of Surgeons last fall? That should take care of any local objections, including those crazy ideas about ability to get along with people and fee-splitting. Maybe you had a bad letter from one of your proctors in residency. Did you make anybody mad there?"

"No. I have copies of every letter of recommendation I requested, and all of them are positive. No, it's nothing from the training program. It has to be someone right here in town."

Gannon put his hands behind his head, leaned back, and closed his eyes. "It is no mystery about who would attack us here. She has hated me since my second summer. She would go after me by getting to you. We're really doing too well. I'm sure we have become a threat to her ego. This surely is the work of Penny Bayard."

"What do you think about my taking a few days off and going to Philadelphia?"

"No. I think I should go. I have the Boards and the College both, and if she is going to attack me through you, I should be the one to ask for the truth. Since I already have the Board, that makes me a professional colleague of the members, and I they have to answer me."

"How soon can you go? The next exam is in six months, and if I'm to make that, I have only three weeks of grace to get this wound up."

Gannon thought a bit and then replied, "Well you're on to do that piggyback aortic graft tomorrow morning. I can be in Philadelphia tomorrow night if that case goes all right. I'll call the Board office midmorning tomorrow and get an appointment with the secretary of the Board. Don't think anything about this affecting our partnership. We're doing just fine, and it's because of that success that this road block is being thrown. Actually, I suppose we should feel good about that!"

Driving home in the dark, Gannon fidgeted and muttered under his breath. *Shit,* he thought. *It was always something.* What was it about doctors? Were lawyers and preachers built the same way? Penny Bayard knew exactly how important being certified as a specialist by the American Board of Surgeons would be to both Matejus and Gannon. In the sixties being "board certified" and "of the College" legitimately set the trained surgeon aside from the average. It was everything. Had she put her accusations in writing? Or had she used the technique of the unwitnessed midnight call? In any event, she had probed for a weak spot and found it.

In Philadelphia two mornings later, his appointment with the secretary of the American Board of Surgery was not until 11:00 A.M., so he took a taxi to the Museum of Art. He had heard that there was a collection of true-to-life scale rooms, exhibiting furnishings and fashions of many different eras in American history. The front of the museum was a huge esplanade of steps, probably a hundred in number, pointed up by enormous statuary, leading into a columned frontispiece, through which the visitors had to pass. At the entrance he turned around and looked east and could see most of the city before him.

Those who had touted him on the museum were certainly correct in their descriptions of the content. The rooms were scaled to the size of the American people at the time in history which each room exhibited. For instance, the beds in the New Salem room were only five feet long, and the door frames of a proportionately similar height. For Gannon, this meant stooping and being careful not to rap his head. While touring the rooms, however, he kept looking at his watch nervously because he knew that what he was about to do, which essentially was challenging the American Board of Surgery, was dangerous in several ways. He was questioning the judgment of an establishment organization whose integrity could not be challenged. Furthermore, he was going to have to rely on the Secretary of the Board to communicate the complaint to the entire Board in complete fashion, leaving out none of the details, so that he, Gannon, was as exposed to criticism as was his partner.

At ten-thirty he ran down the outside steps, took a cab to Fifteenth Street, and an elevator to one of the upper floors. The building was old, old enough so that the elevator doors were of opaque glass, reinforced with wire. The offices themselves were done in dark wood; the floors creaked with age. A counter in the outer office was home to only one office person, and the Secretary of the Board was easily visible through the intervening door to his office.

"Now, Dr. Gannon, I hope you remember that I told you on the telephone I would give you nothing in writing, that this would be a conversation only. Do you remember that?"

"Yes sir, I do. But I feel that it will be somehow different if you speak with me directly across your own desk, because I am certain that I can predict what I am going to hear."

"What do you mean by that, Doctor?"

"I would bet that someone from our local community made a complaint about our activities, in some way. I made an implacable enemy among the surgeons in the community some years ago, but only by being successful. As you might guess, that is the worst crime of any."

"Your partner's application is in a manila file right over there behind me against the wall. I cannot read it to you. But from memory, I can tell you that a local thoracic surgeon in your community says in writing that your partner engages in unethical practice."

Baffled, Gannon chose to sit down at this point. Although he had prepared himself psychologically for exactly this scenario, to hear it repeated matter-of-factly was a real blow. The question was either to argue or not. Gannon decided that if he had gone to all this trouble, he was going to carry it through right to the end.

He would have to rely upon the good judgment of the Secretary of the Board as a whole. it was difficult to keep his voice from quivering.

"Exactly. That's no surprise to me. When someone uses the phrase 'unethical practice,' that is a euphemism among surgeons for fee-splitting. We both know that. If the Board takes that accusation at face value, then they have to take my certificate away. Dr. Matejus and I practice in identical fashion. We would be happy to share with you our original accounting books in any fashion that the Board members would feel they required. My partner belongs to the American College of Surgeons, and has for the last year. As you know they have a local committee and investigate everybody closely for fee-splitting. It seems obvious to me that the doctor would not have been initiated into the American College of Surgeons unless the local committee had cleared him on that issue. The local thoracic surgeon is Dr. Penelope Bayard, and she is actually a member of the local committee for the College. It is possible that she was outvoted on a committee recommendation and that he was initiated into the College against her will."

"I think I understand exactly how you feel, Dr. Gannon. But no one said that the world was going to be fair. At the age of fifty-five. I developed an abdominal aneurysm, which has been grafted, and I felt I had no choice except to quit practice and take this job. So I'm not going to give you any more information, and I'm not going to give you anything in writing. Your partner will have to come here and meet with the Board and plead his case himself. They will be meeting in two weeks to make the final decisions, and I think he should be here in person. This is too important a matter for him to pass up."

"You are telling us that we have no more rights than this, is that right? This reads like a Kafka novel. The alleged culprit has been put on trial for a crime he does not know he has committed, is never told what the crime is, is forced to listen to his accusers, but is provided no means to defend himself. Somehow it does not seem at all fair. I'm sure that the framers of the Constitution in this city two hundred years ago did not have this kind of situation in mind." Gannon knew that he was not concealing his anger well.

"Now cool off, Dr. Gannon. If it matters, I agree with you. The Congress is presently working on a Federal change that reflects freedom of access to information. It won't pass yet for a while, but it will certainly help us here. Frankly, not all Board members agree with me. Some of them come from an old school which agrees with this approach to problem solving, that kind of thing which we used to refer to as the midnight phone call."

Gannon, usually hatless, rose and hovered over the desk, twirling his little used hat in his hands. "Well, I thank you very much Doctor. At least you have opened the gate for us. Dr. Matejus will call right away and will plan to be here for your next meeting. But I'm going to look around town a little bit before I take the evening plane home." Gannon shook hands with the Secretary and took the creaky elevator down to the first floor and strode out into the street. It was now raining. He hailed a cab, saying to the driver, "Take me over to the east side of town toward the river. I want to see the Liberty Bell—I understand there is a very large crack in it."

Chapter 9

Ben Matejus leaned over his bed rail and said, "I think they're going to transfer you out to the floor today. Do you get that?"

Gannon shifted his shoulders and looked at his old friend, now retired. "Yeah, Ben, I get it. But my mind is fuzzy. Is anybody allowed to tell me what happened to me? Or are all of my friends simply afraid to give me the bad news?"

"You can't make me feel guilty, Chris. You have to stop feeling sorry for yourself We did a Cat Scan of the brain while you were still in the ER, showing at least two injuries, and probably a third in the brain-stem. Apparently that's why you quit breathing and then had a cardiac arrest. Do you have any memory of this at all? Do you know that you had CPR for almost ten minutes before the paramedics came to take you to the emergency department?"

"I've had some hints about this from the nursing staff, but I understand that nobody can find a source yet. Blood clots floating into the brain have to come from somewhere."

"You're right, but they can't figure it out. It is all speculation so far. When you get through this early period, and are stabilized, you'll have to have a carotid angio and a cardiac cath. We have deduced that the cerebral injury was from an embolus. But the problem is, where did the embolus come from? Which heart chamber? And are there others still there, flopping around in the bloodstream? I don't have to tell you all these things; you can draw your own conclusions."

Gannon hesitated then came back with, "You are not very comforting, Ben. If they put me out on the floor, I'll have to wrestle my own way out of bed to go to the john. I wonder if they know how many times I get up to urinate because of my big prostate?"

"Well, you're sure going to be on your own tomorrow. I'll drop by and see how you're taking it. The slings make sleeping fun, don't they? I'll see you around."

Christopher Gannon watched him stride out of the Intensive Care Unit. How like him to show up to bail him out in a time of crisis, and to then level the reality of Gannon's situation. They had not been close since Matejus' retirement. He lay for a while, staring at the ceiling, and thinking back to their great times together and the time of growth.

Matejus was holding an official-looking envelope in his hands, with a scrollwork return address in the corner. "Well, it worked. Between us, we beat them down. They're going to let me take the written part of the Boards!"

"Hallelujah," said Gannon. "I wonder what turned them around?"

"I think my fifty cases did it. It was a good book, and it sure covered a wide variety of pathology. We showed them everything; I had a terrific selection of cases. I think they just decided I knew what I was doing and that they should let me take the exam."

"Well in order to do that, they had to refute Bayard's letter. That must have been some bite for them. They must have smelled something sour somewhere, or they would not have changed their minds."

Matejus put the envelope down. "But on another subject; McEwan called me this afternoon and says he has a case with Adams-Stokes syndrome. We've been waiting for a good case for that permanent pacemaker that's put in through the chest. It looks like we have the patient, and we could do it on Wednesday. This is Friday, and I can't think of any other special studies that we would need to do before putting it in. You're on tonight. Would you go in and see the patient and introduce the idea?"

"We'll have to order the unit this afternoon. The stock is in Minneapolis, but they can send us one so that we'll have it by tomorrow at the latest. We'll have a chance then to look at it and see how the electrode is planted on the heart wall. It looked simple enough at that meeting you went to last fall."

The patient, who was a happy-go-lucky fellow, had lost consciousness and hit his head on two different occasions and was ready for anything that would help. He could understand the idea that intermittently his heart rate dropped to about thirty-six and that he had fainted because he was not getting enough blood supply to his head. He had never heard of a pacemaker but understood the principles involved and started to get his mind ready for a Wednesday operation.

But on Sunday at noon Gannon's phone rang at home. It was Matejus. He seemed upset and a little breathless. "Boy, did Bayard do it to us. My golfing buddy, Schreiber, referred her a case of Adams-Stokes last night, and she put the patient on the schedule and did it this morning, so it looks like we have been beaten to the draw this time."

Gannon sat down with a sigh, "Well, I suppose we could have done our case on Friday, but I think we were right to wait a few days and set the stage and train the scrub girls about how to handle the unit. After all, this would have been another first, and we just couldn't afford to make a mistake with this. How's the patient doing?"

"The guy who gave the anesthetic says that he can only see the blip of the pacer on the monitor. He does not see any EKG pattern at all. But maybe that's just a malfunction of the monitor. The patient still has an endo tube in, so the nurses aren't able to draw any conclusions themselves. The blip from the pacer looks a lot like a modified EKG pattern, so nobody really knows what's going on."

Gannon could not keep the disappointment out of voice. Once again, things had been rolling along too smoothly. When that happens, he noted to himself something always seems to upset the apple cart. While Scheiber truly was Matejus's golf partner, Gannon knew that secretly he hated them both and would do anything to trip them up. Everybody in the hospital had known that a pacemaker case was scheduled for next Wednesday, so he had set them up by finding a Sunday case.

When Gannon made his Monday rounds, he went right by the patient's private room. The door was open. He could hear the beep, beep, of the monitor, but he could not see the face of the recording machine itself and he had no choice except to walk on and see his own patients. There was conversation in the nursing station. He overheard words like "pacer" and "monitor," but the discussion seemed to center around the fact that they could not make out an EKG complex that would indicate the patient was still alive. The pacer was working, and the blip was visible, but there was no complex that seemed to relate to a living heart.

Matejus came into the nursing station and crooked a finger at him. They stepped into the hall and huddled together. "I saw a copy of the EKG report done this morning. It's true that there is no EKG complex visible. The patient is still on an endottracheal tube and a closed system. You don't suppose he's lying in there dead as a doornail with that little machine just producing an electric blip and nothing happening. What do you think?"

"It would be too much to hope for. You'd think that if that were the case, they'd shut it all down tonight, and the patient simply wouldn't be there tomorrow morning. I feel sorry for the patient." .

"That's exactly what's going to happen. I'll bet when we come around on rounds tomorrow that room will be empty and cleaned up. Further, I'll bet the patient is dead, and they don't recognize that because of the blip on the screen, and they don't get the idea that there's no complex indicating a beating heart." The partners separated, with no further discussion about the matter on that day. But they were both in the nursing station in the early morning, and sure enough, the patient was gone.

Gannon turned to the collection of nurses in the station and asked, "What happened to the patient in 380? Didn't he make it?"

The supervisor spoke up. "Well, I was on the night shift last night. I watched Dr. Bayard. She came in about nine o'clock and disconnected the electrodes on the pacemaker. Then she watched the screen a little while, and there was nothing on it. It was absolutely black. Then she turned around, went out to the desk, and wrote a final progress note declaring the patient dead. And that was it; no post was granted."

Matejus and Gannon looked at one another, each with a repressed smile. They had been beaten to the draw, but for some reason the patient had not made it. They both wondered if their own patient had heard about this death. The head nurse looked at Gannon sharply. "Yes," she said. "I'm sure you're wondering if Mr. Meyer knows about this. Well, I can tell you that he does. It was not possible to keep this a secret. There was too much activity on the floor and too much chatter among the staff involved. He may get cold feet now."

As it turned out, Mr. Meyer stood fast. He appeared to have that kind of personality which could put up with speculation and adversity and simply move on with life. His cheery approach to life in general was going to stand him in good stead, as it turned out, and the preparations for the insertion of the first successful pacemaker in Waterford Hospital history went ahead.

As he drove across town to his office that afternoon, Gannon was seized by an attack from his conscience. Here he was again, thinking more of his career than the life of the patient, forgetting that the one taking the risks was the patient, not the doctor. He was repeatedly putting himself on the same low level as Penny

Bayard! No wonder she hated him, they were actually much alike, both products of the same extremely competitive medical education system in the United States. "Firsts" were important; they had become too important. But that was how one's abilities and successes were measured; he saw no likely end to the competition. Seating himself at his desk, he began opening his mail. His secretary had placed on top an ominous-looking envelope from a law firm. But it was from his defense attorneys in the Dobnik case, now four years old, a festering sore on his flank. The letter informed him that the case had been thrown out by the judge, after several depositions and a lot of legal billing. Perhaps Caesar had some hold somewhere. His name had never appeared as a defendant; maybe this was the payback.

He thought a moment, then picked up the phone and dialed home. "Helene? I'm a happy man today! Let's take a ride out to the new high school site and check out the steel work in the gym. Let's take the kids and the babies and then go to dinner. The Dobnik case has been dropped!"

Driving home Gannon began to wonder if his civic duties as a member of the local school board were beginning to irritate his partner, because of the time involved. His three older children had helped him distribute flyers on cold February weekends. He had made the traditional appearances before the various teacher's organizations, and it was the latter group who had swept him into office. He never did really understand why the teachers themselves had supported him so vigorously. In the end it was they who controlled board elections.

Why was it that he had gotten into the many controversies involved in educational systems in the early sixties! Once again, as it had so many times before, his ego had gotten in the way. For the twenty years of his childhood and youth, as his family moved from congregation to congregation, it always had seemed that the president of the local school board was also the local town physician. He would have to remind himself not to let it be known that very selfish reasons were really what had propelled him into the field of medicine. He wanted to believe that some element of altruism was a part of his motivation, but he often felt guilty that the economics of being a surgeon had been a prime motivating factor.

So, running for election successfully and participating in the educational system of this city of 70,000 seemed but a natural sequence.

One of the first projects in process when he began to serve his first term was that of construction of a second high school in a city which had always had a single central high school with all of the attendant winning philosophy that entailed availability of a large and strong student body. These were explosive years in the United States, with school systems barely able to keep up with a rapidly growing population. School construction was the most exciting aspect of all of these issues, and there was a lot of fun making the decisions that had to do with educating children, spending "other people's money." Once the construction on this building had begun, it had become a Wednesday afternoon tradition for himself and his wife to visit the construction site. They laughed to one another about having an interest in such a project, one which the general population could ignore and only note when they paid their annual tax bill. Of course, the older three youngsters groaned when he announced that they would stop by and look at the new high school, but the visit had become a ritual.

"See!" Gannon hissed to the three older youngsters. "The steel work for the gym is up! Let's let the babies sleep in the car, and walk inside the steel work and get a feel for the size."

So they splashed their collective way through the gravel and mud in the rays of the afternoon sun, as the workmen were packing their tools and loading their trucks to go home. "My gosh! Look how big it is! When you guys are on the varsity, you'll play in this gym, and we can say we were here when it was still just a skeleton in the sky!"

Diane gave him a chill look, pushing her collar up around her ears. "And what do you propose for your daughter, smart guy? What is she going to do in your fancy gym?"

"She'll bounce around in a short skirt and show off her figure, just like her mother did before her. Which reminds me, daughter dear, around the house have I seen recently something called a 'training bra'?"

His daughter stamped her foot, splashing muddy water in his direction. "You are a fool, Dad. I have grown out of that already, and yes , I am going to bounce around this gym and make all the jocks watch me. Now, it's cold. How about that dinner you promised us!"

The next day he and Matejus were at the scrub sink They had scheduled Mr. Meyer as "John Smith" in order to play down the exciting historic element involved. Of course scheduling "John Smith" for any surgical procedure never fooled anybody in the hospital. Matejus and Gannon succeeded only in attracting, rather than abating attention.

This morning there had been no conversation in the doctors' locker room. Only the slamming of metal doors and the click of locks relieved the obvious tension in the lounge. Penny Bayard had said nothing as she passed through, eyes fixed straight ahead. Caesar and Freudin had given them the "thumbs up" sign at the scrub sink. Finney was silent at the head of the table, squeezing the anesthesia bag.

As Matejus made a sweeping incision over the left ninth rib, Finney spoke up. "Boy, you guys are sure waving a red flag at a mad surgeon today. Bayard did not say a word to me at the scrub sink!"

"Hush, Charlie. We'll talk later." Gannon knew how much Matejus hated idle talk in the OR, and this was Ben's case.

They moved swiftly and were looking at the slowly beating heart within ten minutes of the skin incision. Matejus picked up the transparent covering of the heart with a pair of fine forceps, incised it, and allowed the few cubic centimeters of clear fluid to spill into the chest. "We'll bring the electrodes through the chest wall before attaching them to the heart muscle, okay?" asked Matejus.

"Makes sense to me. That way we won't have any tight manipulations when the electrodes are set."

The foot plate of each of two electrodes was of soft, clear plastic, less than a square centimeter in size. Gannon marveled at the engineering involved in the production of a perpendicular coil spring-like device of metal one centimeter in length, protruding at right angles to the plastic foot. The idea was to bury the metal tip in the wall of the heart and then place four silk sutures at the comers of the foot plate.

"Boy, this is going to be no mean trick," breathed Gannon, as Matejus held the pointed scalpel blade next to the beating heart muscle. "As they say in the directions, 'deep, but not too deep'!"

Matejus, always thinking ahead, had devised a guard for the scalpel blade such that it was only possible to puncture the wall a few millimeters. Gently, but firmly, he moved his hand in cycle with the heart wall, then penetrated the muscle. This was followed by a second puncture, a short distance away. Having pushed each of the two electrodes into the prepared beds, Matejus followed with, "You hold 'em in place, while I tie down the suture. You are a terrible knot-maker." He smiled as his fingers raced through eight one-handed ties. "I think we can both breathe now, Chris," he said, slowly letting his own breath out. Then deftly he made a second incision on the chest wall, developing a pocket of fat to receive the power pack unit, this being about the size and shape of a pack of cigarettes. "When we screw in the two electrodes, that should close the circuit—like throwing a switch and the rate of heart beat should double, just like that." He was right. The batteries fired right off at a pre-set rate of seventy-two beats per minute.

The chest closing was routine. The happiest man in the room appeared to be Finney. "Well you've done it again," he said, laughing. "This is sure going to put a curl in Penny Bayard's tail. Remember your first case with her, eight years ago? She is your unforgiving enemy, that's for sure. She is going to get you, some day, if you both live long enough!"

Matejus and Gannon could not help smiling with self-satisfaction as they strode down the corridor to the surgeons' lounge, masks dangling, a little swagger in their walk.

"Sorry l couldn't be with you today," said a female voice from behind. "I was assigned to Dr. Bayard's chest case." It was Maggie DeLaney. Matejus walked on chart in hand to have a cigarette while writing the orders. Gannon dallied a bit in the corridor. "How about a cup of coffee in the coffee shop? Meet you there after we talk to the family. This was another 'first' for us, you know!"

"Yes, I know!"

Chapter 10

At midnight, Gannon still lay awake, staring at the dimly lit ceiling and thinking. It occurred to him that the dumbest thing to do in bed was to think, because inevitably a train of thought continued, with no ability to displace it from the mind and fall asleep. He was vaguely aware of the need to urinate again. Already this night he had bothered the nursing staff to help him void, but he had dumped over the collecting duck in his own bed, requiring a complete change of linens. He was not going to repeat that; if he could just stand in front of the toilet bowel he would be able to go.

Dumb catheter, he thought. Lying in his bladder for three days it had produced an infection. Seemed like had to pee all the time.

His bed was surrounded by metal poles on wheels, from which were suspended plastic intravenous bags and portable monitoring devices. Just disentangling his feet from the bed sheets made him pant. By the time he had the poles in tow and his feet on the floor, his head was spinning. His shoulders ached; pushing the poles across the room sent jabs of pain into the root of his neck.

My God, I'm weak, he thought. *I'm going down*—He never heard the crash of all the apparatus.

One of the things that bothered Gannon the most was having to do a new surgical undertaking on the afternoon shift. This was magnified by the fact that the operating team did not understand their tasks well. At 3:30 P.M. each day, there was a shift change, and the operators would turn to find that their team of circulating and scrub nurses had been replaced by the P.M. shift. It was much like coming into the middle of a movie and having to see it to the end before coming back to the beginning to know what kind of story had led up to the midpoint.

Instrument counts were sometimes in error, and it was always difficult for the newcomers to get into the rhythm of the procedure. Lap sponge counts had to be repeated, and the personnel updated on volume of blood loss, anticipated blood loss, and whatever operative events were yet to take place.

It was in this state of mind that Matejus and Gannon were scrubbing together on a new type of problem in the end of 1965. "I understand they call this a 'piggy-back graft," Gannon advanced. "I'll bet that's exactly what it looks like when everything's finished."

"Yep," said Matejus. "We did a couple of these at the VA last month. We won't cross-clamp the aorta as we would for removing a plaque from the vessel, but we'll put a side clamp called a Satinsky on the front wall. Once the upper portion of the graft is up and running, then we can put the same clamp on the sides of the leg vessels in the pelvis and complete the out flow by passing around the obstruction in the aorta."

"Well, it's all your baby," said Gannon. "This will be another first for us. Let's put this in your column."

While they completed the ritual of scrubbing, the nursing staff finished draping the patient. Gannon noted that his friend used the same lengthy incision as they would have used for aortic aneurysm and guessed that they were in for a four-hour haul. Going through the routine motions of getting the abdominal contents set up on lap pads and towels, Gannon glanced over at the Mayo table to understand how this new type of clamp was to be applied to the side of the vessel instead of across. He never ceased to marvel at the engineering that went into surgical in instruments. Some tools were badly designed, and no self-respecting carpenter or plumber would use them for anything. It was also true that there was a certain respect to be held toward the tiny chrome teeth of the instruments, with their ratcheted handles, curved to fit the nooks and crannies of the human abdomen.

This particular clamp, the Satinsky clamp, was about eight inches in length. It, like the Southwick before it, had the Willis Potts' teeth. The business end of the clamp was angled in an ingenious fashion, such that, when applied, the channel of the underlying large vessel actually remained open, and the only closed-off part of the vessel was about a three millimeter segment, two centimeters in length, on the side of the vessel. When the clamp was applied tangentially an incision could be made in the wall of the vessel and there would be no bleeding from the isolated segment. "This new clamp is probably named for a doctor, right?"

"Yep. Maybe we can obtain some immortality for ourselves some day by inventing a clamp with our names on it," he smiled.

And so Matejus moved on rapidly, he being technically significantly superior to Gannon. Throughout their entire careers together, Matejus would always be the better operator. He had "hands" and did a lot of finger dissection. Many of Gannon's surgical tricks were learned from Matejus, who knew his way around the body. In all of Gannon's career he had only known two operators who were as good or better than any others in his thirteen years of training. One was their professor-in-common at the VA, and the other was Matejus himself. How had he found this jewel?

He had quickly uncovered the aorta by incising the peritoneal covering and rolling the gut out onto the abdominal wall The dissection of the vessel itself was relatively easy because the arteriosclerotic section had produced a solid vessel and the dissection was essentially bloodless. The one thing about Matejus's work that occasionally irritated Gannon was his passion for detail "Sure is sure," he had said many times. At this point, Matejus stopped and fashioned a plastic woven graft in an inverted position, with the upper end larger than the lower two ends so that the open end, cut on the bias, could be sutured to the incision in the aorta, made possible by the Satinsky clamp. He quickly ran the periphery of the graft with a tiny, filamentous, plastic suture. Slowly removing the clamp, he allowed blood to ooze into the upper end of the graft, and by loosening and then reclosing the clamp on two or three different occasions, with a few moments between each opening, the microscopic interstices in the graft clotted off and bleeding ceased. He then moved the clamp down on the graft about three inches and set about for a similar procedure on each of the iliac vessels at the pelvic rim. At the close of these two sutures, he released the clamp several times. The amount of bleeding did not exceed 50cc.

"Gosh, what a clamp!" said Gannon. What a smart idea! The whole dissection can be done before shutting the vessel off and even then you don't have to shut it completely off. Clot formation inside the vessel will probably be non-existent."

And thus was born the idea of artificial bypass grafting. Bypass-grafting, using the patient's own saphenous vein had been in existence for seven years, but the pioneering efforts to cut down operating time by using plastic-woven grafts had been frustrated by a variety of manufacturing problems. Now, it was possible simply to turn from the table and make a selection from a variety of prostheses from the back table and to apply them practically. On this day, the graft had been cut a little long and had a little kink in it, a difficulty which would be corrected in the future.

The anesthesiologist could not believe the small amount of blood loss, as he had been present at other sittings with earlier plastic grafts, in which the bleeding was similar to water flooding out of the Mississippi River. The case finished in two hours, without a switch in team, which Gannon had so much dreaded. Matejus picked up the chart to write the orders, and the two went down the hall to the surgeons' room It was the end of the operating day, and there was much bustling and scurrying about and clanging of locker doors as the nurses went to their own area to change and go home, returning by 6:30 the following morning for another go-around.

A visitor was waiting for them in the surgeons' room, Holas Vashinski. "Hi," he said. "I have a case for you to see this afternoon. I'm going on to the office, but maybe you can call me about it. I think its a hot gallbladder, and maybe we can do it tomorrow.

"Thanks!" said Matejus as he sat down to begin writing the postoperative orders.

"But that's not really what I want to talk to you about." He glanced around the room, and then into the locker room to see that no one else was listening. "I wasn't going to tell you about this but I think I'd better. I had a run in today with Penny Bayard."

Matejus stopped writing. Gannon, who was drying his hands, stopped the motion of the towel. Matejus and Gannon looked at one another. "More trouble, huh?" asked Matejus.

"Well she made me so mad, she accused me of splitting fees with you fellows. I knew that when I switched my referral work to you people there would be trouble. But I didn't think she'd stop me right out there in the hallway and shake her finger at me in front of everybody!"

Said Gannon, "You mean she stopped you in front of the nurses? What was her beef?"

Vashinski stood up to his six-foot-two, blond and blue-eyed Lithuanian frame. "Boy, she shook that finger right in my face and shouted at me about 'unethical practice.' She has a real thing about that."

Again Matejus and Gannon looked at one another. "Yeah, we know. We felt this before. This is just an extension of the same ides."

Vashinksky blustered, "Nobody ever did a thing like that to me before. She just stood there in the hall and read me off. She said she had proof because of some billing that we made together, but she began to shout, yelling that you fellas were doing ghost surgery and charging money and sending it to me without the knowledge of the patient. She claims the patient was Mrs. Christianson. Remember her?"

Gannon held up his hand, suggesting that he had heard enough "Well, I'll look into it. I don't remember much about it. I remember what she had and what we did, but I don't remember anything unusual about the billing. I'm certain we will hear about this in another way. But today we did the first 'piggyback graft' in Waterford Hospital history. And it is running like a dream. Come on, we'll buy a cup of coffee before you go to the office, and we'll tell you about it.

As Gannon and Vashinsky stepped into the stairwell on the way to the coffee shop, Matejus moved down the corridor to find the family to review the surgery with them. At this hour, the coffee shop was jammed with people getting off on shift change. The room was the most garishly decorated recreational area Gannon had ever seen, contrasting so much with the similar facility in the VA. The tables and some of the chairs were trimmed in a bright orange plastic material set off against a distribution of bright yellow and green drapes hanging in the glaring sun coming in the west windows. The designer, who had spent practically his entire career repeatedly decorating Waterford Hospital, had really stretched it this time. The interior seemed much like the interior of the clown tent at the circus. There was no relief from the blinding reflections off the tables and chairs.

As Vashinsky tore off the top of a new pack of cigarettes, he ventured, "I suppose you guys are feeling pretty good these days, right? Almost every week, you have something new on the schedule. You must be driving them crazy."

Gannon smiled a little, trying not to look self-satisfied. "Yeah, we have been pretty lucky now for a year or so. It is about time for something awful to happen again. If we don't come-a-cropper here at the hospital, almost certainly I'm going to put my foot in it in civic work. I got burned in the Boy Scout movement, and I rather suspect I'm heading for a fall in my own church. "

Vashinsky smiled. "I remember you telling us about the famous horse battle at the scout camp. How did that all end?"

Gannon laughed, ruefully. "One day, the new president of the Boy Scout Board, a lawyer friend of mine, got a telephone tip that the Scout executive was not at home anymore. So he and I shared one of the truly dirtiest events that I have ever touched. We sat in a darkened car in front of the house of the alleged paramour and waited for him to come out. Poor fellow, he did. So in the end, the pageant people and the land-holding board got all of us right in the ass—the school teachers, the lawyer, and me. But we deserved it. We had been too self-righteous."

"So, did you get out of that?"

"Right away. But we definitely were left holding the bag."

Vashinsky laughed loudly. He was a garrulous man who had always worn fashionable clothes purchased in a Chicago shop. His greatest and most startling story was telling of his method of getting into a German medical school right after the war. He had bribed his way in with a ham and a bicycle tire, which he had wrapped around his body beneath his shirt. Gannon had commented many times that there was one thing certainly true that he had learned from all the displaced doctors from European countries: "When all else fails, fold up your diploma and conceal it in the heel of your shoe and start walking west." Thus it was that so many blond and blue-eyed Baltic peoples had ended up in Chicago, by way of Montreal. He affected a peculiar way of holding his cigarette, tilting his head back when he was enjoying someone else's story and laughing.

"I understand that you have been teaching in your local Sunday school for several years now, in addition to putting time in on the local school board. How does Ben react to your giving up that time? You must have to hurry and do Sunday rounds early and make Monday evening rounds before going to the school board meeting. Am I right? Does that make Ben a little peevish?"

"Yeah, Holas. I don't think Ben likes it much. He devotes his entire time and interest to the practice, and I am sure that he thinks I should too. My rationalization has been that I am keeping our names in the public eye in the way of public service and making an additional contribution to the general welfare of the practice at the same time."

"Do you think Ben understands that? This country is so different from the way it was at home. I bet that Ben doesn't have any idea how you fit into these things." He looked down at his coffee cup and then up at Gannon. "By the way, why do you do those things?"

Gannon hesitated. "I suppose it is an ego thing. I confess that I like to be out in front of groups and in leadership positions. For instance, one Sunday, after a particularly exciting meeting of an adult class, one guy said to me leaving the church basement, 'You need this more than we do!' That really gave me a jolt. I have begun to think about how presumptuous it is to think that I can teach comparative religion just because I was brought up in a minister's home."

"I'm glad you see that about yourself" said Holas. "Penny Bayard has a huge ego, as I certainly saw today. But so do you. Actually, you are much alike."

Chapter 11

"Oh, Dr. Gannon, why didn't you call for help? My heavens, what a mess!"

"I...I...I'm sorry, Polly. I just didn't want to have you make my bed again."

Gannon was stretched out on the floor, leaning against the toilet door frame, IV poles across his body, his face splashed with sticky glucose solution.

"Idiot! Do you think this will be easier to clean up? Besides, everybody on this wing heard the crash and were sure that somebody died. Golly! Your subclavian IV is hanging loose; let's get you back in bed. I don't care if you do have to pee. Do it in bed, use the duck!

So together they managed to get him rearranged and cleaned up. "Here, Dr. Gannon, I have some Valium for you; that ought to hold you till dawn."

Merciful oblivion—he dreamed of Ken Adams.

Ken Adams was born to privilege. Gannon had been in Waterford only a couple of years when he was approached by Adams, who, when he first introduced himself in a corridor conversation, said, "You're from Northwestern, huh? So'm I. Finished just before the war. Great school, great school! We should have a lot in common..."

Subsequently that element of "commonality" never bloomed. And not because Adams did not try. Clearly he regarded himself as one who had gone to all of the right schools and, in this later time, belonged to all the right clubs. At one point he had even persuaded Gannon to join a local country club, a membership which lasted only a few months because of Gannon's negative feelings about the matter of privilege. He simply could not get by the idea that it would be bad for his youngsters to spend their summer weekends growing up on a private golf course and sunning themselves next to a country club pool. Adams took this club resignation hard and let him know about it in no uncertain terms. At every turn Gannon had frustrated Adams's efforts to involve him in social life among the physicians, so after a few years, Adams had essentially given up. Their professional relationship was also cool.

One summer evening in 1965, Adams called Gannon for a consultation. They met in the corridor outside a patient's room when the evening trays were being picked up.

"I did a prostatic resection on this old fellow yesterday," said Adams. "Today he had some chest pain in the afternoon, and an EKG showed a pulse rate of forty-two. He fainted twice this afternoon. I asked Mark Silver to see him after office hours, and he said he was having episodes of Adams-Stokes. Haven't you done something with pacemakers in the last year?"

"Well, yes. As a matter of fact, there's a new catheter type of pacemaker to put in through a vein in the neck under local anesthesia, for bad risk patients. So far, the ones we have done have all been done the hard way, through the chest under general anesthesia."

"It sounds like just the ticket. Do you have one of those things in the hospital? He sure would not stand any chest surgery under general anesthesia."

"As a matter of fact, we do. Ben Matejus brought a sample home from a meeting, and it's been sterilized and is waiting in the operating room for just such a case. I'll leave him right here in bed and take care of it tonight."

They parted, and Gannon hurried around the corner of the nursing station into the surgical storeroom. He poked around among the shelves and boxes for a while and then came upon a wrapped package labeled "Transvenous Pacemaker." Stepping back into the corridor, he pushed ahead of him a cart on which sat a large metal box, light metallic blue in color, with a six-inch electronic screen on its face, and control buttons, switches, and electrical terminals in its lower half. Putting a sterile surgical equipment tray alongside the box, he returned to the patient's room.

Darkness had settled outside, and the only light in the room was a single, subdued floor lamp next to a visitor's chair. After his eyes had adjusted, he noted that the patient was snoring gently. He guessed his age at eighty or more, his face deeply seamed and discolored by years of outside work. His head was covered by a shock of unruly white hair. From beneath his bed sheet extended a clear plastic tube, draining out into a large bottle taped to the floor. The content of the tube was a cherry red, which Gannon knew to be the faintly bloody urine passed after prostatic surgery.

"Mr. Rogers, Mr. Rogers," he whispered loudly, touching the patient on the shoulder as he was lowering the bed rail.

The old man opened his eyes slowly as the accompanying floor nurse elevated his bed to thirty degrees. He seemed to be only faintly aware of what was going on, probably because of narcosis, Gannon thought.

"Mr. Rogers, I'm going to put a little tube in your neck. It won't hurt except for the local anesthetic. It will sting a little, but the tube is going to help your heart. You won't have any more fainting spells."

He turned to the nurse, and asked, "Have you seen this Electrodyne monitor before?"

"No, not really. I heard a little about it from some of the other girls on other floors. Is it safe? What does it do?"

"Well it's obviously supposed to be safe, but honestly, I got a shock from it a month ago when I was applying it to a patient on the fourth floor. I never did understand why. The instructions say it is totally grounded, but it does use electricity to stimulate a heart that is beating too slowly. Just stick the ends of these three electrodes in the three buttons there on the machine, and I'll hook him up with these straps."

So Gannon busied himself with setting up the monitoring device, experiencing no shock similar to that he had sustained previously Then he turned his attention to the patients neck, on the right side. After gloving, he prepped and draped a small area on the side of the patient's neck, filled a syringe with local anesthetic, and quickly injected the skin of the middle part of the right side, roughly in a one-inch square. He made a one inch incision in front of the long visible strap muscle on the right side. During this, the patient only muttered to himself and jerked his arm when the needle penetrated the side. Gannon felt for the front border of the muscle and made a further, deeper incision into the soft tissues of the neck. Using blunt dissection with the index finger and a hemostat, he spread apart the tissues until he visualized a vertical column of blue, it was deep, behind the previously visualized muscle.

"I've got the vein. But we need more light. Could you just go get a flashlight from the nursing station and hold it for me so I can continue?"

So the rest of the procedure was done by flashlight. As he worked, he muttered under his breath, almost to the room at large, expecting his assistant to pick up his conversation on her own. "I've never done this type of pacemaker before. The others have all been major surgery, placed with an open chest. The demonstration at the College meeting recommended using the external jugular vein. But this is the internal, and it's as big as my thumb. I'm going to isolate a piece between ligatures, put a purse string suture in, and thread the catheter electrode in through that hole. If I do it right, we won't lose a drop of blood. If I do it wrong, it may be messy. I'll apologize now, in case I get something on your clean uniform." He raised his face and smiled at his assistant holding the flashlight, which seemed to have developed a nervous tremor of its own. As for himself beads of sweat were gathering on his forehead. He thought to himself, *Ben and I are the only two that can do this. Why am I so nervous about it? So, if it's never been done before here, so what? This'll be just another "first."*

After isolating the one inch segment of internal jugular vein, he passed two silk ligatures around the vein at separate points, one inch apart, so that when they were pulled down, the segment of vein between them would have no flow. Then he took a fine silk suture and made a circle of stitches with a single thread, about a quarter-inch in diameter. "Well, I think we're ready now." Then he opened the electrode package and removing a piece of green plastic an eighth of an inch in diameter and about two feet long; the tip was encased in a small chrome electrode. "Now, when we're all set, I'm going to have you plug the ends here into the machine on the table and throw the switch. I'm going to stay sterile until the wound is closed."

At that point he tied the two silk ligatures with a single knot only, picked up the previously placed purse string and with a pointed scalpel blade made a hole in the vein wall just big enough to admit the one-eight inch tip of the electrode. With a quick maneuver, first loosening the purse string, passing the catheter in, and then tightening the purse string about the length of the catheter, he was able to pass the tube into the isolated segment of vein and to tie down the purse string. Then, loosening the isolating silks, he was able to pass the catheter further into the vein, down through the neck, and into the patient's chest.

"Well, I that's it. We're about ready to throw the switch." He looked at the screen one last time, seeing a standard normal electrocardiographic pattern working its way across the screen about forty times a minutes.

"I set the rate at seventy-two, so the pacer should take over right away and boost the rate to that number. Plug in the electrodes now, and I'll move the electrode tip around inside the vena cava until we find a spot where it takes over. I'm sure this will work as soon as I get it set in the right place."

He turned to the screen one more time as the nurse plugged the electrodes into the power box. Then he began to maneuver the electrode inside the vein by advancing slowly and then retreating when suddenly a vertical blip appeared on the screen, followed immediately by a standard electrocardiographic pattern of successive beats.

"I think we've got it," he said excitedly. "According to the written material about this, this should take over now and it won't make any difference whether his heart slows to forty or not because it'll just keep beating at seventy-two. There is a battery pack that the manufacturer sells, which we don't have. We have to get that and hook it up, so it will be portable, since now he's still stuck to the bedside. But, so far, we've got him."

Finishing the wound closure, he applied a dressing, burying the electrode in a towel around the patient's neck. He could not escape doing these latter things with a bit of a flourish, saying to the nurse, still patiently holding the flashlight, "Well, we made history again. Put that down in your little black book at home because we might want to write this up twenty-five years from now."

"Did we bother you, Mr. Rogers?" The patient was awake, but still staring off into space, really unaware of anything that had taken place. He certainly had no grasp of the significance of what had been done and probably had no idea at all that his life had been on the line, in the hands of a young man who "had never done this before."

Turning to the nurse, Gannon said, "If he begins fiddling with this in the night, you may have to put restraints on his hand; let's try to avoid that. Come on, let's go. You'll have to check on the monitor here periodically and see if it's still in contact and beating at seventy-two times a minute. If you lose that little vertical blip there and the rate drops, call me at home and I'll come back and readjust the tip. This looks like a great idea to me. It is certainly much easier on the patient than putting something in through the chest. I'd say there's a great future for this kind of device." The two, feeling a little like conspirators, then turned and slipped through the door into the corridor, each with his or her sense of elation associated with the historic event.

Within six weeks Adams called on him again. As usual, being a junior surgeon, Gannon was seated in the surgeon's waiting room, preparatory to doing a late scheduled case. Through the intercom came the voice of the charge nurse, "Dr. Gannon, Dr. Gannon? Dr. Adams would like you to come into room nine. Can you hear me?" a call from other surgeons working in an operating room had become an issue producing fear and apprehension. It usually meant that a surgeon was in trouble and was asking for help. To be requested by surgeons who had rarely referred work was a step beyond the usual "open" consultation. *Nonetheless, duty calls,* he thought, as he walked down the corridor toward the door to room nine. A doctor in trouble was a doctor in trouble. This usually meant that a patient was in trouble, also. He had to go, no matter how much the two surgeons in question might dislike him.

He was greeted by the voice of Adams when he pushed the door open. "Well you say you are a vascular surgeon. Compared to what we have here today, what you did for me a few weeks ago was a cinch. Almost the entire left kidney is replaced with cancer, but I can feel an extension of the tumor into the main kidney vein, the tail of tumor turning upward in the vena cava for at least two to three centimeters. It seems to be free, though. Why don't you put some gloves on and see if you can figure out some way to get everything out, along with the kidney?"

Standing at the scrub sink one more time, Gannon had a feeling at the nape of his neck that somehow he was being set up. This pair of surgeons had always used other general surgeons for such problems. It seemed to him that someone was simply throwing a bone down before him, hoping he would be stupid enough to pick it up, yet from the description of the problem it should not really be difficult. it would require setting things up a little bit, but it should be possible to retain control of the blood within the vena cava and left kidney vein and slowly extract the tumor as the kidney was pulled away. The more he thought about it, the more he smiled to himself, thinking it really should be a cinch.

In 1965 kidneys with cancer were still being removed in the traditional fashion. That is, the kidney and its contained tumor was freed from around all the adjacent tissues in the back of the abdomen cavity and then the blood supply taken care of where it came together at the middle part of the kidneys, the so-called "hilum." Surgeons isolated the organ and its contained tumor on this pedicle of vessels, both the major artery and the major vein, and then simply put clamps on those vessels and cut the tumor away. Apparently the situation was a little different today, and that was the reason for the request for help.

Gannon gowned and gloved rapidly and stepped up to the table next to Adams. The tumor was huge; there was no doubt about that. The kidney, located in the deepest part of the abdominal cavity to one side of the spine, had been loosened well and was hanging free by the pedicle of the vessels. As he poked around the artery and the vein, he could feel a column of tumor passing through the vein. By retracting the kidney it was then possible to actually see the tumor mass through the thin vein wall and to confirm that it did indeed make a right angle turn, somewhat resembling a snake's tail extending upward and dangling loose within the much larger channel of the vena cava.

"Let's just take care of the artery first as a separate structure. After we've done that, the inflow will decrease and the whole organ and cancerous mass will decrease in size. It will be easier to handle then and we can hold the mass within the vein by closing the vein against the tail of the tumor between my thumb and index finger and slowly pull the whole thing out. I really don't think it will be too difficult."

Adams laughed. "You mean you're going to pull that thing right out of there with nothing more than your thumb and index finger to control it?"

"Yes," was Gannon's confident reply. Following his own suggestion, Gannon applied an arterial clamp to the kidney artery, which measured about five millimeters in size and followed that by oversewing the cut end with a running nylon suture. Then he placed a "safety" free ligature of heavier silk placed in the wall of the vessel itself. The remainder of the pedicle was only the kidney vein, and this contained tumor, so grasping the whole combination between his fingers, he took a small pair of scissors and incised the wall of the vein, carrying the incision around the entire vein circumference, leaving the exposed snake-like tumor mass visible.

"Now, Ken, if you'll just lift the tumor and the kidney and start drawing it up toward yourself, I think the rest of it will come along behind that." He was right. Adams stood fast, shaking just slightly and slowly pulled the large tumor mass upward onto his own chest wall while the snake-like collection of tumor within the vena cava and kidney vein came behind it; it was well over eight inches long. As soon as the last fragment of tumor came out of the end of the vein, Gannon closed his fingers and then applied a vascular clump to the balance of the pedicle. The vein was treated similarly to the artery, and the procedure was essentially over.

Under ordinary circumstances, there should have been congratulations and smiles of appreciation all around. Gannon did not detect any feeling of elation on the part of those who had called him in. As a matter of fact, he thought perhaps there was some disappointment at the fact that he had not been defeated by a difficult technical problem. Once before he had had the same feeling, when he had resected and grafted the abdominal aneurysm at the beginning of his time in Waterford. With his back toward the two men who were engaged in irrigation of the wound and cleaning up prior to closing, he stripped off his gown and gloves. He wondered if he had made another enemy or if somehow there was an alliance between Adams and Bayard. Obviously, something was wrong. He wondered if, actually, there was not a group of physicians who might be developing as an opposing force.

He was aware that he was being recognized as someone who could be relied upon to develop policy. "Policy" and "political" were certainly derived from the same roots. He would have to be careful that the practice was not hurt because of political and social issues among the staff members. He had already made some mistakes, and probably an opposition was developing. Gannon's continuing refusal to socialize with Adams and his friends, his failure even to reply to invitations to physicians' parties, was probably about to come to a head, he realized. It fit with his personal history from childhood, when he had sat in the front pew in a succession of churches and listened to the preaching of his father. He had always been a social misfit at college, in medical school and in residency. He was a teetotaler, competing in a profession in which liquor was all too common. He was going to be hurt, of that he was certain.

Going to the scrub sink to do his own case, he began to reflect on these elements. Oddly enough, Matejus fit better than he. Already he was accepted where Gannon could not seem to fit in. Gannon saw himself as the civic and community leader, whereas his partner, who had absolutely no interest in such matters, was in greater demand to flesh out foursomes in hostess' tables.

And he could not change—why was that? He had to admit to himself that he felt above it all, honestly snobbishly superior to his colleagues and their wives. The former he regarded as men with limited view, the latter as shallow and self-centered. In a social setting he never knew what to say. His interests, the great books, religion, were political taboo, not fit subjects for the average Saturday cocktail party. Helene moved easily among the guests at such gatherings; Gannon fled from groupings and sat alone in a corner. Rarely did anyone sit with him; indeed, he was boring!

What had his father said so many times? "Lose yourself in other's problems, and you will find yourself " He was trying, but somehow this approach made him feel isolated, guilty of something. Was he just guilty of being born? Did everybody feel the same way, and how was he affecting his own offspring?

Barbara Raven had come into Gannon's life just when he moved to a larger office. She came to him with an abscess on her finger, accompanied by a pair of unruly Golden Labradors. She was a free spirit, a lover of dogs, and Gannon was immediately attracted to this high school student. He encouraged her to continue her education and was pleased when she was accepted into a nursing school.

When she returned several years later to work in the expanding Waterford Hospital emergency department, Gannon depended on her common sense in evaluation of clinical problems. So when she called one summer evening, asking him to come and treat a state policeman for a gunshot wound of the abdomen, he took his time driving in, because she did not seem to feel there was urgency.

This was confirmed when he examined the patient. He had been in a seated position in his patrol car; the shooter had aimed downward, and the bullet had entered his body just above the genitalia. At trial a couple of years later, they learned that this had been a lover's quarrel and the gunman had intended to strike a little lower.

The wound of entrance was barely visible and not bleeding. There was no apparent exit wound. Two opposing x-ray studies suggested the bullet lay free inside the rectum; it had to have traversed the bladder.

Gannon smiled and looked at Barbara. "Give me a glove and some lubricant . He slipped his finger into the officer's rectum and rooted around a little in the ampulla. Then he smiled again and withdrew the finger, with the bullet neatly crooked in its flexion crease. The patrolman grunted. "Cancel the OR, Barbara. There'll be no colostomy tonight. Our only surgery will be to insert an inlying catheter. What luck!"

"You always speak in riddles, Chris. Even 1 have trouble understanding you sometimes. You are," Helene paused, searching for the right word, "opaque."

"People should just assume that I try to make my speech colorful; they should look behind the obvious. My examples are not all riddles: they are parables, or fables, or myths. They should make for more interest, and my fun is making up the allegories as I go."

"Like a dark shot, that is?"

"No, like a shot in the dark

Two large shiny-black Dobermans were dashing back and forth at the fence, baring their teeth, growling and barking furiously. Helene and Chris Gannon backed away, thankful that their host kept his guard dogs behind a high fence.

"Boy, they look mean!"

"Maybe we should forget dinner with Domonic and his wife!

"Surely he will hear them and come to our rescue. Nice doggies, nice fellows," he said soothingly.

Dominic stepped out on the patio, calling to the dogs in a gibberish. "Nothing you say will work. They only understand Lithuanian." As the dogs lay down quietly, he began to laugh. "Come on in to dinner."

Angelo had a middle-European accent almost as thick as that of C.K. Moon. He blurted rather than spoke. His practice was very successful much because of an untiring office staff who explained his directions to the patients. It was a form of translation.

At a formal dance one spring, Angelo was seated at a table near Gannon. Penelope Bayard, wearing a deep-blue strapless gown, stopped before Angelo and began scolding him

"I saw you on the C.K. Moon vote yesterday. I saw you stand up for him!"

Angelo put up his hands, gesticulated vigorously, in a defensive mode, while answering loudly, but unintelligibly.

Shaking her index finger directly in Angelo's face, she hissed, "One day you will pay for that! We'll be watching you!"

Poor Angelo, thought Gannon. *Such a nice guy to be punished for having done the right thing!*

Holas Vashinski liked large automobiles. And he liked to drive them at high speed. Probably he relished settling in a small town fifteen miles west of Waterford because it meant at least one round trip daily on Big Woods Road to the hospital Additionally, when he had a patient in labor, he could look forward to several round trips on this hilly, narrow, winding picturesque route.

For years, Gannon expected Vashinski to smash himself up, but he seemed to lead a charmed life. Holas's wife, Nina, probably had the same thought, for she began to nag her husband about moving to town for his own safety. Gannon's thought that the couple were from the Lithuanian aristocracy was often reinforced by little incidents and observations. Gannon compared Vashinski's big car and the country house to scenes from *Zhivago*.

Nina, a very smart woman, should have seen what effect the move would have on Holas, Gannon thought. Somehow, something went out of him. His tall, straight figure seemed to shrink, and his tailored clothes no longer hung well. He stopped using a cigarette holder! He exchanged his soft, cream-colored shoes for hard brown wingtips. His practice was off. He no longer lived in the big doctor's house among the oaks and hickories north of town.

He still drove a big auto, but it was unkempt. He still made the daily round trip, but in the opposite direction. More importantly, he drove slowly. I liked him better when he was willing to take a risk, thought Gannon.

Gannon first became a member of the Waterford Hospital Staff Executive Committee in the mid-sixties. Having spent his spare time in the first ten years in

Waterford with community service, he let his ego persuade him that he should make an effort to lead the hospital and that he could do it. He had certain plans.

He had observed that of the one hundred physicians on the staff, only forty lived and participated in the community of Waterford. One day, in an effort to inspire the doctors to become civic leaders in their own towns, he gave a short speech to his fellows.

"We cannot abdicate our responsibilities where we live. As a class we are intelligent, educated, and experienced. On our staff there are only two of us who have run for elected office. There are presently no physicians in Congress or in the Illinois state legislature. That is a shame. We are at fault.

"Recently I visited the USS *Yorktown*, a World War II carrier now serving as a floating monument in Charleston Harbor. I was onboard her in the Sea of Japan in the winter of 1952 so I had a feeling for her as I toured the interior gangways and walked the flight deck. I looked at the battle markings painted on her stack, and I could feel the sense of history of which I had been a part. I could remember the awful news of the sinking of her predecessor at Midway in 1942. I was silent and in awe at the memory.

"Compare that now to the group of us here, finishing luncheon. We can be going into battle in each of our own communities and have here in our own hospital! There are medical horizons yet unseen and yet untouched!"

On that note, quite pleased with himself Gannon sat down. Not only was there no applause, there was absolute silence! Had they not understood? No they had not. Was his illustration that cloudy?

Then he understood. No one at the table was born in America. There was the barrier of language and the barrier of history. They were all thinking of their own Korean, Chinese, Persian, Lithuanian, Hindu, Pakistani—and probably crying a little.

Chapter 12

"What? You say I need a cardiac cath? What's the deal? Do you think this thing in my head started in my heart? Gannon was truly alarmed at this turn of affairs because, for the first time, he perceived there might be some additional problems requiring a future solution.

"Look, Chris; you are not out of the woods yet. We do not have a satisfactory explanation for this sequence. You have at least two holes in your brain on the CT scan and probably a third in the respiratory center. The best bet is that these were floating clots, most likely from one of the two chambers in the left side of your heart. We can check out the vessels to the brain at the same time."

Gannon looked at his good friend, Irving Wren, who was the best of that generation of cardiologists who passed tiny catheters though the arteries of the body and took x-ray studies of the small vessels to the heart wall. He was constantly moving, bobbing about, pacing back and forth, possessing a great sense of humor, but always with a speck of dried food on his tie. "Well, I suppose if you must, you must. When do you want to do it?"

"Late this afternoon. I can get you on the schedule. We really need the knowledge. Maybe we can do something to prevent another episode."

"'Your conclusions, Irving, as usual are irrefutable. Just give me something by hypo so that I don't remember the ride to the cath lab. I'm just beat to death."

Said Irving, "Stop feeling sorry for yourself. Take a walk down the hall and look at real trouble."

Gannon grimaced and turned toward the wall keeping his shoulder tight to his trunk. "Okay, Irving, you cannot make me feel guilty for being sick."

The evaluation of stroke was a mine-run problem for Gannon to analyze. He had dealt with them for twenty-five years; and had listened to his own neck vessels before, and there simply was no indication of narrowing. The likelihood of emboli breaking off from a silent plaque in either vessel in the neck was remote.

So he was forced to consider the, other possible sources. An undetected abnormal quivering type of rhythm of the inflow tract, called the atrium, was a common event. But he felt he would certainly have recognized such a rhythm. The best bet was a "silent infarct." The probability was that he had sustained a minor coronary artery occlusion with development of a clot on the inter ventricular wall, which had subsequently fragmented. Painless, or "silent." Infarcts were not common. The cardiac catheterization should clarify that issue and would affect management over the long term.

Meanwhile, he was recovering his appetite and was hungry for the noon meal But this was to be denied because of the late afternoon heart study. By the time the nurse with the pre-operative injection had appeared, the sun had swung around and the area outside his room was beginning to darken. The onset of the hypo was swift and accompanied by more dreams of the past.

Matejus and Gannon were just finishing rounds on three south. Neither was scheduled for any surgery this day, so they were cleaning up loose ends. Methodically. they had sat down to talk with every patient, changed all the dressings themselves, and completed a series of charts. With that, they swung down the corridor toward the elevators, bound for the coffee shop.

They were still standing, waiting, when they were approached by Bob Rockwell and Richard Whiting. Theirs was an obstetrical partnership , with a duration of about ten years, whereas Matejus and Gannon had only been working together for about six years. A strong social relationship had developed among the four, both in the living room and on the golf course. Whiting, the older, had been kind enough to help Gannon build his practice, both by referrals of his obstetrical patients with gallbladder disease and breast problems; and also he had tried somewhat in vain, to establish Gannon socially in the community. Rockwell was one of those fellows whom everybody liked and who was, in turn, everybody's friend. It was Rockwell who spoke first: "Boy, do you guys have enemies! Does either of you know anything about the Fox Valley Medical Travel Club?"

Gannon looked at Matejus, then "Yeah, we've heard something about it. No Jews, no blacks, no foreign medical graduates need apply."

Whiting flushed a little bit. "No, it's more complicated than that. This is more like a physicians' travel club."

Gannon answered abruptly. "Travel club, my eye! I heard that the only traveling is a few steps to the local bar. I also heard that it was some kind of far-right political action group!"

Rockwell stepped between the two doctors. "Now, now don't get upset. But the fact is that you guys were both blackballed last night when your names were up for membership. That has never happened before. Who have you made that mad?"

Matejus folded his arms and smiled, "There is no mystery here. Penny Bayard tried to keep me from taking the board exam, so she certainly is not going to let us join some social club. She accused me of fee-spitting the past five years. Tell me, are there any women in your club?"

Whiting and Rockwell looked at each other. Even Rockwell was getting a little tense by now. "Well, yes, there are. I suppose could say that that is the one minority group that is represented."

By now Gannon was thoroughly angry. "Well, Ben, it looks like this is going to dog our careers forever. Surely you guys know I would fight for the right for any club to exist, even one with purple and scarlet ears, just as long as they let me alone. I never asked to join their damn club; I hardly knew it existed!"

"Just settle down," said Rockwell "The way this works, your name is put up by someone, and then they pass the box for 'white-ball–black-ball' votes. Since I counted the balls last night, I happen to know that you each had two black balls against you."

"Since you have women in your club, it's easy to guess who put the first one in," said Matejus. "But I don't see the identity of the second."

"You fellas have been moving too rapidly," said Whiting "I shouldn't have sent you so much work! One idea you've got to get used to in medicine is that nobody minds you unless you're successful, and then everybody minds. Funny, though, we never had this happen to anybody before, and this club started just about the time of the Kennedy election, about when Ben came."

'Well, just in case the two of you have any doubts about us, this whole matter was cleared up officially, first by the local committee of the American College of Surgeons and secondly the American Board of Surgery," Gannon began. "Ben was vulnerable when he asked to take the Boards, and somebody stuck it to him with an accusation of fee-splitting. We think that had all been settled. Most likely, the source of the complaint to the Board is the same person who dropped one of the black balls. Do you think I have that correct?"

Rockwell spoke next. "I think we have said enough. We were there, and we thought you ought to know about this. I doubt that it'll have any long term effect."

"You are probably wrong about that," said Gannon. "Ben and I have been feeling plenty of pressure, even from before the time that he came here. In the past two years we have been getting squeezed from all sides. There is expressed bitterness every time a general practitioner switches to us for surgical referral. Our competition refuses to see that the vascular work has given us an advantage. Penny Bayard sincerely believes we're just splitting fees with the GPs and that that is why we're getting the work. What gets me is the origin of the other black ball! I'll bet Charlie Peterson is a member, but Charlie is too nice a guy to cast such a vote just because we are competitors."

"Better start looking over your shoulder now, every day," said Rockwell "But you're not alone. Dick and I have our troubles, too. But you are a first. If there's trouble brewing for you in the Fox Valley Medical Travel Club, then there's trouble brewing for you elsewhere."

"Yeah," said Whiting. "You're smart enough, maybe too smart. You'll both be ready to be staff officers in four or five years, but if you continue at this rate, you won't be able to be elected. You're stepping on someone's toes in some way you don't understand or realize. Or maybe you do realize and you just don't want to tell us about it. Gannon, you've got to warm up to people. You're a tight-ass. You can't sound and look as though you're better than everybody else. Maybe you're becoming a focus of controversy without even knowing it."

Gannon answered stuffily, "you should know by now that Ben and I will not compromise ourselves just to be popular. Were going to keep slugging away. Furthermore Ben is going to a place where there is something called an 'intensive care unit,' and we intend to push that through. We've already hinted to Administration about it, and I think they'll set the money aside. The cost seems high, but a ten bed unit would go for only three hundred and fifty thousands dollars. Maybe the real beef is that the one who cast the second black ball thinks we're gaining control of the administrators by bringing good ideas to the hospital. Maybe that person believes that the status quo was to his advantage. Perhaps he believes that his privileged position is being challenged."

Rockwell and Whiting were beginning to back away now and left with one parting piece of advice. "Just don't screw up. Bob and I will back you up so long as you don't do anything that hurts patients. Definitely the hospital needs a change in direction. What did you call it last summer, Chris? The lighthouse hospital? Just don't let the light go out because you've been blackballed once. We'll put your names up again in one year. Meanwhile, see if you can improve your images with the doctors.

Play poker with a few of them."

"It's true, you know Chris, you are a bit of a snob. You act like you are better than everyone else," said Matejus, starting to ease his way down the corridor, "but it's okay. I enjoy a nice, cool glass of wine. Let me be the social butterfly. You can stay alone on your island of purity. I'm pretty good at poker too; all kinds of poker!"

Gannon waved good-bye, then walked slowly to a dictating booth in the nursing station. His head was throbbing. Was this complex of skirmishes becoming a full-blown war? How far off was the ultimate confrontation, and what form would it take? Well, how many times had he been told by someone describing a Cubs ballgame that "the best defense is a good offense?" Maybe it was time to bug the chief of the x-ray department about something new that he did not want to do, the creation of a room for special x-ray procedures.

Attack, attack, he thought, as he hurried down in the elevator to the x-ray department. As he entered the office of the chief Jack Murphy, he found Penny Bayard reviewing films with the radiologist. Bent over, heads together, they literally jumped apart when Gannon pushed the door open. Dr. Bayard flushed, picked up a jacket of films, and hurried out the door, saying, "We're through, Dr. Gannon! He's all yours." Was there a guilty expression on her face?

Dr. Jack Murphy was crisp in speech, dapper in dress, and short. He chain-smoked all day, every day, holed up in his dark cave for interpreting films. His manner toward Gannon had always been one of diffidence and tolerance rather than frank dislike. Gannon, on the other hand, was afraid of Murphy. Radiologists saw all of the problems in each doctors' complications; in a way, they had access to too much information for Gannon's taste.

"Jack, do you have a little time? I have mentioned before that I think your department should have a room designed for special x-ray procedures. Have you thought about that?"

Murphy's speech came in clipped, short sentences, with an accent that could not be placed, faintly akin to a mixture of New England heritage. "Too expensive. No need for it in a community hospital. Needs a rapid cassette changer. That's a lot of money."

"A Sanchez-Perez is only $25,000 bucks, Jack. It can be fitted to any x-ray machine you already have and any room lined with lead. No extensive remodeling is necessary. We can schedule in the afternoon so you can generate twice the income from space that otherwise is downtime. I've worked all the economics of the project. It will pay for itself in ninety days. You will see."

"Okay, Chris; I'll take it up with my bosses. But, I'm not promising anything." He put up the next batch of films ostensibly to show that the conversation was over. "Don't call me. I'll call you."

As Gannon retreated down the halt he thought, *Well, that guy is a member of the Fox Valley Medical Travel Club, also, or I'll eat my hat.*

"Hey, doc!" a voice hailed. "Why so down in the mouth?" It was Maggie DeLaney. He was actually grateful when she put her hand through his arm. "Come on. You can cry on my shoulder, whatever the trouble is. Let's talk!"

Chapter 13

Warmed by the afternoon sun shining on his heavy blankets, Gannon was staring sleepily at the screen of his monitor. Housed now in this newer step-down department for observation, he was no longer prevented from ambulation by a complex of wires from chest leads to electronic devices, the communication between these inanimate objects now employing radio waves. The train of thought initiated by observing his own endless electrocardiographic pattern on the oscilloscope took him back to the early days in this field, when the whole idea of constantly monitoring the heart action of a patient was a new concept. Comfortable in the warm sun and mesmerized by the moving green pattern, he dozed intermittently and remembered the beginnings of it all.

A few days later, Ben Matejus stopped him in the hall on rounds and said, "I've got something for you. A letter from Kansas City. I don't think this is all just public relations and a lot of breast beating, but really is a good idea. Come on, I'll buy you a cup."

The coffee shop was manned by pink ladies, volunteers, and a couple of older waitresses. It was common social ground for attending staff and nurses, and it was not unusual to see clumps of three or four bent over coffee and doughnuts, heads together, engaged in some kind of planning. And such was the case at mid-morning on this day, when Matejus and Gannon met to discuss the idea of "intensive care" for the first time.

"I want to go to Kansas City in about two weeks," said Ben. "There is a collection of eight beds out there in a university setting, devoted to the idea of what is called "intensive care." It is a new concept aimed at a constant, running EKG pattern kept under observation at a central nursing station, twenty-four hours a day, on all of the patients in the unit. The idea is to pick up changes in cardiac rhythm and treat them with medicine before their condition declines too drastically."

"Is this strictly electronic monitoring or are other parameters also under close observation?" asked Gannon.

"Smart guy," said Matejus. "With laboratory and x-ray equipment and personnel concentrated in the same area, all the blood chemistries can be closely watched, when it counts, and serial x-ray studies done on short notice. Also, I understand that an accompanying feature is a small laboratory specially designed for measuring oxygen and carbon dioxide in the bloodstream, so-called blood gas studies."

"Is this in line with some reading I've been doing regarding increased usage of pacemakers and defibrillators by nursing staff, under the right circumstances?" asked Gannon.

"Right. We both are aware of how difficult it has been to teach these concepts to physicians. But I think it would be much more accepting by nurses because they would have increased responsibility. For this to work, nurses would have to be trained in interpretation of electrocardiograms so they can make instant decisions. If they have to call the physician for diagnosis and approval for action, the whole purpose would be defeated, because of that eight-minute time limit without oxygen that the brain cannot tolerate. This is really aimed at heading off, preventing and treating cardiac arrests. I think we would have to construct an additional training course for nursing staffing and follow that up with some legal documentation transferring the decision making from M.D.'s to RN's."

"Certainly sounds revolutionary to me. But will Bayard and Adams and that gang let us get away with it? Surely they will throw road-blocks. I'll bet it's expensive. All the equipment may yet be in the 'research and development' stage. How do you think McKee will react to the money factor?" asked Gannon.

"Funny you should mention that. He agreed to pay my plane fare to Kansas City. I heard there's another similar unit in Miami and a four-bed unit in Philadelphia. Maybe you could arrange to go look at one of those. They're both in the university setting, however, and I don't know of any similar unit in a community hospital anywhere in the United States." Matejus's voice was intense and beginning to shake with excitement as he speculated upon this totally new approach to patient care.

Gannon was thinking along the same lines and voiced a question, "Do these eight beds in Kansas City have a mix of illnesses or are they all surgical as opposed to all medical?"

"Good question. So far, the units are mixed. Two or three beds of each type of illness. The units house patients after injury, complications of severe diabetes, coronary occlusive disease and critical states after surgery. And apparently occasionally there have been people who have been revived from cardiac arrest and ended up on a respirator for a prolonged period. That might be a problem over the long haul."

So it was just a brief three weeks after that when Matejus dragged Gannon by the hand down to the coffee shop again, saying, "I've asked Paul Irish to join us in a little bit. We have to go ahead with this. We cannot wait. With any luck, we could be the first community hospital in the United States to have such a unit. I saw people in Kansas City that would surely have been dead if the nurses had not been empowered to intervene. Here comes Paul."

Paul Irish was the medical photographer for the hospital. He had done many illustrations for over ten years in this practice, most of those pictures going into exhibits; he was also known for his home-produced medical movies that were exhibited across the United States at major surgical meetings. He truly had a knack for setting up a surgical field and getting just the right shots and had been partly responsible for Matejus and Gannon winning prizes at such exhibits. He was a chain smoker, so the first thing he did was lay a full pack of cigarettes on the table. Over the next thirty minutes he went through half of them while Gannon and Matejus discussed the options and the idea.

"First, Paul," said Gannon, "You've got to keep quiet about this. Even when you're shooting pictures for some of the other surgeons, you can't talk about this. We have to get it through the Administration and the Board before the staff has a chance to organize a negative campaign. You know how much trouble Penelope Bayard has given us, and she'll do all she can to block this."

"I get what you mean," answered Paul "I'll keep my mouth shut. Do you have any drawings or photographs of the unit in Kansas City?"

Matejus responded, "Yes, I have more than that. Look at these photographs. You see, in their unit, the eight beds are only separated by curtains. I think we should partition our unit in such a fashion that each bed is actually a private room. Chris and I both think we should go for ten beds. See this bank of black boxes over here?" he asked, pointing to a set of eight units, side by side, each about one foot square, lined up on a desk in front of two nurses.

Said Matejus, "You can't see them, but on the other side of each of these boxes is an electronic screen, an oscilloscope, each screen reflecting the EKG pattern of one of the patients in the eight beds. There are wires everywhere in this room, because nothing was buried in the floor; they all connect to EKG leads strapped on the patient's chest and extremities, so there is a constant, running pattern. Where there is a change, the nurse knows it instantly and can take action."

Paul Irish had had a tremor for years. This was exacerbated by the cigarette trembling in his hand. "Know what? If we are going to go for broke, I think we should make a model. I'll make some notes today and come back in a week with a cardboard model. It won't cost us a nickel. We'll put in the beds, the glass partitions, the chairs, the location of the monitors, and the nursing station and then move everything around as we figure out how to do it most efficiently. Does McKee know about this yet?"

"Just a little," said Gannon. "McKee paid Ben's expenses to Kansas City, and I presume he'll do the same for me somewhere else. But he doesn't have much information about it. We've quoted that each bed, with all its equipment and so forth, would cost about $35,000. That makes a $350,000 bite for the Board to chew off. So if Penny Bayard gets to any of them we could be headed off because of the size of the project. But Ben and I are going to suggest that McKee look at it as just ten private beds, so that if the idea fails and does not become a used item across the country, he simply has ten private beds. I think we can put it up on top of the second floor off the third floor south wing."

Paul Irish looked at them steadily through the curling murk of his cigarette. "Let's make a few sketches now, and I'll bring the model back in a week."

A week later they met again in the library to look at the first edition, and they continued meeting regularly for the next few weeks, turning the model over to Sam McKee and the hospital architect to begin engineering drawings.

In the meantime Gannon received consent from Presbyterian Hospital in Philadelphia to go visit their four-bed unit. As he was driving to the airport, he thought to himself about the last trip he had made to Philadelphia and smiled a little, as this one was going to serve more than one purpose. Not only was he going to establish some concept of the validity of intensive care, but he also planned to light a dynamite fuse that had potential for blowing up Penny Bayard. The battle was on...

The hospital in Philadelphia was very old. It was so old that the various wings were not even consistent elevations. It had been built in sections over a period of one hundred and fifty years, and as he walked down the corridors, he had the feeling that there always was yet another older part of the hospital The four-bed unit did not look very promising. No design changes had been permitted to give the idea of "unit" or to give the feel of a separate nursing care entity. The four beds were located at the end of a hallway. The setup was remarkably like Matejus's photographs from Kansas City, with just hanging curtains among the four beds. Nothing about any of the monitoring equipment appeared to be ready-made. Electronic leads and electronic cords crossed and re-crossed the floor in what Gannon thought was a dangerous manner. The cords were held down by tape, presumably so that people would not stumble over the connections. The four monitors were simply arranged on a long table and appeared to be from a different manufacturer than those seen in Kansas City.

The physician who ran the unit seemed as old and decrepit as his institution. A cardiologist, he had been working on the idea for over twenty years. *That has to be almost half a career,* thought Gannon. Here is a man who had staked his entire professional reputation on one basic idea, and it had not yet taken hold in university centers, except for Miami and Kansas City. He grinned to himself He knew enough about negative medical politics to realize that this old fellow was working in a similar situation. Someone was sitting on this idea and keeping the older internist buried in a back corridor in the old hospital so that his ideas could not get out.

"Well, Doctor, could you give me some reprints of articles you have written so that I can read them on the plane home?" asked Gannon. The internist, a tall graying, stooped man who had introduced himself as Dr. Koenig nodded his head vigorously and said, "I can give you a half-dozen articles and re-prints. Finally, I am getting some attention. Greatbatch and Chardack and a man named Zoll have small practical external pacing devices to go with the monitoring equipment, and I think we'll be able to put the whole thing together into a functioning package yet within this year. "

"Dr. Koenig, you mentioned external pacing. Does that mean that our intensive care unit would be not only for intense observation but also for intense treatment? I'm not sure I get the idea. "

"But of course. Not only is external pacing available, but so is defibrillation. When a patient fibrillates here, the nurses make the diagnosis, put the paddles on, and shock the patients themselves within seconds of onset."

"Aren't there a lot of legal issues involved? I mean, the nurses are making a diagnosis of a life threatening complication and treating the patient without conferring with a doctor. How does that work? What do the lawyers think of that?"

Dr. Koenig answered quickly, "You will have to design and implement written protocols covering these issues before you open."

"Do you think this could be considered for a community hospital as opposed to a university setting? I mean, most of the bugs are worked out in universities, before the rest of us are given a shot," said Gannon.

"No, I don't think you will have to wait. Electronics manufacturers are very much interested in this. There is a lot of competing equipment becoming available that can be used for monitoring and a dozen or so companies are eager to make them for public use. The basic idea is simply an oscilloscope. Oscilloscopes have been in use for several years in industry, so it's simply a matter of making the application to the human body."

On the plane home Gannon produced notes from all the things that had occurred, particularly the comments from Dr. Koenig. It really did appear that most of the kinks had been worked out and that practical application was simply a matter of finishing the model and hiring the right personnel. If they moved rapidly, they could have the unit functioning in one year. As a concept, it was going to be an absolute necessity for the kind of work that Gannon felt his partnership would begin to do within five or six years.

Implementation of the concept was not easy, as it turned out. Inevitably, a physicians' planning committee had to be appointed, and Ben Matejus conducted night meetings for six months with this committee, at the end of which time they produced the protocol which legislated decision making by the nursing staff and aggressive treatment of heart rhythm changes. After many meetings with the architect, it was still necessary to conduct meetings with the engineers and the contractors. As it turned out, there was simply no example to follow elsewhere in the United States and no prior drawings. The cardboard model became engineering drawings, and the ten-bed unit opened for surgical patients, patients suffering from acute coronary occlusions, trauma, and severe diabetes, within the year.

Chapter 14

Gannon was annoyed on Monday afternoon. It was one of those bright, sunny February days with a harsh wind blowing skiffs of snow around the feet of people on the street below his room, all walking with their garments pulled closely about their bodies. The sun was misleading; it was a very cold day. The frost on the inner surface of his north window had not even begun to melt. His annoyance centered around the fact that he was going to miss another lunch, as he was to have another "study" later in the afternoon. He was losing weight. There was plenty of evidence that his physicians were having trouble explaining his illness to themselves, much less to their patient. What ever had happened had almost killed him.

"The cardiac cath was normal," Irving Wren had said. "No residual clots are in the ventricle. But we need to check that with an echo cardiogram."

"Shit, " Gannon had said.

Here again came his nurse to check his blood pressure and blood sugar. And he supposed that a part of the attention would be some kind of an injection culminating in somnolence. Having finished her other duties, the nurse picked up a previously prepared syringe and needle and injected the contents into his subclavian line. He had learned that IV Valium had a merciful effect on him and this time it was almost instantaneous. As he drifted off into sleep, a memory from approximately 1968 was rekindled.

Gannon was in Sam McKee's office. McKee had asked him to make a presentation to one of the service clubs at a meeting that would be held in the hospital. "I understand that you fellows have a black-and-white film on pacemaking. I think I heard that you presented that at some meeting somewhere. Am I correct?"

"Yep, you are right," replied Gannon. "Actually, we've shown it at several different meetings. Why do you ask?"

"You probably don't know that we invite one of the service clubs annually to hold one of their monthly meetings here. It costs us a bit for the lunch, but I've always felt that it was well worth it. Yes, it is a public relations gimmick. I was hoping that you would be willing to show your film, with a live description by yourself," said McKee.

"Well, sure," answered Gannon. "But you should know that one or two of my competitors may lodge a complaint against me about advertising. I'd be glad to do the program, but you may have to defend me, if there's some official squawk. Would you do that?" Actually, Gannon was smiling as though such a problem seemed improbable and remote.

Anticipating doing the program a month or so later, Gannon was in a good mood when he left the administrator's office and moved across to the physicians' cloak room, which also doubled as the mailroom. This combination made it a place in which one could cross paths with both friend and enemy. The handshakes of the former were counterbalanced by the curt nods and noncommittal looks of the latter. Most conversations were inconsequential, for the traffic was too high to permit any kind of confidence or trust. Smiles were often masks for venomous ideas.

On this day, Mark Silver, who had been affable enough through the years but had continued steadfastly to refer his surgery to Penelope Bayard, waved him over as he was going through a stack of correspondence. "Sit down a minute, Chris. Let's talk a little."

Gannon accompanied Silver with some care putting his guard up against saying too much that involved commitment. Silver was a Jew and almost certainly not a member of the Fox Valley Medical Travel Club, yet because of his continuing pattern of referral to his chief competitor, Gannon was never certain as to the political alliances of Dr. Silver.

Silver spoke first, "I hear that the nominating committee is going to put you up for staff secretary at the March meeting. You must have greater political impact than I suspected."

"Not really," replied Gannon, "but I do believe that some of the staff think I could lead the hospital in a different direction, away from the present establishment. I don't exactly have the support of the administrators, because they can't afford to make my opposition angry. But my ideas about the future affect their future, also."

Silver tilted his head back, put his fingers together in front of his chest, and spoke softly. "Aren't you afraid of some negative reaction from the rest of the staff? You've only been here ten years. Surely anybody against you could get the support of the elder half of the staff. You might have a lot of trouble if you let yourself be nominated. Maybe you should think it over and tell them "no" for the time being. Maybe this is a time to be patient."

Gannon hesitated a bit. He wondered what Silver really wanted. "Well Mark, maybe you and some others feel that my ambitions are too radical for this hospital. I do have a large program in mind, one that would involve only a modest investment by the hospital at this time, but which would yield millions for the institution in the future, and this is income for further dispersion and dispensation by the Board of Trustees into other fields. I'm not ready to share the specifics with you yet, but I believe that you will support me when the time comes. Don't you think that if I were an officer, I would have less trouble beating my way through the Executive Committee for support for this program? I think I must let the nomination stand."

Silver stood up and stuck out his hand to shake. "Well I don't mind telling you that I think it's a mistake. I think that it is too soon for you, and I think the staff will react badly and you will lose.

"I admit that I have been learning recently that I have enemies, Mark," said Gannon. "But the only people who do not have enemies are those who do nothing and those who are not successful. I believe enough in myself to believe that I'm in the cat-bird seat, not only with my program, but also positioned to change the direction of the institution. I certainly hope I can count on your support at the ballot box." He shook Silver's hand and strode out the door, seething in anger, his face hot and undoubtedly red, giving away his reaction to this conversation. He knew that he had always had a problem trying to mask his emotions. Anyone could read his face.

In personal matters he simply could not be confrontational. In matters involving groups of people or principles, he had no trouble defining the issues and making his case. He simply could never speak for himself, and now he had almost been told out-right that it would be better if he were not a candidate because he was going to be made to look like a loser by the very people he had come to dislike the most.

At that moment, one of those stepped out of the stairwell and bumped into him. It was Ken Adams. "Oh, Chris, good morning. I've been thinking about coming to talk to you about something of a political nature. I understand that you are going to be up for election to the chairs this spring, and frankly, I'd like to make a deal with you."

"Well Ken, I don't know. You and I are not known as bosom buddies. Of course I would like your support in any election. But what is the price I am going to have to pay in order to have that?"

Adams chuckled and looked at the floor with his hands on his hips. "Well that's frontal enough. You only have to be one of the good ole' boys. In return for that, you can have the support of the establishment men on the staff. I'm going to let you in on a secret."

Gannon smiled, leaning against the door frame. "If it's a secret, it would be better if you did not tell me. My partner tells me that I'm no good at secrets. So, what's the deal?"

Adams shifted his hands to his pockets and gazed at a spot on the opposite wall. "I suppose you know that the other hospital in town, St. Benedict's, has been condemned and that they either have to close up or put up another building. Are you aware of that?"

"Yep, a technician in the x-ray department told me they were having trouble getting water to the fourth floor. There have been electrical problems in the operating room for the last five years at least. It does look like they're approaching a crisis. Didn't I hear something about a quiet city-wide money raising effort in 1966? I don't think it went anywhere."

Adams stiffened his back before he spoke. "You are right. The pledges were very small and I don't think they'll ever put together enough of a campaign in this city to rebuild. There are not enough monied Catholics. But let's get on to what I want you to help us do."

"Who do you mean by 'us'? Who do you represent other than yourself and your partner?"

Adams looked him straight in the eye for the next bit of speech. "'Us' are those who control Waterford Hospital and this does include some board members. Later on, you will understand the business relation. What I want you to do is help us close St. Benedict's as soon as possible. The easiest way is by not admitting patients. Patients are the lifeline of any hospital and if we deliberately cut the admissions, they will fold. Under those circumstances; we can control medicine in the whole town. You're young, and I think you should be in on the ground floor of this. By controlling the practice we can refer patients to one another and freeze everybody else out. What do you say?"

Gannon was amazed at what he was hearing, not for the actual information so much, which he had long-since guessed, but because this man was foolish enough to openly explain the strategy. To confess that he was the ringleader in such a destructive move was idiotic to Gannon and further informed Gannon that Adams had no appreciation or understanding how Gannon and his friends would react to this kind of betrayal.

"Well, I don't know, Ken. I will have to talk this over with Ben and our friends. Personally, I don't see how doctors' freedom can be preserved by having only one institution from which to select. Putting the practice of medicine and the care of patients in the hands of a few doctors is certainly putting a major burden on that group. I would need to know more about the identity of your supporters and why they think this would work before I could make a decision. Just offhand, it is my Judgment that most towns are better off with two grocery stores two newspapers, and probably with two hospitals. Of course there may be some other elements that neither one of us knows at this time."

With a wave of his hand, he slipped through the stairway door and down the steps, tears of frustration blinding his eyes. First of all he was angry because he had now become certain that Mark Silver had been sent as a messenger by Penelope Bayard for the sole reason to persuade him not to be a candidate. Additionally Ken Adams had extended an invitation to him to join their political ranks. He thought of all the other similar kinds of people he had known before, at the college level, again in medical school and finally in his residency. It seemed like there was no escape from greedy schemers and planners. This seemed to be a special affliction of those born to privilege and determined to hang on to it, no matter what it took. He wondered what other events had already taken place, leading to some kind of boycott of St. Benedict's. The strategy was correct, patient admissions did keep a hospital alive, and restriction of that would simply cut off the life blood of the institution.

Gannon kept thinking of these things as he traversed the stairs, went to his mailbox, put his coat on, and walked out of the building. He guessed that he had three years to turn this situation around. There was not a chance that they could ally themselves with Adams and Penny Bayard, attractive as that possibility might be from a financial perspective. He would have to participate directly and vigorously in a leadership role in any money-raising campaign for St. Benedict's and somehow find an issue to attract the attention of the staff. And what would that look like to Sam McKee and his associates?

As he thought about it, he wished that this was all out of altruism. He knew there was a significant element of selfishness because he also knew that he would never be in a controlling position at Waterford Hospital and that he could force the competing institution to keep the first one honest. *Well*, he thought, *this has been some day. It looks like I have my issue for the election, if I choose to exploit it. First, I'll have to see if they nominate someone else to run against me.*

Secretly, after his corridor conversation with Mark Silver a month before, Gannon had become convinced of the likelihood of his own election. When, at the spring quarterly meeting in 1968, Peter Freudin was nominated to contest his own nomination by the staff nominating committee, he still did not feel in any way threatened or have an indication of the possibility that he might not win. Gannon did not realize how politically naive he was or that power was a much more driving motive than money. He should have recognized that something was afoot when the nomination was made from the floor by Ken Adams. He had turned Adams down on his request for a deal and the enmity of Adams for him was now an open and confrontive issue at Executive Committee meetings. When Adams came up with the name of Peter Freudin, Gannon should have recognized trouble ahead.

Because Gannon and Freudin had shared clinical responsibility, particularly through the emergency department, Gannon considered him a friend, or at least as much as an older and established surgeon in a community could be a friend to a new, younger challenger. Furthermore, his specialty was orthopedics, being in partnership with Michael Caesar, and there had been the shared emergency room responsibility with Gannon with mixed results.

Freudin looked like a doctor. He was six feet tall, about fifty-five years of age, and had wavy silver hair. His winter attire in the operating room area was a navy-blue, single-breasted jacket, worn with gray pants, and he looked every bit like a surgeon as conceived by nonmedical people. He wore metal taps in the corners of his heels, and since it was his wont to stride up and down the terrazzo floor in the corridor outside the operating rooms while waiting for a case to begin, everyone within ear shot was conscious of his presence by the clicking of those heels on the hard marble-like floor. Tap, tap, tap—he strode up and down, snuffing and snorting like a purebred bull, clicking his heels and folding and unfolding his arms on his chest, while glaring down the hall at the nursing staff with a poorly disguised look of disgust because, yet one more time, they had failed in their duties and he was going to be held up for his scheduled operation.

It was these very qualities which made Freudin attractive to his colleagues. He not only looked like a doctor, he acted like a doctor. Anyone but a young fool like Gannon would have had the common sense to withdraw his nomination when Peter Freudin's name was put up.

Over the three months between quarterly meetings leading up to the election, Freudin, who had never shown any evidence of political leadership, simply went about his business on a day-to-day basis. Gannon thought that he was not campaigning and did not want the responsibility of the series of offices over three years, beginning with election to the position of staff secretary. Gannon, on the contrary, was actively soliciting votes. He knew that a block of votes would go to Freudin, simply because of his age group. Gannon felt that he had demonstrated the ability to plan and had shown that he could lead the staff

While the intensive care unit planning was generally accepted by the staff to have been carried out by Ben Matejus, Gannon still had been given some credit for this, by reason of the association between himself and Ben. The unit was up and running and was a financial success. It had attracted much attention to the community. Gannon thought he had proved himself to the administrative staff in terms of ability to create new ideas and to follow up with implementation. The real strategy had not yet been announced and was known only to a small circle of close friends.

He and Matejus had made the decision to go ahead with a program of open heart surgery. Pumps were now readily available, and a specific surgical procedure for relief of coronary artery occlusion was becoming a day-to-day clinical undertaking in many hospitals across the country. For years surgical innovators had been working on different approaches for the relief of angina. Finally, some applied exactly the same principles as Gannon and Matejus had learned in the mid-fifties for the bypass of obstruction of large vessels in the limbs. A method had been developed by which venous channels were removed from the limb of a given patient and transferred into the chest, attaching one end to the aorta at its root and the other end to the far end of the narrowed coronary artery, thus introducing a bypass of blood supply to the heart wall by going around the occluded segment. Coronary bypass surgery was well on its way to what would become one of the common operations in the United States by the mid-'70s. For the past year Matejus and Gannon had been conducting a quiet search for a young man who could do this kind of cardiac surgery. As much as he had wanted to make this information known to the staff in general in order to reap some of the harvest of credit for planning, Gannon had had to stay silent and say nothing about this possible venture.

On the day of the election, there was not much evidence of excitement at all. Gannon was unaware of any unusual pressure. When the votes were counted, he had been squashed like a bug and was greatly surprised. When Mark Silver had said, "You must have a great deal of strength," he had felt that he was on the right path and with the right people. It was evident that the establishment had decided that he did not have those qualities which rendered him a singular potential for leadership and had turned in favor of the older, wiser head. Gannon was not devastated emotionally. It was just another in a series of bumps during this era. In general he was getting what he wanted at almost every turn.

In the subsequent summer of 1968, he and Matejus went to see Sam McKee. After a self congratulatory review of the opening and functioning of the intensive care unit, they indicated that they were there to show evidence of a future program Then, for the first time, they told him of their plans to do open heart surgery at Waterford Hospital. Characteristically McKee was not surprised and was helpful. Would they need any additional personnel? How much money was necessary for capital and how much would be needed for operating expenses? There did not seem to be any hesitation regarding their ability to accomplish the stated goal. They had shown him of their abilities to plan and proceed. They opened by indicating their need for another surgeon, a younger man, with the right kind of training, and that seemed to satisfy any questions that McKee might have had.

Discussion then centered on the x-ray department. As chief of radiology, Jack Murphy indicated his personal resistance to a room dedicated to special procedures. He had dragged his feet and done everything possible to prevent the opening of the special procedures room, which was accomplished about the same time as the opening of the intensive care unit. Murphy simply did not want to get involved. It was a technical advance with which he was unfamiliar, and he was certain would cost more than it could return in terms of dollars. The fact that he was a close personal friend of Penelope Bayard was not lost upon either Matejus or Gannon. Bayard spent time daily in Murphy's viewing room, and there was no doubt that Murphy applied influence to other referring physicians when he had knowledge of a surgically correctable process that could be referred.

Gannon and Matejus knew that there was another level of sophistication necessary for the diagnostic aspect of open heart surgery, above and beyond those things available already in the pioneer special procedures room. Gannon was encountering resistance at every level for establishment of coronary angiography. Having lost the secretarial election, for the first time Gannon began to suspect that he was being hemmed in by a still-hidden collection of staff members, perhaps representing a majority. Putting that together with the information he had been given by Bob Rockwell a couple of years before, Gannon and Matejus agreed that there was a collection of physicians to whom they began to apply the name "American Legion." They were certain that they themselves were included in the opposition group, many of whom were displaced physicians who had survived World War II and were surely identified by the term "Foreign Legion."

Chapter 15

"Come on, Chris," said his friend Wren. "Let's get you into this harness. It's a combination of electrodes for a little portable monitor, combined with a sling and bag to carry the unit. Now walk around today and see what cooks up. On the big monitor in ICU, you never showed a fibrillating pattern. But you may have had something in the days or week before the stroke."

"Well, Irving you finally said it. You used the word 'stroke.' Gannon was staring at the wall. "What does my brain look like on the CT?"

"Since day one we've known that you had three holes in your brain. The smallest was in the respiratory center, which is why you arrested. You had respiratory arrest first, followed by cardiac arrest. If your guest on the radio program that day had not been the RN who runs the cardiac rehabilitation unit, we would not be having this conversation today. She saved your bloody neck. Enough of that. Now take up your bed and walk around here with the monitor running and see what you can produce."

"Well that is easy for you to say. I gather that you are trying to trigger a fibrillation of the atrium in order to explain the source of emboli to the brain."

"Yep. You've got it right for once. This is just a diagnostic test."

So after dangling on the edge of the bed a few moments, Gannon stepped toward the hallway, somewhat hesitantly, hugging the wall.

During this era in the summer of 1968, Gannon and Matejus reached the peak of their combined skills. Both were still young enough to take the long and late hours, yet old enough to have gleaned sufficient experience to know what they were doing in most situations. Clinical diagnosis came easily and was helped more and more by additional advanced diagnostic machinery. They were responsible for the introduction of many of those advanced techniques and for recruitment of young people with certain specific skills. Their operating times decreased steadily each year. Removal of a fractured spleen was accomplished easily in forty minutes. The usual operating time for removal of the average gallbladder was similar, and it was not unusual at all for appendectomy to be accomplished in ten minutes. They were still naive enough to measure their skill in terms of time and felt that if they were working rapidly and efficiently and safely, the blood loss and trauma to the patient would be less. They thought together and complemented one another at the operating table.

One day that summer they were stopped in the corridor by Whiting and Rockwell, the two obstetricians who had informed them of the existence of the Fox Valley Medical Travel Club. Rockwell touched Gannon on the arm and said,

"Well you've done it again! Can't you guys stay out of trouble?" He laughed good naturedly and poked Gannon in the ribs.

On the other hand, Whiting bristled a little saying, "You have done it this time! You were on the pan before the counselors of the County Medical Society two weeks ago. One of your competitors filed a complaint about unethical advertising. What do you know about it?"

Gannon smacked his fist into the palm of his hand. "Nothing. This is the first we have heard of this. Are you telling me that a hearing was held by some outfit and decisions were made without our knowledge? Boy, how crooked can those guys be! What was the complaint this time?"

"The complaint in writing was that you presented a movie about pacemaking a year ago here at Waterford Hospital using your own film and personal discussion. Did you do that?"

"Of course. McKee asked me to do the presentation. The hospital does something for a service club every year. I was the program. I used the same film that we put into the College library in 1965. Everybody had a good time. Why in the name of heaven would anybody squawk about that?"

Rockwell spoke soothingly. "Now, now, settle down. It sounds worse than it really was. It was an official meeting, all right, and minutes were kept and later signed by the participants. A hearing was offered to the plaintiff, who is a close friend of your old buddy, Penelope Bayard. Frankly, we thought she put him up to it. Since she is one of the counselors this year, she was able to sit in judgment in a perfectly legal fashion. Anyhow, they did make you look bad.

"How come I never was informed of the hearing? How come I was never allowed to speak for myself and give evidence? What a fouled-up situation that County Society is. I can't imagine a gang of thieves at the lowest level doing anything like that. How did it turn out? Is there some kind of permanent record?"

"Well, you have more friends than you know. The guys from the neighboring towns were so shocked and surprised at the complaint and the unethical way in which it was given they all voted in your favor. But you never heard anything about it, huh?"

"No. And I'll bet that this was before the quarterly meeting here at Waterford Hospital. I bet it affected some of the votes at the election in June. Well, I guess it's going to be hardball from here on. I should raise a fuss about doctor freedom, but I'm not going to right now. On to other things! Ben and I are telling you right here in the hall that we are seeking a third partner who can do cardiac surgery. Boy, will they squawk about that! And half of the complaints will come from hospital-based physicians from the x-ray department, and the laboratory. I don't think McKee can control them, even though he pays their salaries. But we do have his support!"

Whiting looked at Rockwell and grimaced. He spoke last as they were retreating down the corridor. "Well good luck. Just don't put us in a spot where we have to choose between you and somebody else. I mean it. We may have to vote the other way the next time." They stepped on the elevator as they gave a departing wave.

"Looks like it's going to get nasty, Ben. And you've probably taken along some heat, indirectly, that you haven't told me about. If you want out, just say so. But

I'm going to keep on with the idea that we have put together. We've done the vascular work; we established the intensive care unit and trained the girls there, so we've paid our dues to Waterford Hospital and have to move on. If either of us gets cold feet, he has to share it with the other. See you tomorrow? We have an 8:00 gallbladder."

The practice went on into the autumn. The annual meeting of the American College of Surgeons was being held in Chicago, just forty miles away, that October. On the Saturday afternoon of the last day of the meeting, Gannon received a call from a man with an Irish accent. He introduced himself as Brian Casey and said he understood from a friend at the College meeting that Gannon and Matejus were looking for someone to do heart surgery. He said he thought he would be available in a few months and wished to come out and interview for the position, if this could be done on short notice.

Next day, on a hot Sunday afternoon, with broken air conditioning in the building, the three men sat together for the first time. They hit it off easily and comfortably from the beginning. Casey had brought his wife to look over the town, wondering if she could get used to a small community as opposed to the international atmosphere in which they had both grown up. They had met at college in Switzerland, she being the granddaughter of a famous sculptor from Norway and he being of high rank in the Irish community. She did not appear to be dismayed at raising their children in a small town.

On the other hand, Casey clearly had some hesitancy. Apparently he had an offer to go to a university in the northeast, to head up a cardiac surgical program in its infancy. But he would be only a department member and not the head and owner of his own service.

So Matejus and Gannon built on that fact, and the discussion centered around what Casey thought of the opportunity in a community such as theirs. He agreed that the correct foundations had been laid with angiography, pacemaking, and arterial surgery and that this strong base had been reinforced with the opening of the intensive care unit, one of the first in the United States in a community hospital. He was surprised and gratified at what the two general surgeons had done. When they stepped out into the late afternoon sun, where it was a little cooler, Casey said, "I think there is a terrific situation here. You are at a 'Y' in the road. I will call you back within a week while you think over what you could pay me to come and work here. We have only one youngster so far—a girl who seems to have talent in the entertainment field."

The two young people waved as they drove out of the parking lot. Matejus said to Gannon, "I don't think we'll have any trouble with him. But she is different." The two men looked at one another, then smiled and shook hands. It looked like a major step along the road had been accomplished. Casey joined them in six months.

At about this same time, Gannon became involved in a couple of events that changed his direction in the political life of the community and in the political life of the hospital also. The first episode involved urban renewal money, a federal program in which participating municipalities were provided monies for buying up distressed properties and turning them into "renewal" of certain urban districts.

The opening shot was the delivery one evening of an edition of the local newspaper, upon whose front page there were two stories. The first was across the bottom of the page and described a "new" hundred-person committee of local citizens whose objective was to create and manipulate the methodology for the redevelopment of the north half of the downtown district, which was essentially a slum. Gannon read the article with some interest and then was amazed to see his own name listed among the membership. It was the first he had ever heard of the program, and no one had requested his participation. The second article, on the same page, was a description of how certain subcommittees of this larger committee had already met and made the decisions as to what properties were to be purchased in the program, the prices that were to be paid, and what elements of the renewal program were to be put in place, including a post office, a library, a city hall, a fire station, and an appellate court building, all surrounding a civic auditorium that was really the product of a wise investment made by a local citizen many years before.

While Gannon always had trouble confronting problems involving himself and personal situations, his sense of social responsibility was such that the obvious conflict of interest at this level was so gross as to require a letter to the editor. It was the first he ever wrote. In that letter he attacked the mayor, the salaried head of the Chamber of Commerce, and the local real estate industry, having learned that the chairman of the one hundred person committee was a real estate agent, of all things. The episode was climaxed by his resignation from the committee on the very first night of its assembly, accompanied somewhat by a mild apology for having raised such a fuss. Privately, he learned that the real estate agent chairing the group had referred to him as a "son of a bitch." With the exception of one or two other simpler matters, this was the end of his involvement in civic life in Waterford. The establishment no longer trusted him and he certainly did not trust the establishment. This ended ten years of community dedication. Later on he learned that "so much had been expected of him."

The second episode at this time was the case of Dr. C. K. Moon. C.K. had been brought to Waterford by gynecologist and obstetrician Roman Fox. Fox had had previous trouble working with partners, but he was trying again by employing C.K. Moon.

The constitution of Waterford Hospital provided for a period of two years for the new physician to remain under observation by his colleagues prior to being appointed to the active staff and being given the vote. Idealists would assume that this was a period of time for older and experienced physicians to guide the younger men toward a successful practice. Actually, it worked absolutely the opposite way. His would-be mentors were looking for mistakes, the kind of mistakes that would effectively put such a new competitor out of business. What set C.K. Moon aside was the fact that he was the first Oriental to apply to the staff and to come under consideration for advancement to "full attending" status.

In the spring of 1968, after two-and-a-half years of being under observation, C.K. was being bounced around among the advancement committees. The obstetrical department was small in number, so that often there was no quorum and therefore no meeting, and sometimes a meeting was held in which the feelings of the majority were known and votes were taken, the outcome of which was determined prior to the meeting. Some staff members attended and voted, even though they did not belong to the obstetrical department. C.K. stopped Gannon in the corridor one day to complain about his lack of advancement. C.K.'s thick accent was the most difficult that he had been called upon to understand. He could never reproduce it.

"I don't understand the trouble, Chris," he said. "I should have been advanced and my recommendation for full attending status been sent to the Board of Trustees six months ago. No recommendation has been made for advancement, and I can't make full attending staff. I've been through an appeals committee in my own department, but the doctors on the committee were the same ones that voted against me in the department. I took my case to the Executive Committee, and they appointed an ad hoc committee to review the matter. But the ad hoc committee were the same from the OB department that had been my appeals committee, so the outcome was again the same. What the hell do you think about that?"

I'm sorry, C.K.," replied Gannon. "It's a shell game I've seen before. You are a member of what is called the Foreign legion a round here and the first Oriental, if I am right. Some of the others, displaced doctors after World War II who came here in the late fifties, had some troubles for a while too. But they represented a referral base for all the specialists, so they were ultimately accepted. They represented money in the bank for the specialists. But you are a primary doctor in obstetrics and a competitor, and I'm sure they'd like to find some way to put you away. Did you have any bad cases for them to base the lack of advancement on?"

"They have four OB cases which they feel I mismanaged. But the critical vote was five to four, which is almost equal on both sides of the question. When I was present, they had endless arguments about what the correct management should have been. No, I don't think they have a thing. They're just giving me trouble because I'm an Oriental."

"Well maybe you are right, C.K.," responded Gannon. "Do you think it has anything to do with the fact that Roman Fox has had other partners ahead of you and that the rest of the department is fed up with him? Maybe they are trying to get at him through you.

"I thought about it," replied C.K.. "You may be right. This may be the beginning of a long division in the staff caused by failed partnerships. I may be in the wrong place at the wrong time."

Over succeeding weeks Gannon carried out a private investigation of the issues, and he became increasingly convinced that this represented a political matter involving two factions in the department, neither group being large enough to control or manage the other. Corridor and nursing station discussions began to lead the staff toward a split among the entire group. When reviewing department minutes, Gannon noted that Ken Adams had cast votes on several occasions, although he was not an obstetrician.

At the close of the September quarterly staff meeting, Gannon was seated toward the back of the room when the presiding officer called for "any additional business?" C.K. Moon stood up. Gannon cringed. He withdrew further into himself as C.K. described what had been happening to him for many months in the obstetrical department. Ordinarily he had no trouble getting his meaning across in spite of his thick accent, but on this particular day he was tense, and his thick words made his expressions difficult to understand and interpret. However, at the close of his speech, there was no missing the final question: "Why me?"

Gannon was immediately ashamed of himself He should have been the one to speak for C.K. He sat silent, afraid to precipitate another major battle, having been stung once already that summer in his own lost election. Nonetheless, the fact was that this man stood alone at the microphone in the presence of his colleagues and complained about now he was being treated by the staff leadership, and he, Gannon, had not had the courage to stand by him and support his cause.

The presiding officer called for a vote from the whole staff. After some wrangling about how to express the motion and some difficulty getting the positives and the negatives phrased correctly, a stand-up vote was taken. The count was almost evenly divided, but what was more important was how the lines were drawn. The separation was the group of American graduates on one side and the foreign graduates on the other. Gannon's observation was, however, that the latter were of sufficient numbers to produce a controlling vote at any staff meeting.

Gannon did not feel good at all upon leaving the meeting. He didn't think anyone else did either. Everybody was silent and looked guilty at the floor as they left. Only a couple shook C.K.'s hand for having taken this stand alone. *Well,* Gannon thought, *there still is time to do something.* The final decision has yet to be made by the Board of Trustees, who presumably have no vested interest in any of this. He reminded himself however, that some of the people influencing board members were in business with those same men, and only time would tell whether or not the Board would support the justice of the individual doctor or would succumb to economic pressures from the physicians who were against him.

Chapter 16

"Morning, Dad. How ya doin'?" Gannon blinked in the early morning sunlight. Standing next to his bed was his oldest son, now in his early forties. Always the athlete, this middle-aged man still looked thirty-ish: handsome, with a broad forehead, prominent cheek bones, and a straight profile. What a good looking man, thought Gannon.

The two of them had not understood one another for twenty years. Until Bill had left for the university, Gannon's relationship with him had seemed to be that existing between two mutual observers: Gannon had watched him in Little League, cheered him at high school football games, gone crazy in the stands as he scored the winning points in a basketball game. The situation was reversed as Bill had watched Gannon leading Cub Scout cheers giving addresses at sports banquets' giving interviews about local board of education policies. Gannon could not remember if he had ever told this boy that he loved him—admire, yes, but love? he was uncertain.

"Better, son. I can walk and talk, and that's a lot. Come here, closer!" They embraced awkwardly, as though this were not a habit, then spoke of Gannon's grandson, a punter for a nearby college team.

"I congratulate you on how you have brought him along. You did better with him than I did with you. I did not seem to know which button to push!"

"Aw, come on, Dad. There were just too many of us to get your attention. By the time I got to college, you had two more in Little League!"

Gannon sighed, "Anyway, you seem to have overcome an underprivileged childhood. You have become a good person, in spite of me. I do love you, you know."

"I always was a good person, Dad. You just did not notice. You would be happier now if you had listened to me when I told you that many people hated you because you would not let them be your friend!"

Gannon was reminded of a signal event bearing that out.

Gannon was wondering how he had let himself become involved in the present mess. Ken Adams had set a trap, and he and Matejus had fallen in.

"We'll have the meeting at the Hammer club, up the river a bit. We'll invite thirty of the leading staff members to help decide about hiring this—what do you call him? Cardiopulmonary physiologist for your heart program." Ken Adams further volunteered to pay for the dinner.

It seemed to Gannon too good to be true, and as things were developing on this evening, it was. Rockwell had to prepare him by explaining that the meeting would be held in the lair of his enemy, a private "key" club owned by Adams and his friends, including a couple of hospital board members. "You'll see," Rockwell had said. "None of your friends will be invited. At least you'll know who your enemies are—they will be everyone else in the room!"

How right he had been, thought Gannon, as he looked across the bar on the night of the meeting. Penny Bayard was hoisting glasses with an admiring group of her referring doctors. Adams seemed to be telling stories that made another group laugh, gesturing intermittently toward Gannon. The guest of honor, the physician to be interviewed for a position that had recently been created by Sam McKee, was surrounded by another group of internists. McKee himself was holding forth in a group of junior administrators.

"Ben, we've been had," said Gannon. "Stay sober. We'll both have to be able to think clearly. This is a setup, and Adams is keeping everybody in the bar, drinking on an empty stomach. They won't be able to decide anything!"

This prediction was soon confirmed, as the group lurched into dinner, stumbling against chairs, laughing at one another's antics. Gannon was seated between two internists whom he despised and shortly one simply fell asleep, head down on the dinner table. Efforts by McKee to conduct a business meeting were frustrated by his babbling audience. Michael Caesar and Peter Freudin were not interested in interviewing a new type of cardiologist. Why were they here? *Window dressing*, thought Gannon. Sprinkled among the tables were several general practitioners—*heavy admitters*, thought Gannon whose opinions were important to McKee for economic reasons but whose knowledge of this advanced technology was very limited.

Juan Gomez, the guest of honor, could not get the attention of anyone and could not be heard. Everyone howled in glee when Ken Adams slid off his chair and beneath the table. McKee lost control of the meeting, and Dr. Gomez gave up trying to be heard. The internist on Gannon's other side was now dozing.

It was a disaster. One month previously Matejus and Gannon had introduced the idea of the need for an invasive cardiologist, someone to do the special dye and x-ray procedures. They did so because they thought they had found the right man for the job. Looking at one another across the dining room, McKee just shrugged his shoulders. Certainly Gomez was a lost cause. It would be months before they could find another.

Ken Adams had beaten them by delaying the heart program indefinitely. On the other hand, he had exposed the cards in his hand and hinted at just how far he might go to defeat them The question was, Why would Adams go to so much trouble? Gannon still failed to see what it was that he wanted. Somehow, Gannon had to get the presidency; there was no other way to get his program off the ground.

A few days later, Matejus and Gannon were scrubbed on a night case. "What makes you think that this kid has appendicitis, Chris?" asked Ben Matejus. "I checked his belly before he went to sleep, and it was not very impressive.

"Well Ben, you'll have to trust me on this one. I admit that he does not have many belly findings. But he looks pale and sick, and his white count was still over fifteen thousand. Funny thing, though, his red count was only three million, and his hemoglobin was ten grams. I can't explain that," answered Gannon. "But I'm sure there is something surgical going on here, and there is no sense waiting overnight to face the same decision tomorrow."

"Hah," replied Matejus. "For a guy who is a little uncertain about what the diagnosis is, you certainly are making a statement by beginning with a McBurney incision."

"Well, we'll soon see." Gannon had indeed made the classical McBurney incision for a patient with certain acute appendicitis. So to the unwary, this was a commitment. This incision, which had been around for sixty years, was designed for appendectomy only, and was an angled short incision in the right lower quadrant of the abdomen, oriented to make it possible to divide the three underlying muscle layers bluntly with the fingers, so that when the wound was closed, these fell back together in the manner of a gridiron, making a strong wound. However, the overconfident operator who employed this incision for entering the abdomen with intention to do an appendectomy, and found a different diagnosis in another part of the abdomen, was indeed hard put to it to solve the problem surgically.

The time consumed with the muscle splitting incision was only a matter of a couple of minutes, and then, to his chagrin, Gannon noticed that the peritoneum just before the incision, was blue in color. "Look, Ben," he said, "a blue peritoneum. What the heck is going on? It looks like there's blood under this, and there is." He held up the peritoneum with a couple of mosquito clamps and inserted an aspirator, which promptly pulled the old liquid blood and clots up into the suction bottle.

Matejus laughed gently, under his breath. He did not say, "I told you so" because he had made similar mistakes himself before. Had he not, he would not have challenged the incision at the beginning, realizing what a headache it was to have the wrong incision for exploration of the abdomen in a small, five-year-old youngster. Following the bloody aspiration in the right lower quadrant, which was the explanation for the abdominal physical findings, there still was no obvious explanation for the blood in the abdomen.

"Was there any history of injury?" Matejus asked.

"Well, yes, a little. He did mention bumping into the newel post at the foot of the stairs at home two days ago, but he remembered only after I pressed him with conversation. He did not get sick until yesterday. Furthermore, he bumped himself on the left side, not on the right."

"Maybe that's the trouble," answered Ben. "Do you suppose he cracked his spleen with such a minor blow?"

"Well, we're going to have to find out. Shall we close this wound and make a second incision or should we extend the present wound?"

"Why don't you extend it upwards in a vertical fashion, toward the rib cage? At least we can see if there's blood coming down from above or coming up from the pelvis, and we'll be able to get a couple of fingers inside," Matejus offered.

Gannon quickly cut a vertical arm up toward the margin of the rib cage for a distance of about two inches, producing what could be called a hockey-stick incision. This did not help much. They had the impression of still-liquid blood coming down from above in the upper part of the abdomen but could feel nothing with the examining finger because the wound was still too small to admit a hand. "Come on, Chris," said Matejus. "Let's suck out the rest of this blood and see if we can't figure out which direction we are going to take."

As he aspirated the pelvis, Gannon said, "Well, it does not appear to be coming up from the pelvis. Besides, there's nothing down there that would bleed that I can of think of. Let's bet the percentages. I think we both figure now that he has a cracked spleen, possibly from that minor blow on the newel post."

Matejus nodded, so Gannon extended the upper end of the vertical arm of the incision across the abdomen to the left and up toward the other rib margin. This produced essentially a U shaped wound, which was in the nature of a flap of the abdominal wall which could then be turned over. When this was done, the problem was obvious. The young child's spleen was split into five or six pieces and lay deep in the left upper quadrant. There was no longer any active bleeding, presumably because the blood loss had produced a drop in blood pressure and consequent thrombosis of the venous circulation. Matejus pulled the rib margin back, and Gannon slid his left hand down along the wall of the diaphragm until he got behind the fragments of the spleen high in the abdomen and pulled those fragments and the rest of the left upper quadrant down and up onto the abdominal wall Then, he quickly put several clamps on the remaining vessels, leaving the center of the spleen, asking for 2-0 chromic catgut on a needle. This took care of the blood supply to the spleen, so the abdominal contents were returned into the abdomen.

Gannon was disgusted with himself and muttered under his breath throughout this part of the procedure. As he pulled down the abdominal wall flap he continued, "Well now, we can close up this mess. What a ridiculous situation! We have a three-sided incision on a five-year-old kid, and we're going to have to explain this to the parents. Well, as usual, truth is stranger than fiction, and the truth is the best explanation. Perhaps the parents can tell us about some other trauma we don't know about."

"You know what, Chris, I bet the boy has mononucleosis, with a friable spleen, and that this minor injury cracked it. I'll put a mono test on the list of postop orders, and I'll eat my hat if it's not positive tomorrow. Come on, let's close."

During the wound closure, Gannon spoke softy, "Say, Ben," he said. "We haven't had a chance to talk about today's Executive Committee. You were there. Anything of interest happen with regard to C.K?"

"I can talk more when we are in the locker room. But I can give you a couple of quotes that tell us in general where things are. First of all, the appeals committee report from the Board of Trustees came down and gave him a pass. Tough thing about today's meeting was that C.K. himself was present, and so was Ken Adams. Roman Fox came in a little late as usual as he probably knew that a contentious item like this would be the last item on the agenda. Everybody stuck around for the fireworks.

"C'mon Ben, what happened?"

"Not so loud, Chris. First of all, Fox dragged out an original letter signed by Ken Adams and read it to the group. Essentially it read, 'Congratulations on your new partner. He can take care of the transverse cunt part of your practice!' Ken Adams was present and did not deny that he wrote it. He looked like he was going to blow up. I would guess that this was the first time the Medical Travel Club has been successfully challenged."

"Is that all?"

"No, not quite. When Fox stood up to leave the meeting, he had to walk right by Adams' chair. I was sitting just two seats down. I could not help but hear. Fox looked right at Adams and hissed, "Shithead!" Adams fired back at him with "Fuckhead," and that was the end of that. Everybody in the room heard this exchange, and we all just filed out, trying to get away as fast as possible."

"You probably think we have not seen the end of this, right?" asked Gannon.

"No, we haven't. As a matter of fact this is just the second round of this battle. I would say that the war is still a few months off. But there's going to be a lot of heat between now and then." Gannon motioned to the scrub nurses to apply a dressing.

Chapter 17

"Well, Irving, I guess I'm going to have to go home, whether I want to or not, right?" asked Gannon. Staring disconsolately at his breakfast tray, he continued with, "Somewhere in this hospital is a bottomless container of green jello, made with low calorie sugar. Oatmeal has been on the menu every day now for six days. According to a recent television ad, it's the real thing! "

Irving was looking at the tray also. "Yeah, you're going home in a day or so. I agree that your tray is not very appetizing. But you are going to have to make some adjustment in what everybody calls your 'lifestyle.'

As Gannon picked up his spoon and spread some of the low calorie sugar on the oatmeal, he muttered to himself about the blue milk he was given to use to dilute his breakfast. "As a matter fact, Irving, everything on this tray is fake. There is fake sugar, fake fat, fake wheat, and I'll bet a dollar that there's somebody somewhere planning to send me turkey disguised as bacon."

Wren was standing with his arms akimbo, a far-off look in his eyes. "The most I'm going to suggest for you is 'an aspirin a day will keep the cardiologist away,' That is, no heparin!"

"Hah! We both remember the last time I had a relationship with heparin. Every time I look at the skin graft on my forearm, I think of that sequence. "

But Irving was not going to let Gannon get him down. He was a man who was always "up" psychologically, even during the worst personal problems of his own life. Gannon had always respected him as a man who kept his head in a crisis and could not be talked into doing things against his better judgment. Not only was he the most intelligent doctor on the staff, but he also had a lot of common sense and a great sense of humor.

"So Irving, what else are we going to do? Am I sitting on a keg of dynamite or not?"

In a few months, a series of events developed which confirmed Gannon's suspicion about the existence of a hidden political group whose purpose seemed to be the maintenance of the status quo, this group apparently feeling it was being threatened by Gannon. He repeatedly had experienced the sting of the Fox Valley Medical Travel Club, who initially blackballed him and Matejus in the sixties. This pattern was refined and enlarged upon in the hearing before the Valley County Medical Society in the matter of his showing the film on pacemakers to the service club meeting. And then there had been the disastrous meeting designed to defeat the recruitment of a salaried cardiologist.

While Gannon had put himself in the position of the central figure in Kafka's novel *The Trial* he soon could see that C.K. Moon was being run around the horn in much the same way. Only he and Ben Matejus placed much significance in these events. Then a close friend of Penelope Bayard had lodged a complaint about the movie presentation and Bayard sat with the counselors who were the judging group for the County Medical Society. In the matter of the inaction of the obstetrical department, in addition to casting unauthorized votes, both Bayard and Adams, would have had to have been exerting influence on some of the committee members. There were close social and business relationships in the group, so Gannon concluded that the Travel Club again was the true cause of C.K. Moon's troubles. As the weeks passed, Gannon decided he could kill off the Travel Club and take away their control of the Waterford Hospital staff leadership.

One of the weaker links in the club's circle was Ken Adams's partner, Bob Urbanawicz. He seemed to Gannon to be less-than-committed to the group of bigots that made up the club. As a matter of fact, Gannon was relatively certain from his own observation that Urbanawicz would not participate in these kinds of things if left to his own thinking. Therefore, he was vulnerable. He had been elected staff secretary in the preceding spring and would shortly be the establishment nominee for vice-president. However, there was nothing automatic about election to the vice-presidency from the position of secretary. Gannon decided to get himself nominated from the floor in the meeting of March 1972 and to try to beat Uzbanawicz in the June annual meeting. In conversation at one point Matejus warned him, "You will have to watch it, Chris. You've got to consider the possibility that you could not upset him and that might hurt our practice. Don't forget that we're fighting for open-heart surgery, and there may be one or two showdown votes before the big one involving yourself for vice president. You don't want to become known as a loser. Maybe you should back off."

Gannon shook his head. "No, I can't show weakness now. I've got to go out and get them. I don't see anybody else that can do it, including yourself. If and when it gets down to the voting, it will be the American Legion versus the Foreign Legion. Do you think there are enough foreign graduates who would help me win?"

"Don't count on all of them, Chris. We don't know who has been taken in to the Travel Club membership, and there may be some out of the foreign graduates who are there already and who will not support you. The emotional strain will be terrific. The question is, can you take all of that at the same time we're trying to get open heart started?"

"Ben, I'll never be any younger or any more ready. The establishment beat me in 1968, but they're going to have to work awfully hard to do it again four years later. I think I know how to create a major issue."

"I'll bet I know what you are thinking," said Matejus. And as was usually the case, Gannon had to concede that Ben was right, "You are a liberal Chris, disguised as a conservative, and what you have in mind is a new constitution, changing the rules about doctors. Am I right?"

"Yes, Ben. I read that throw-away booklet from the Joint Commission that you brought home from the spring meeting, and the major issue in there relates to the freedom of physicians. In the opening paragraph there is a concession that physicians do not have much freedom. The case that's cited seems to be exactly like the situation here in our hospital. C.K.. Moon's case is a classic example. The control lies with the smallest group of establishment doctors, in league with a few board members and administrators, who themselves are squeezed economically because of declining admissions. I'm starting right now to make reprints and to begin dragging it through the various committees. It will take months, right up to next spring, in order to get this seriously considered. Voting will take place on the same day for a new constitution and for a new vice-president, me being the challenger of the establishment candidate. As we both know, everybody needs an issue. Well, I think I've been handed one, and I think I can use the new constitution as the basis of a platform of candidacy. Ben, you're a member of the bylaws committee this year. Are you willing to help me wade through that?"

On occasion Gannon had felt some guilt about asking for the support of the foreign graduate doctors. Ben Matejus had been the first of a new generation of these men, and the first to become a part of an established partnership. There was some degree of conflict of interest in asking Ben to help. But someone had to drive the new constitution through the bylaws committee, and Ben would have to be that person. There were only eight months left before a new constitution could be approved at a first reading.

"Go for it, Chris. I'll do my job with the bylaws committee, and you can take the new constitution to the annual meeting next June as the major plank in your platform. But we have to clothe the issues in the idea of physicians' freedom. The Foreign Legion certainly understands that element."

Gannon looked at him with lowered lids. "There is something else, Ben. There is a St. Benedict's Hospital finance campaign about ready to be launched. I have some ideas about that. There are some hangers-on in the voting group from us here in the annual meeting next year. There may be a couple of power plays yet to be applied, and I will catch hell for that. Are you sure you want to take some of the punishment?"

"Absolutely," said Matejus. "Like in everything else over the last ten years, we're partners. We will take the rewards and the punishments together." He stuck out his hand, and Gannon wrung it warmly.

Less than one month later Gannon nosed his car into in a parking space in front of St. Benedict's Hospital. His path into the building took him right by the open door of the administrator, David Arlington. His door was open, and the administrator hailed him into his room. "Come in here, Dr. Gannon. I want to share something with you. A few months ago I made a move without talking to my Board of Trustees, and it may have been a mistake."

Arlington was a pink-cheeked young fellow, and he had been at St. Benedict's less than two years. For some reason, the Board had hired a Protestant and he came with very little experience in administration. Gannon had always guessed that he was there because he came at a low salary, an item which always seemed to attract the Board of Trustees of this hospital.

Arlington motioned him to sit down while he opened a drawer at the side of his desk. "Sam McKee and I signed an agreement about six months ago regarding a cobalt unit. You wouldn't have known this, but such a unit has been included in the engineering drawings for the new hospital, a responsibility which we took on several years ago."

The document was a simple one page agreement. In the opening paragraph it recognized the prior existence of a future-planning group identified as the Valley Planning Commission, an organization of fourteen hospitals within a forty-mile radius, including St. Benedict's and Waterford Hospital. The second paragraph identified the existence of a disagreement between the two Waterford hospitals in the matter of installation of a unit for the radiation treatment of cancer. The third paragraph was an agreement between the two administrators assigning the right of decision regarding the issue of which hospital should assume the burden of the installation of the unit, the assignment to be made by the above-mentioned Valley Planning Commission. Gannon read the document with increasing disbelief, astonishment, and anger. He felt himself getting hot and red in the face, and the paper began to shake in his hand. He rose rapidly to his feet, lifting his eyes from the paper and looking directly at Arlington, asked, "Did you sign this agreement willingly?"

"Of course. Nobody had a gun to my head. I thought it was a good idea. Since we have not launched a finance campaign yet, I thought that perhaps this planning commission would dig up some money for us and give us the right to build a unit."

Gannon strode across the room and closed the two open doors. Then he returned and sat down, sitting forward on his chair, confronting Arlington. "You have been had, David. By signing this agreement, you simply gave away what you already had. All of these administrators will hang with Sam McKee, and you will lose any kind of vote, thirteen to one. You don't have a chance of keeping this. And you have to keep it, because it's one way of continuing blood flow into this hospital for the next twenty-five to fifty years and, something around which to build your finance campaign. Don't you get that?"

Arlington looked at the floor. "I haven't told you the worst. The next meeting of the planning commission is tonight at a restaurant down the valley. But maybe we still have a chance if someone will lead the way. I have a couple of letters in the file, dating back to 1966, five years ago."

He ruffled around in his drawer, then pulled up a manila folder and handed the contents to Gannon. Gannon noted two letters in the file, back-to-back, both signed in 1966. One was signed by the chairman of the then radiation-therapy committee, no less a person than Penelope Bayard. The content of the memorandum stated flatly that Waterford Hospital was not interested in radiation treatment, and if St. Benedict's wished to go ahead with their own project, they were welcome to do so. The second letter was signed by the chief of radiology, Jack Murphy, who stated the same thing. Although Gannon was amazed that Arlington had been stupid enough to sign such a letter and put it in the hands of the administrator of the competing hospital; he had been no more foolish than Bayard and Murphy on the other side of the issue.

Gannon slapped his thighs and jumped up: "God damn it! I'll lead the way. I have some trading material that you don't know about. We have to organize a team and crash the meeting tonight. How many representatives does each hospital have? How big a group is this?"

Arlington looked down at the papers in the file again. "Each hospital has three votes, one from the administrator, one from the president of the Board of Trustees, and the third from the president of the staff."

Gannon thought a little bit and then asked, "Who runs the meeting?"

"The presiding officer is an administrator from down the valley. He is a lawyer, however."

Gannon laughed. "Never mind. Lawyer or not, I know exactly the gambit we will use to get into the meeting. People used it against those of us who worked on the Board of Education in the sixties. We will beat his ass first and then Waterford Hospital's second. Before I leave, how is the finance campaign going?"

Arlington smiled broadly and gave the thumbs-up sign. "All ten of the physicians teams have reported in , including yours. Each team has generated pledges of over one hundred thousand dollars from the staff doctors. That makes a neat one million committed before the open campaign has even begun. The doctors' pledges are money in the bank because they have a vested interest in what goes on here. And the public will know that. We can make an announcement about this in the winter quarter before the general campaign begins in town. It should be a cinch!"

"Don't look so pleased with yourself David. We have to get over this big hurdle. I will call five other guys this afternoon, and we'll get into the meeting somehow. I can delay by getting someone to table any motion for at least a month, so we can organize a campaign to retrieve this. Five years have passed since these negative letters were written unless there is something else in correspondence since that time. I we can hold their noses to it. We both know that cobalt therapy is a big deal. The fact that they did not recognize this five years ago and rejected it is their headache. You probably have heard that Ben, Casey, and I have been working for three years on a cardiac surgical program at Waterford Hospital. We're going to be ready to launch that in March this spring. Maybe we can make a trade, and everybody will end up looking good.

He put his hand on the door knob and then turned around again for one last parting shot. "And don't be upset at anything that happens tonight. It may get rough. I'll probably yell at the lawyer, but that's just my way of venting a general feeling about that profession. This looks like real fun. See you then."

Chapter 18

Two people were in the pick-up party to take him home; his spouse and his least conventional, most loving son. James was the third of the older three and had always been the most loving and attentive, whether in crisis or not. He and Gannon had shared failing hopes and aspirations several times; they always seemed to reach higher than they could attain. This had probably produced a situation that was unfair to the three younger siblings. They all loved Jim in spite of the fact that he was consistently a misfit. He had been unable to find a way to slide into the middle-class society, of which the rest of the family was a part. Once Jim had asked Gannon, "Am I expected to work an eight-hour day like everybody else? Why can't I work a sixteen-hour day one day and four hours the next?" He followed that with a statement, "I think everybody else is out of step with me, rather than the other way around."

So Gannon was not at all surprised when Jim and Helene were the two trying to organize his departure. *It is amazing how much junk one can accumulate in two weeks in a hospital room*, thought Gannon. The OR crew had brought him a running suit, which was fine in its lower half for the trips to physio therapy but was impossible for covering his upper half because of the slings. He slipped on a light windbreaker in red, white, and blue with a Cubs insignia on the pocket, then sat in the wheelchair. He picked up a box of bills in his hands, the collection measuring six inches in depth. He had tried to sign some checks for payment a couple of days previously, but his developing hand tremor was simply so much that no bank would honor his shaky signature.

Big problems were going to come from the six weeks of lost income, he thought. In "retirement" he was living on such a level, paying for contracted land purchases, that the family had been living on a very narrow margin. That balance was about to be upset, and probably it would take months for payment. Worse than that, he could only guess what his hospital cost had been; he guessed-two thousand dollars per day.

Jim began to push his wheelchair toward the elevator doors, when they were approached by a young woman in a business suit waving some papers. Her high heels clicked to a stop next to his chair, as the group hesitated at the door. "Just a minute, Dr. Gannon. You are on Medicare, right?"

"Yes, I am but just by six days. My birthday was February 7, and the stroke came February 13. 1 think I just got under the wire in late January."

"Do you want to know the size of your bill as of today?"

"Not really," replied Gannon. "Furthermore, I almost let an excess medical care policy lapse. But I made the payment while I was still in a grace period. What am I looking at?"

"Thirty-one thousand dollars."

Gannon gasped in disbelief. "I wonder if any human-being is worth that amount of money?" His spouse answered, pushing the wheelchair, "Shut up." The elevator door closed behind them.

On the same afternoon following his discussion with David Arlington, Gannon went straight home. He spent his time pursuing five other doctors to go with him to the meeting of the Valley Planning Commission. He received acceptance from the St. Benedict pathologist, the St. Benedict radiologist, a strong Catholic family practitioner, and C.K.. Moon, who was rapidly becoming the strongest obstetrician at St. Benedict's. It is a good group, he thought. He was certain that they would be representative and would not be afraid when the crisis came. Apparently each of them trusted him enough to accept his request with only a brief explanation when they met in the parking lot outside the restaurant down the valley.

Everyone was on time. There was a palpable tension among them, but Gannon was sure his strategy would work. It was the kind of situation where he could turn lawyers' strategy against lawyer. What he intended to do was not a bluff and should put the balance of members of the hospitals making up the planning commission into a state of reasonable doubt. It was his intention to only push so far and then produce a delaying action, providing relief to everybody in the room. He was certain they would all be delighted when offered a deferring solution; they would grab the opportunity and run for home.

Walking in tandem, the group went together across the lobby of the hotel in which the meeting was taking place, toward the dining room in the far corner. The door was closed and fronted by a functioning decorated black iron gate, heavy with sculptured metal.

Gannon picked up a single chair, directing each of the other five to do the same, and pushed the gate inward and stepped inside. He found himself at the extreme right end of a room occupied by a collection of dining tables, at which were seated approximately fifty people. Facing him was a speakers' table with about six occupants, one of whom was addressing the commission.

As it turned out, Gannon's people had arrived just in time. Possibly the group had been forewarned that there was going to be a protest at this meeting for the matter of the radiation center was at the top of the agenda. Gannon chuckled to himself, he had caught them in the act.

Gannon and his followers had to sit in the aisles between the tables because there was no room for additional attendees. Meanwhile, the presiding officer continued to address the audience, choosing to ignore the visitors. Finally, he had no choice but to note their presence, so he addressed the group. "This is a private business meeting of the Valley Planning Commission. No one but members may attend. We cannot proceed as long as you people are here."

Gannon spoke first, emphatically. "Sure you can. There are fourteen member hospitals of this commission, self-appointed. Unless I have miscounted, I bet that everyone of you has spent Hill-Burton funds in recent years, right up to and including the present. I know of two hospitals in Valley City that are in construction phase using Hill-Burton money also. According to the federal law such meetings must be open, and that means that anybody can come in and sit down and listen and participate. We are here to seek the floor."

The lawyer, whom Gannon had been told was a president of the board at one of the valley hospitals, was tight-lipped for a moment as he thought over this challenge. "It is possible that you are right, sir. On that outside chance, I would ask that you introduce yourselves and state your business, and we will see if there is any subject on the agenda this evening that is relevant."

After each of the invaders had introduced himself Gannon stated, "We're all from St. Benedict's hospital. We are staff members or hospital based employees. The matter we are here about is the matter you were just discussing when we came in."

The presiding officer once again faced his audience. "Whether or not the group of men who has entered the meeting here are legally present or not may have to be decided by the courts at some future date. However we can insert their names and their business in the record, and I shall rule, as chairman, that they have a legitimate presence here. As I was saying when they came, I have in my hands here a copy of an agreement made between St. Benedict's Hospital and Waterford Hospital regarding the installation of a cobalt unit. The agreement is signed by the two administrators. It concedes the power of the group of which we are all a part, the Valley Planning Commission, to make the choice about which hospital shall have the responsibility for radiation therapy in the future. Do I have the understanding of this matter correctly, Mr. McKee?"

Gannon had noticed the representatives of Waterford Hospital in the back row in the far corner, leaning in their chairs against the wall McKee did not speak, choosing instead, simply to nod his head. Gannon thought, *he is so sure of himself he doesn't even have to comment. Well we shall see.*

The presiding lawyer spoke again. "Do we all agree as to the validity of this document?"

"No," said Gannon. "We don't think that agreement is valid at all. It is signed only by the two administrators, and furthermore this represents a shift in position by Waterford Hospital on this matter."

"What do you mean by that?" asked the lawyer. All three of the Waterford Hospital members now had their chairs planted squarely on the floor.

Gannon continued: "I have here in my hand two documents signed by officers of staff committees at Waterford Hospital dated 1966. One is the statement by a person who was then chairman of the radiology committee, Dr. Penelope Bayard, and another document signed by the chief of the radiology department, Dr. Jack Murphy. In both of these letters, prepared at the same time, they make the flat statement that Waterford Hospital is not interested in any way in radiation therapy. Based on that, St. Benedict's Hospital has chosen to include a separate wing for a cobalt unit in its plans for new construction. As you all should know, this is a very expensive commitment, necessitating inclusion in the engineering drawings. What kind of planning is it when those plans are changed half way into a construction phase?"

The presiding officer seemed confused. "Well we would like to see the documents and file them in the minutes. I would like to take a vote on this issue tonight and resolve it. We had heard that St. Benedict's was not going to build a new hospital. What do you have to say to that?"

Gannon smiled. "I also have here tonight a record of the pledges of ten teams of ten doctors each totaling building pledges of one million dollars. That is the nut upon which the public finance campaign is about to be built. We are certain with that beginning, we can get pledges for two million more. In that case we can borrow the rest and construction can begin."

The room was silent. There was some clearing of throats and shifting of chairs. This was certainly a new dimension and something unexpected for those who had felt they were in control.

"Does anyone else want to make any comment?" asked the lawyer.

Various members of the meeting seemed now confused and disorganized. Uncertainty was on the face of almost every person present. By now they were wondering if perhaps there was something shady going on.

Gannon filled the vacuum "I think we have supplied you with more information than you can digest at this meeting. I am not an official member of this body and have no vote, but I strongly urge the presiding officer to ask for a tabling motion until at least one month hence. The members can prepare themselves adequately and perhaps, in the end, endorse the commitment of St. Benedict's to cobalt therapy in Waterford.

The lawyer hesitated, "Does no one else have any comment?" There was still silence in the room. McKee himself looked a little guilty, probably he had succumbed to pressure from the Travel Club. The chairman of the Board of Trustees was simply angry. The hospital staff president was looking at the floor, embarrassed.

Then came a voice from the far end of the room "Mr. Chairman, as a member of this body, I should like to put a motion to table the issue. We have received far more information tonight than we had at any time before and did not realize that there was contention over this issue. My tabling motion would put a limit of days on the decision, so we can meet again within a month."

Gannon suppressed a grin of triumph and looked at his associates. They were still all seated on their chairs in the aisle, nervous about the whole thing. Gannon had crawled out on the limb alone and pulled them along with him. They were somewhat fearful about having the limb sawed off by the Board of Trustees or by their administrator. Perhaps the administrator was embarrassed, but he deserved the embarrassment. He had made a bad agreement at a bad time. Gannon was not depressed at all. The tabling motion passed. Gannon had one more ace up his sleeve.

By now McKee looked mad. But Gannon had some salve for McKee's wounds, and he was ready to see him and enlarge on his plans for open heart surgery at Waterford Hospital. He was certain that it would more than balance the cobalt unit. So his group turned and walked out, shoving the last ignominious element into the faces of the rest of the body by carrying their chairs out themselves.

A month later Gannon was driving into the country club parking lot for the next meeting of the Valley Hospital Planning Commission. He purposefully showed up late, certain that the dinner would be over. The idea of a meal with a meeting had always been repugnant to him, as he felt that engaging in social enterprise at business meetings resulted in dropping one's guard, as though there was any such thing as a free lunch. Gannon was not a drinker, which had also tended to make him a social pariah all his life. He could honestly say, after many years of meetings of all kinds and in many different places, that he owed nothing to any administrator in any professional area. He always felt that being massaged by having a full stomach was a cheap way of being bought off.

As he was hanging his coat in the closet, he noted lined up across from him were three nuns in the classic full-length garments. His contact previously had been quite superficial. In the middle sat the mother superior, Sister Maria. All three were solemn, and they only greeted him with a nod of the head. Almost certainly they had been invited to the meeting also. But equally certainly, they had chosen to stay outside until decision-making time came. Gannon laughed to himself. He slipped through a side door into the dining room to observe an unusual setting. There was a single damask-covered table, at which were seated approximately forty members of the commission, all lined up on only one side. The electric lighting was dimmed, most of the light being supplied by a series of candles displayed down the middle of the table. In the center sat the lawyer that had presided at the meeting one month earlier, and immediately adjacent to him were the three Waterford Hospital representatives. At least two of the latter looked very much self-satisfied, as though the proceedings of the meeting were predictable and unnecessary. Gannon had had no occasion in the intervening time to discuss the issues with anyone, and he had been careful during this time specifically to avoid Sam McKee.

After running through the tiresome parts of any such meeting, the lawyer announced that the single item on the agenda was the disposition of the cobalt unit. Then he turned to Gannon and asked if anybody was present representing St. Benedict's. Gannon replied that they were "waiting in the wings." He went to the dining room door and crooked his finger at the group of three seated on the bench outside. Sister Maria was the only one to respond to his beckoning, and she arose to her full height. The latter was plentiful as she was just under six feet tall. On this occasion, she entered the room slowly and with great dignity, stopping finally just in front of the long table. Almost everyone present was of Protestant persuasion. This was certainly true of the Waterford Hospital representatives. Gannon himself had always been in awe of the garb of nuns, and frankly, was simply afraid of them. To see this tall, dignified woman crossing the floor was enough to make Gannon sit down hard on his own chair. He noticed also that the response of the people in the middle of the dinner table was to slide forward toward the edges of their seats. The flickering candles produced an eerie setting, and to see the nun's shadow floating about, with her huge flowing sleeves and skirts, capped by the classical white wimple of her order, was scary indeed. The entire room sat silent and transfixed. It was as though an official representative of God had caught some school children in some kind of skullduggery. And of course, she had.

She addressed the group in a soft, cultured voice. She did not display any hostility as she discussed the effort of Waterford Hospital to take the cobalt unit from St. Benedict's. Dispassionately, she reviewed the history of the issue covering the preceding five years, emphasizing the economic commitment of St. Benedict's to radiation therapy.

There was no response from anyone at the table. Sister Maria elected to stay in the room, not moving from the spot where she stood. She was daring the group to turn down her request for designation of St. Benedict's as the home of the radiation center. She had but one vote, as the president of the Board of Trustees, so her presence meant little in the count. But when the vote was taken, the representatives from Waterford Hospital were the only three granting the cobalt unit to their own institution. The rest of the vote was unanimous in support of St. Benedict's. Saying nothing, she simply turned and flowed out of the room, Gannon following. When outside she still did not drop her dignity and make any comment regarding this enormous victory. Not only had she beaten Waterford Hospital but she had beaten the planning commission.

Gannon walked out to the parking lot in silence along with the three nuns. They stood aside and did engage in a couple of good humored chuckles, glancing his way. Well, he was in the record now, and he actually had been the cause of their winning. He was certain that the planning commission would die after this single event, and would never return to complicate anybody's planning in the future. He was going to have to play his ace with Sam McKee as soon as possible.

Chapter 19

It had not snowed much in the latter part of the winter of 1990, so there was just a skiff around when the nursing staff pushed Gannon to the curb in his wheel-chair. There was bright sunshine on this morning, but a chill wind blew the light collection of snow around his ankles. Gannon had vowed in his own mind not to get wobbly or to look weak as he walked from the curb to the car, but his brain whirled every time he stood up, and he was certain it was apparent to any observer.

As they turned onto Liberty Street, heading south into the low-hanging sun, one more time he looked at the arch of trees shading this street for most of each year, now stark naked, except for an occasional flapping leaf on a red oak. It was a street which he had traveled at least twice a day for thirty-five years, but would not be traveling again yet for a while. He wondered what cause-and-effect rela-tionship might exist between his stroke and retirement from private practice six weeks previously. He had seen this phenomenon many times but always pooh-poohed it, as he did most things of a psychic nature. As the car turned left on Chicago Street toward the football field at the edge of town, he slunk down in his seat so that the two passengers with him would not see the tears in his eyes. This was the second time he had taken such a ride home from the hospital, and he was not anxious for another.

A decade before, he had returned from the hospital so relieved at being alive that he sat down on the living room couch and sobbed uncontrollably. He did not want to repeat that performance and had all he could do getting through the front door, heading for his big chair in the living room, breathless. He knew that he was weak, but he had had no idea the extent of his weakness. His wife, using that eter-nal gambit of womankind, displaced his attention by putting next to him the box containing all of his letters and notes of good will from colleagues and friends alike. He had been through them once, upon the arrival of each but remembered absolutely nothing of their content. He fingered them idly, then pushed the box away. Today was not the day to wallow in ancient history and self-pity. He sim-ply lay back in the chair and fell asleep. That he should dream of old events seemed only natural, because now he was just a sick, impotent old man.

It was a Wednesday in December 1971, traditionally the afternoon each week when Gannon went home early. As was usually the case, there was still something going on in the operating room, and Ben Matejus was late to meet him in the doc-tors' room. Having put on his overcoat and muffler, he sat down with a cup of cof-fee to wait. His mind was down in the x-ray department, in the special procedures room in which their newly-hired cardiophysiologist was doing the first angiogram on coronary vessels.

A moment later Ben hurried in, still in greens, to say, "there is another long meeting of the constitution committee beginning at 6:00 P.M. tonight. We're getting into the guts of protecting doctors' freedom now, so if there is anything you especially want, now is the time to speak up."

"No, Ben, we've been over the Joint Commission guidelines together, and I think that if we follow that general pattern we will have what we want. It will just be my duty to make a case for this at the first meeting in March. That will also be the meeting for nominations. Good luck tonight. I'll see you in the A.M. for tomorrow's 7:45 case." They waved good-bye as Gannon went out toward the parking lot.

As he was pushing open the door going out of the south wing, striding toward him, coat flapping in the wind, was Sam McKee. McKee spoke first. He was obviously distressed about something. "Chris, I've been looking for you all morning. Where have you been?"

"In the OR. Where else? I have to tell you that this dumb beeper system you fellows recently bought hardly ever works in any place that has steel girders in the wall, and that's particularly true in the operating room. Then the secretaries confuse what we do get."

"I'm going to ignore that," said McKee. "We have something more important to talk about. Come back in the building with me to my office. I've got to show you something." He strode down the hall waving Gannon into his office and then rather elaborately closing both doors to his space. "Now sit down, Chris. I have some bad news for you, which I cannot understand or figure out myself. I have asked Don Floyd to meet us here shortly, so he can participate in this conversation too and serve as an independent witness. As staff president he will have to deal with this. Somebody is after you, directly. Here, look at this, and see if there's anything you can understand in it." He reached into his vest pocket and pulled out an envelope, handing it to Gannon.

Gannon found himself looking at the enclosed letterhead, the design of which he had never seen before. It was a piece of office stationery with his name, office address, and phone number on it. He said to McKee, "I have never had office stationery with only my name on it and certainly not this small billhead size. My stationery has always had the names of my partners right with mine. Where did you get this?"

"For the moment, never mind where I got it. Why don't you read what's written on it? You are starting at the wrong end with these questions." Gannon looked down again at the paper, and there was a short message written on it, with a date that had only been one day previously. The words read, "I will meet you at the Red Rooster at 11:00 P.M. tonight." At the bottom was his own name, hand-written, but clearly by someone else.

"This a fake, Sam. It's addressed to Owen Bird, but I never wrote this. Why would I want to have a late night meeting at a restaurant with Owen Bird? He hasn't even been around here for a couple of years."

"Exactly my thoughts," said McKee. "I could not believe that you had written this, and that's why I called you. I believe Bird has been doing anesthesia in Rockford since he left here. Is that what you heard?"

"Well, yes. As a matter of fact, I wrote him a letter of recommendation to a hospital in Rockford a year ago, even though he left here with a blight on his name. Frankly, I always thought there was some kind of fakery in his trouble here. Many disliked him because of his deformity and disability, and then he made a misstep with the drug business."

"Well," said McKee. "We knew he was hooked on something, probably just plain old morphine. In the hearings about his management of the case he lost, he indicated that at one time he had become dependent on morphine after the bad auto accident in which he was involved while still in his training program at the university, but nobody ever found any confirming narcotic records in the anesthesia department. Apparently he was able to cover the usage quite well."

Gannon had been reading the sheet over and over, trying to make sense of such a peculiar message. "Why would anybody go to such trouble? I have not told anybody that I was intending to be a candidate in the spring. Do you think that somebody guessed that or mentioned it, and that my enemies are trying to discredit me already?"

"Yes, Chris, no doubt about it. I hear you are squeezing the practices of a couple of doctors right now, and they're going to pull out all the stops, even before you announce you're a candidate. They are going to do everything to put you away, if possible for good, in the June election." There was a knock at the door, and McKee admitted Floyd, staff president. He stood six foot six and weighing over three hundred pounds. But he had always had a positive attitude toward Gannon and had sent him some work from one of the adjacent small towns in which he was the only physician. McKee reviewed the issues to Floyd, explaining that he wanted Floyd to see the letter and know of the incident because it was something he was going to have to deal with as the presiding officer of the staff.

Floyd turned to Gannon. "So you are suggesting that you never have seen this stationery before and that it's something somebody made up especially for this purpose?" He smiled openly and then chuckled. "That seems ridiculous to me. Why would anybody care that much about a hospital election? There has to be more to this than that, unless you are both suffering from some refined form of paranoia."

"We're not both paranoid," said McKee. "Gannon and his partners are pushing a couple of our surgeons pretty hard. Furthermore, Ken Adams was made to look foolish in the C.K.. Moon case, and I don't think he is very forgiving." He turned to Gannon, "Chris, you'll have to run this matter down yourself. See if you can find who printed this single sheet of paper. There are only a dozen or so printers in town, and one of them surely did this. He will remember setting type for a single sheet of paper. You must call Owen Bird and discuss this with him, also. Meanwhile, Don and I will look upon this as just an aberrant incident."

"Could I make a couple of copies of this?" asked Gannon. "You never know. This one just might disappear. You never did tell me how you got it—"

"Somebody shoved it under my door while I was still in the office late yesterday afternoon," replied McKee. "Whoever it was wanted me, as the hospital administrator, to believe you were somehow involved in some crooked business with Bird and to discredit you with the old theme of guilt by association. I am really sorry. I know that you would not do something as stupid as this." Gannon waved his hand at the two men as he left them, huddled together in McKee's office.

Owen Bird was a cripple with whom he had sympathized, taking the part of the underdog, as usual. In a terrible auto accident in the middle of his anesthesia residency, he had sustained a severe head injury, along with two broken hips and had had to fight himself back into working condition in order to finish his training. In his own defense later he claimed to have gotten hooked on morphine because of using it for many weeks after his hip injuries. He had always walked with a stumbling gait in the time that Gannon had known him and sometimes he had trouble manipulating anesthesia equipment. At Waterford Hospital he had lost a case, resulting in a major lawsuit about two years previously. It was the hospital review of this case that had led to pressure for him to resign from the staff, which he had done.

What an odd selection, thought Gannon, *for someone to pick on Owen Bird, in order to discredit me.* Yet it was a well-known fact that bigots, who hated black people and Jewish people, also hated the deformed and crippled. Only a bigot would believe that the way to discredit another person was somehow to associate him with one of the world's misbegotten. Gannon reviewed the list of those who hated him most. Who was obviously the most prejudiced? He decided that he would have to find Owen Bird and arrange to meet him and warn him about this. He wondered how directly Bird was involved—he always was a queer duck, no doubt about that.

Only a few days had elapsed when Gannon visited Sam McKee the next time. Sam leaned back in his executive chair, folding his hands behind his head and finding Gannon with his eyes. "Well, Chris, anything further on the Owen Bird business?"

"Actually, yes. Although that's not why I'm here today."

He continued, "Nonetheless, let's take that up first. I'm going to see Bird next week in Rockford. Oddly he did not seem particularly surprised by this. He runs a sideline antique business up there, and I'm going next week to meet him. I'll take the original of the letter. He wants to have a handwriting expert analyze it and see if that person can come up with a description of the character and personality of the writer. Personally, I think it's a nutty idea. Black magic, and all that. But he is a smart guy, and he's willing to pay for it because he is involved."

"Anything else?" asked McKee, leaning forward into the upright position in his chair.

"Again, yes. You know I have a scalawag of a son-in-law, so I don't know how much credence to give this information. Mind you now, I had not told anyone else in the family about this episode involving the forged letter. Tommy called me last week to warn me of something. He goes to the YMCA almost every day. He described having overheard a conversation in the locker room between Bob Urbanawicz and a man named Woolly who runs a printing business in Waterford.

The story related to me by Tommy was that they were talking and laughing together about some 'practical joke' that had been played upon me by Urbanawicz. Tommy described the conversation as being one involving the fact that Woolly had printed a letterhead with my name on it. Now, honestly, I don't exactly trust all the things that Tommy tells me, and it fits a little too neatly. Nonetheless, I know that Tommy had no prior information about this from me. Remember, we have a couple of doctors that think it is funny to mail boxes of dog turds to one another at Christmas time."

"Were there any witnesses to that conversation?"

"Tommy didn't mention any. But I can ask. Meanwhile, on to other, more important things."

"Okay, Chris. I've had the feeling for some time that you've had something on your mind. But after that business at the country club with Sister Maria, I haven't really felt very good about you personally. You've had enough of my blood this fall. Do you want some more?"

"No, Sam," replied Gannon. "You have always been in my corner. As a matter of fact, I want to offer a transfusion. I know I stepped hard on your toes over that radiation center business, but you and Woodruff simply left me no choice. I have to assume that he talked you into it because I think you are above conning that young Arlington into such a deal. You and I cannot help the fact that you had a reactionary chief of radiology and that he was in league with Penny Bayard, and neither should have been stupid enough to put those thoughts in writing. No, what I have for you is much bigger.

McKee leaned back in his chair again, this time folding his arms across his chest. There was an element of testiness, as he said, "Well, out with it. What do you have up your sleeve?"

Gannon sat down and put his hands on McKee's desk. "We're ready to go with our first open heart case in less than three months. Do we have the go-ahead from you and the Board?"

McKee stood up and let out a deep breath, and walked toward his outside window, gazing out between the blinds. "Well, I never thought you would give this program to us after the radiation center business. I'll take it to the Board on Monday." He turned and strode back to his desk and stuck out his hand. "I've always had a blank check for you fellows, and you have not let me down yet. You have been working on this project for upwards of fifteen years. Are you really ready?"

Gannon stood up and wrung his hand warmly, much relieved. "We did the dog surgery two weeks ago. Maggie DeLaney and Johnnie Stork have been traveling to Loyola for a year, which I think you know about. I have found the right patient for the first case: my own pastor. I think he has an inside track with the good Lord. Both we and he will need a little luck."

McKee assumed a more friendly attitude. Gannon was certain there were very few community hospitals capable of handling the enormous burden of undertaking cardiac surgery. He also was certain that McKee was taking a big risk with his Board of Trustees. Penny Bayard and her friends could not only make trouble for Gannon, in the course of this and other matters, but could certainly make life difficult for the administrator also. Added to this was the unknown threat of Ken

Adams and Bob Urbanawicz in their manufacture of forged letters, and he was a little bit uncertain as to what direction things were taking.

McKee spoke, "I'll be backing you to the end of this, because I believe the future of our hospital depends on it. But I'm going to have to take a lot of heat and open myself widely to the Fox Valley Medical Travel. I think I can , but not if you fellows make any mistakes. They will be lying in wait for you in the audit committee."

Gannon put his hand on the doorknob, preparatory to opening it and leaving. He hesitated. "I know that at least as well as you, Sam. But one last item: you observed that Ben Matejus has been guiding the constitutional changes through the committee. Can I count on you not to be against it, simply because it has some guarantee of physicians' freedom in the future?"

"No, Chris. I won't oppose you on that. I know of your intention to challenge Urbanawicz in the vice-presidential election. Probably Urbanawicz and Adams heard the same thing and are trying to scare you off with this letter business. As you say, it all seemed just a little too pat. But you and I are both going to have to suffer through this spring quarter. I'll stick by you in the background as much as I can."

"I sure would appreciate that, Sam," said Gannon. "On occasion I've been a little uncertain about how you felt about me. Do you remember the episode with the pacemaker film and the service club? Well, I took a licking from the Fox County Medical Society about that. I did not hear your voice sounding any defense. Since I did not know about the accusations until after it was over, probably you did not either. I took a big rap for helping you out with your public relations."

"It won't be the last time. You'll have to face at least two votes of approval of the cardiac surgical program yet. You are not home free. Good luck!"

Chapter 20

Gannon had been at home one day when he received his first neighborly visitor. His wife was out and about, as was her wont, probably detailing and at the same time exaggerating aspects of her spouse's illness. He had spent the morning puttering around the living room which had been rearranged as an office for writing and accounting. During that process he had learned how much was missing from his memory, as he was forced to retrace his business steps by reading the checkbook stubs and trying to remember which bills he had paid and which were still pending. One stub that was a little unnerving had been written to an exotic lingerie store known as "Victoria's Secret." It was dated on the morning before his stroke, and he had absolutely no memory of the event. He must have purchased something, but what did he buy, and for whom? Had he already given it to the recipient on the day of its purchase or had he put it away somewhere for a Valentine's gift? While there might be some humor built into this, it was possible that his family might draw the incorrect conclusion. He was tapping the checkbook with his pencil, trying to remember, when the doorbell rang.

When he swung the door open to the inrush of cold air, he saw before him that minute fragment of protoplasm known in the neighborhood as "Irene." Irene was everybody's neighborhood favorite because she seemed to stand the ravages of age with such great dignity. Her inherent younger beauty still shown through the crows' feet at the corner of each eye, only seeming to emphasize further the deep lines around her mouth when she smiled so prettily. She extended her hands to him, holding a large crockery bowl.

"Good gosh, Irene. What's up?" Chris ventured.

"This bowl is what's up, you dumb bunny. This is a variation on a theme of boiled chicken and dumplings, as made at home in Czechoslovakia."

"Come in, come in," said Gannon. It's bitter out there. Boy, this hot soup will just hit the spot. I'm still a little wobbly, so you'd better carry the pot to the table yourself. Would you like to share some while you are still here?" As she set the bowl down, she turned and faced him frontally. "Sure, I'll taste some of my own product, and while we're eating, you can tell me about some of the more interesting parts of your time in the hospital. Believe me, we've had some experiences too!"

As she sipped her soup ever so delicately, she looked into his eyes with each spoonful, letting her own deep brown irises flash back at him in the light coming from the flames in the fireplace. "Would you like some wine?" asked Gannon. "I'm not sure what color, red or white, goes with chicken soup. Do you have any suggestions?"

"No, just skip it. Having chicken soup in front of the fireplace is just close enough. Even though you've been sick, you might get ideas."

It was late afternoon when Gannon arrived in Rockford. He had been given an address for Owen Bird's antique sales building, but he had only a vague idea of its location. Finally he found the right house, which was a white frame Victorian home set in the middle of a city block, surrounded by oaks and maples, well landscaped with junipers and yews, and probably with a lovely green lawn coming up from the river in the summer time. Bird must have gone to considerable effort to get the zoning change in a noncommercial neighborhood, Gannon thought, but the house looked like anything but a business. He walked up the long cement drive to the front door and turned the handle.

The sun was just setting with flaming red in the southwest, so it took a bit for his eyes to adjust to the lower light inside the hallway. There appeared to be five or six rooms in this converted dwelling, two of them toward the back of the building were lighted at the present, but the hallway was darkened. Then a door opened on the left, and Owen Bird stepped through.

Bird had always reminded Gannon of certain characters from one of the novels of Victor Hugo, unwillingly and unwittingly so. In the dark of the still-unlighted hallway, this was exaggerated significantly. His walk was a flailing type of gait, the right leg flung out to the side with each step, very much like that of a palsied child so frequently seen on the street. He was well over six feet in height, and Gannon estimated probably he did not weigh over one hundred forty pounds. This was a fortunate circumstance, as had he weighed much more, he would certainly have fallen with every step. Along with the stork-like figure came a pair of flying wings, which suspended from any other body, would be called arms and hands. Gannon had observed them many times struggling to hold a laryngoscope while searching for a patient's vocal cords, then struggling with airway connections between and among the various parts of an anesthesia machine in order to establish an airway.

Owen Bird had not been trusted by some of the surgeons at Waterford Hospital, so Gannon had gone out of his way to refer him work, as he was still in the rehabilitation phase after his head injury. He had always seemed competent enough, but the death of the one patient had resulted in a complex investigation, followed by pressure to resign from the hospital staff, putting Bird on the shelf for a while. It was not without some reservation that Gannon had sent a letter of recommendation when he had applied to the hospital in Rockford. Although he was reasonably certain that he was competent in his work, there was always that nagging doubt about whether he had or had not been hooked on morphine after the prolonged hospitalization.

Today, he seemed alert enough and greeted Gannon warmly. He thanked him for the letter of recommendation and explained that it was truly giving him a second chance. Gannon reached inside his breast pocket and took out the folded sheet of paper which had been identified as the forged note from himself to Owen Bird. "This is the original Owen. I'm giving it to you rather than giving you a copy, because if the handwriting is to be reviewed by a professional, I think he or she should have the opportunity to see those tiny squiggles only visible in an original sample of writing."

"Let's defer this for a few minutes, Chris," said Bird. "I do appreciate being given the original, and I promise you that I will not mess it up. This particular piece of paper may mean a great deal to you in the future, somewhere else. Come on in, and let's have a cup of coffee. Also, I want to show you around this project, so you'll better understand what my partner and I do."

So they wandered from room to room, each of which had its own unique set of furnishings, all of them being quality antiques. "My heavens, Owen, you have an enormous inventory in this building Where did you get enough money to buy all of these antiques?"

"Actually, this has been a side business for me since I was in training. I got a settlement from the driver of the car that hit me five years ago, and that allowed me to add additional furnishings. Actually I'm doing all right in anesthesia, also."

Gannon turned toward his guide, "I told you about the business of the conversation overheard at the YMCA, didn't I? As I mentioned, this was a questionable source, and it seemed a little too pat and simple to be true. What do you think?"

"I think it is absolutely consistent with those guys in the Fox Valley Travel Club. Over the two years I worked at Waterford, they never sent me a dime's worth of work. And I heard them in the physicians' locker room snickering about my physical condition repeatedly. I also know they started some ugly rumors about morphine addiction. They alleged that they had some secret source of information from the university hospital. Actually, I was hooked for the last three months of hospitalization and had to go through a special withdrawal program to get off it. But it was not a self-induced addiction; it was the result of large dosage of narcotics because of slow healing of my hip fractures. Surely you know that bigots despise cripples as much as blacks."

By this time they had completed the round of the first floor and wound up in the corridor at the front beneath the stairs, the anteroom now being well lighted. "Now, Owen, I'm going to give you two other things. These are writing samples I picked up in the physicians' locker room from notes written by the two guys I think were involved in this. This one is labeled Urbanawicz, and this one is labeled Ken Adams. I am betting that the writing sample will match with Ken Adams signature. How long do you think this process will take?"

"The expert is coming down from Milwaukee tomorrow," said Bird. "She will complete the examination in just a couple of hours. I'll get a written report, in case we need it later for some other action. I will call you at home tomorrow night. With any luck we will have an answer to this by then. I'm very nervous about all of this myself l am sorry that someone is trying to tie you to me and my problem. The only possible motive would be to discredit you. I am gone from Waterford Hospital."

Gannon turned as he was buttoning his overcoat and shook Bird's hand warmly. The latter was still having trouble using his right arm, and there was a tangible tremor at the time of exchanging the handshake. "I'll hear from you tomorrow night then, right?" asked Gannon.

A little over twenty-four hours later, the telephone rang. The voice on the other end of the line was Owen Bird. "Chris? I've got the stuff for you. The analyst says it definitely is the hand of Ken Adams. Honestly, I want to get rid of this stuff tonight, if possible. I'm willing to drive over from our home in Kirkland if we can arrange a place to meet. How about the Red Rooster, the place identified in the fake letter?" He chuckled on the other end of the telephone.

Gannon did not share the laugh but agreed to the meeting place. "I suppose it's a reasonable idea. Frankly I have never been there for anything. It looks kind of scuzzy from the outside, but maybe we should meet there just for a laugh, if nothing else. What time do you suggest?"

"How about 10:15 tonight yet? The wind is drifting the snow on the east-west roads out here, and I'll have to take that Big Woods Road in order not to have to go out of my way. I'll bring all of the material including her written and signed opinion. Okay?"

"Okay. I'll be there."

Gannon's heart had quickened at the information he had been given. If any validity could be given to the handwriting analyst's opinion, then this so-called practical joke could be wound up. The question was, what to do about it?

Later, driving into town, he considered his options. Should he confront Adams and Urbanawicz? Should he accuse them privately or publicly, as at a departmental meeting? These were smart adversaries, and he had concluded by now that they were also dangerous. Why did they care so much? What was their motive in making so much effort to discredit him? He concluded that they must really be nervous about what he could do politically about the Fox Valley Travel Group. But why would they worry? Maybe this was just a part of a habit pattern, a method used by them before in other matters.

All of these thoughts were bombarding his mind as he turned into the lot at the small restaurant. There were a few customers sitting at the counter, sipping coffee and smoking in a desultory fashion. Conversation was in low tones, mostly about the late weather. Gannon ordered pie and coffee and settled in to await the appearance of Owen Bird.

He never came. After an hour of waiting, Gannon got up in disgust and drove home, leaving a message with the waiter in case he showed up at a late hour. He could hear the kitchen phone ringing as he drove into the garage, so he hurried inside and picked it up. A strange voice at the other end of the telephone asked, "Dr. Gannon?"

"Yes, this is Dr. Gannon. Who is speaking?"

"I am Sergeant McCoy, with the Illinois State Police. A man was killed on Big Woods Road tonight, in a single car accident. I found an envelope lying on the seat of his car, addressed to you. Today's date is written on the outside of the envelope, along with your phone number. You know anything about this?"

"Do you have any identification of the driver? Was this man by any chance someone named Owen Bird?"

"Yes sir. How did you guess the name? Tell me what you know about this.

"He was coming from Kirkland. I was supposed to meet him tonight at the Red Rooster, a few blocks from the hospital, but he never showed up. Yes, there have been some funny things going on among the physicians in our community in recent weeks. It's too late to go into all of this now, but if you're going to be the investigating officer, I'd like to stop by in the morning and see if I may have the envelope. It may have several answers, not only for me but also for you."

"Well, doc, if you expected some help, you're not going to get much from me.

The envelope had been ripped open, and there was just one sheet in it. Can you come in about 9:00 A.M. tomorrow? I'll be writing this up at that time. I can review with you the skid marks, what it was that he hit, and a couple of other things that don't add up. Personally, I have the feeling that this was made to look like a suicide, but there may be more to it than that. I'll see you in the morning, doc."

Click. Gannon slowly put down his own telephone. So someone had stolen the handwriting expert's report. Now what?

Chapter 21

It was noon. Gannon sat at the counter in his kitchen, staring out the south window at the falling snow. Another of his neighbors, Rosalie, had just appeared at the front door, delivering a Jewish preparation of boiled chicken. Meaning to do the right thing, she had prepared it without salt, apparently it being her perception that he should not have excess sodium in his food. Rosalie was number two of the triumvirate of the neighborhood women who hung out together, and her appearance this day suggested the probability that there would be a third tomorrow. He reached for the forbidden salt shaker, thinking that perhaps he could liven up the dish with a few sprinkles placed on top of the carefully distributed herb preparation applied by Rosalie in an effort to create the flavor which he was sure she incorrectly believed to have been a part of his daily habit.

The new snowfall was a disappointment. For the preceding three days, he had limited himself to walking around the house, trying to gain enough confidence in the familiar surroundings, hoping to get up enough courage to go outside. He was afraid to leave his home. He dwelt on the idea of falling in the snow and freezing before his wife came home, or worse, getting lost in the neighborhood and being unable to get back to familiar surroundings. Fifteen years before, when he first became significantly hypertensive, he had had a series of cerebral fugues characterized by mental confusion, becoming lost while driving his car, so that he was very familiar with the frightening aspect of being awake but not understanding who one was or where one was. These episodes had not occurred for years, until the recent stroke.

He munched on the chicken, noting that the added salt was not doing much, but consuming the contents of the pot because Rosalie had gone to so much effort. Rosalie's husband had been a friend, an ear, nose, and throat surgeon, killed in the prime of life by a malignancy of the pancreas. One evening, Manny had called him from his office to ask him to come examine him because he had turned yellow, seemingly overnight. The onset of painless jaundice was a sentence of death. Rosalie and her group were able to continue the same lifestyle, because her husband had prepared the way much more successfully than Gannon had for his own group. It was just another depressing series of thoughts. He waited for the sound of the family car pulling into the garage, placing his forehead on his crossed arms on the counter and weeping.

"This is all that was in the envelope, sergeant? Nothing else? No other sheets of paper inside the car?"

"No, doctor. As a matter of fact, most of the car burned up. This envelope was stuck under his hip on the seat: Otherwise I doubt that we'd have found it. The envelope had been opened and had your name on it. The only thing in it was a copy of a note. I remembered you from the old ambulance-training days, so that's why I called you last night."

It seemed to Gannon as though the sergeant wished to say more but was somehow waiting for some response from him. "Well, he was coming to Waterford to see me. He had called me early in the evening and we were going to have a cup of coffee at a restaurant on the north side. He said he had additional information about a certain matter. That's why I'm puzzled that the only thing in the envelope was a copy of a fake letter I gave him in Rockford several days ago. There should also have been the original note plus an analysis of handwriting." The sergeant put his fingers together in front of his face and stared out across the desk. "Come on, doc. There's more to this than you have told me. If you don't want to get any deeper at this point, you can stay quiet, but that will guarantee some further discussions. Something about this business smells funny. Do you think someone could have swiped whatever else was in the envelope? This was a one-car accident, and he hit a big oak at the side of the road at high speed."

Gannon sat down and looked across the desk at the officer. "Most people would say he was an odd duck. Further, from what I know, he has been under a lot of pressure for the past two years. You'll have to search out his family and pursue the possibility of suicide."

The sergeant shifted his eyes and made contact with Gannon. "This was made to look like a suicide, I think. He was driving a sports car, with a steering mechanism that was simple and entirely mechanical. One bar looked like it had been sawed through deliberately. Now can you tell me anything more?"

Gannon hesitated, "Well, I suppose I have to get this over. The only content of the envelope was a copy of an original note. You can see that it has my printed professional letterhead on it, but I swear that I have never had a letterhead of my own in all of my years of work. I believe that someone went to a great deal of trouble to reproduce this sheet of paper. For confirmation, you can interview the hospital administrator and the president of the medical staff who actually were the people who gave me the letter. We believe it was printed to discredit me before an upcoming staff election this summer. From Mr. Bird's family you will get a history of a nasty auto accident some years ago, with a severe head injury, that left him crippled and barely able to complete his specialty training. Also he admitted to me that he had been addicted to morphine at the time he was getting well from pelvic fractures. Now how's that for a bunch of variables to untangle?"

The sergeant smiled, then separated his fingers and spread his hands on the desk. He shrugged his shoulders. "About like the diagnosis of abdominal pain whose cause is unknown, I would guess. All the facts are there, but they are concealed. If this involves something of the interior politics among you and some hospital staff members, it could get messy. What I will want from you over the next few days is just the facts. Don't surmise anything on your own. Guesswork will take us nowhere. In the meantime you are not really a suspect yourself but you might become so. This letter puts you in this up to your neck. don't leave town without letting me know. I'll get back to you in a few days." He stood and stuck out his hand and Gannon returned the handshake, but not without misgivings.

He walked out into the bright March sunshine. A chill wind was blowing snow around his ankles, forcing him to close the top button on his coat and to push up the collar. He drove up the hill to a park. He walked slowly over to a bench and sat down, turning his hatless head up to the warm sunshine. He had to think.

It was difficult to accept the idea of a successful murder of Owen Bird having been completed. Gannon's trip to Rockford had only taken place a few days before, and Bird's decision to make the trip to River City could have only been a few hours old. There was no way a hit man could purposely have damaged his car on such short notice. If this were the case, the purposeful damage to the steering mechanism had to have been coincidental, the killer just knowing that something would happen on the next trip or so. It could have been done days before and just broken on this trip. If he were to pursue this further himself he would have to establish a motive. The fact was that the death of Owen Bird and the loss of any written evaluation of the handwriting created a dead end. Bird must have shared this sequence with another party, someone among the hospital staff who was aware of the event. Gannon himself had informed the administration of the hospital about the pursuit of a handwriting expert seeking to tie Urbanawicz or Adams to the fake letter. Certainly there was an employed assassin involved, with at least one person between himself and the producers of the letter. A telephone call could produce a professional killer. There were hundreds available in Chicago every day.

Suicide remained a possibility. A coroner's jury could develop a case for that, based on a history of addiction, depression, continuing physical disabilities, and the recent added stress of the incident of the fake letter. Unless he, Gannon, gave additional information, much of which was conjecture and circumstantial, almost certainly the decision would be for accident or suicide. The investigating sergeant did not have much to go on other than a steering apparatus which appeared to have been deliberately damaged. There were too many loose ends. What a mess.

He looked down the hill to the center of a decaying community. At 10:00 A.M., the streets were bereft of traffic, and the newly built city parking lots were empty. Most of the stores on the north-south streets were closed, with last autumn's leaves still blowing around in the entryways. As for himself he would have to choose between pursuing the matter or letting it go. Even he could see that it was difficult to accept the idea that personal jealousy combined with injured ego could produce enough ill will among professionals to result in the hiring of a killer for the sole purpose of destroying a chain of evidence. Should he try to find the handwriting expert in Milwaukee or should he make a trip out to Owen Bird's home and business and nag his family for additional information? Gannon had to assume that there was still somebody out there, on a retainer fee as it were, and that he would be the next target.

As he kicked at the snow pack beneath the park bench, it occurred to him that he had better make a record of all these events and give copies to a couple of independent friends, should anything happen to him in the near future. He drove quickly to his office. The nurse and receptionist were just locking the door as he came up the ramp. "Just leave it open, girls. I'm going to do some lengthy dictating this afternoon. I'll leave the tapes by your typewriter, Bernice. But you must not repeat the contents to anybody else. The matter is too long and too complex for me to put in handwriting, and I do wish to keep it a secret." The two young women looked at one another. Bernice came back with, "Anything you say, boss," and then the two walked away. This was a Wednesday, his afternoon off. He hoped Ben did not come in to do extra work, so that he wouldn't have to explain why he was there. He wanted to keep Matejus out of this so if indeed something did develop, Matejus need not necessarily come into the sights of whoever was holding the rifle.

He sat down at the dictating machine and related all of the events which he felt were relevant. Already dates and time and places were fading into the amalgam of seemingly unrelated events The further he went in the description, the more he began to question his own degree of paranoia and to ask himself whether he was not supplying the glue, manufacturing some of the events just because of thinking about them too much. Had these events really happened? Perhaps the death of Owen Bird the night before was just a coincidence.

He asked for an original and two copies of the dictation. On the next day, he would give one to Bob Rockwell and the other to Henry Kasinowski, both of whom he had come to trust over the preceding twenty years. They could be relied upon to keep the record according to his instruction, each in his own personal safety deposit box, for recovery and submission to the state's attorney, should anything happen to Gannon.

The dictation took a long time. Much introspection and thought was necessary as the production of the documents progressed. The sun was golden and just setting in the west as he went out to the parking lot. The wind had died down, but he was chilled to the bone. There was nothing about the review of all these events that was sufficient to warm the body or spirit. And there still lay before him the most severe trial of his life.

Chapter 22

Gannon boosted himself onto the gurney somewhat awkwardly because his left shoulder hurt so much. A facial grimace and vocal grunt did little to help the pain. He looked at the two doctors standing opposite in the curtained-off room in the emergency department, and said, "I'm sorry, Henry, I know that you warned me about this. But I just lay my arm on top of the couch, and when I slid it off, I could feel that head of the humerus sliding into what felt like a leather tube."

Henry did not seem upset, as he stood with arms akimbo, "It's out, all right. The same anterior dislocation as you had before. We will go with a little IV Valium, and I'll reduce it right here." He nodded to the nurse who had started the IV and she pushed the plunger on the syringe. Oblivion.

Fortunately for the balance of Gannon's outlook on life, he never realized that the peak of his professional career occurred in March of 1972. The team had selected a Saturday morning for the first open heart operation, because in those days there was less activity around the hospital on Saturdays and they could do the surgery unscheduled and unannounced. The great problem was not that they just might fail and the patient might die, but they were also working against the element of case review by Penny Bayard. They wished to do this work as anonymously as possible, until there was enough of a history of success to go public. The blood vessel disease in this particular patient involved only one occlusion among the three major possibilities. Even if things did not go well the chances were good that the patient would survive anyhow.

As he parked in the dark and crunched his way across the lot and into the back door of the hospital, he thought back over the last two months, to the last-ditch efforts of the Travel Group still to scuttle the open heart program. Penny Bayard had been in her last year of a three-year term on the Executive Committee and had put a motion in January to kill the cardiac program, making a case that it would reflect badly on the institution. However, her motion simply died for want of a second from any of the fifteen members. Still she did not understand the message being sent by her colleagues, so she put yet another motion, to hold a formal extraordinary staff meeting, the purpose of which was to take a staff vote on whether to go ahead with the program or not. Perhaps because they felt sympathy with the physician, or perhaps because the balance of the Executive Committee simply wanted a staff endorsement of the program, the other members agreed to this special evening meeting.

Casey, Matejus and Gannon had approached the meeting with real apprehension because they were uncertain about the staff being stampeded into a "no" vote at the last minute. On the night of the extraordinary evening meeting, Penny Bayard took the podium and spoke for an hour. She quoted all of the available negative literature and all of the reports which were not supportive of such a program, and which, in some instances, actually condemned this kind of case being done in a community hospital. She took the argument to the point of quoting two telephone calls that she had placed to authorities in the western part of the country, saying that no such program should be undertaken in a community hospital without support of a resident staff. The three on the team sat at the same table through this long discussion.

Gannon was suffering from the dry mouth syndrome as he sensed that perhaps the tide was turning against them. He had deliberately chosen a table at the front of the room in order to be in a position to watch the emotional reactions of the various staff members. There were sixty-eight voting members present, at the end; Penny Bayard played her last ace, which was to put a motion for a stand-up vote. The staff stood fast and trumped her ace. When the president called for the vote, sixty-four members voted "aye" and only four voted "nay." The four nays were Penny Bayard, Ken Adams, the chief of the hospital radiology department, and the chief of the laboratory. They were all seated at the same table, suggesting that they had planned together.

Gannon shot a hot look at McKee on the other side of the room. Had he realized that he had so little control over his hospital employees? Here was a situation where fifty percent of the "no" votes were from salaried, hospital-based physicians, who presumably should have been at the beck and call of the hospital administrator. Probably McKee had known their position all along and had chosen to stand by Gannon and his crew through official and unofficial meetings of all kinds. The lack of support from his employees must have been a disappointment for him, but he was stuck with them because of a long history of social engagements of one kind or another, and he would have to live with that. McKee must have known that a successful open heart program at this hospital would be an enormous feather in his own cap, and the thought of losing it must have given him a great deal of frustration. Gannon hoped that Sam McKee was as relieved as his own team was at the sixty-four to four count.

And now, weeks later, he was on his way up the stairs to the operating room, and this was the moment of truth. As he had passed the light board at the entrance, he noticed three lights on already, that of Ben, and Casey, and Charlie Bartlett, who was to give the anesthetic. The latter had finished his training just two years previously and had spent three months giving anesthesia for cardiac surgical operations and was a logical choice of the department for the first few cases.

Standing in the doorway of operating room three, tying his mask behind his head and neck, Gannon noted that Maggie DeLaney had the patient already spread-eagled on the table while she did the surgical shave to the chest and both legs. Charlie Bartlett had already intubated the patient, and Gannon was relieved that he did not have to share preoperative pleasantries with the patient, who was his own minister. Ben and Casey were already scrubbing. Gannon turned toward the sink and opened a brush. None of the three spoke. Gannon was facing away from the other two, or they would have seen his head bob gently and his eyes close, as he thought a silent prayer.

Gannon's own religious life had been in disarray in recent years, and his belief in God was marginal at best. Still, it couldn't hurt anything, he had thought as he closed his eyes.

Maggie handed him a towel to dry his hands, and the circulating nurse came in behind to tie his gown. Casey would be the operator, as he had the credentials and the experience, and Matejus would be the first assistant, as he had the technical knack. Gannon was well aware that he was the least of the three in terms of skill and training and that he would be delegated (relegated?) to taking the vein graft needed for the bypass. They would be working in two fields, his other partners engaged in the chest, while he was left to his own devices on the legs.

Casey picked up the electrical sternal-splitting saw and after a midline skin incision from the notch of the upper end of the breast bone to the rib cage margin in the upper abdomen, split the sternum in half, then inserted a mechanical retractor to hold the rib cage apart. As he ratcheted open the chest, Johnnie Stork pushed the pump through the door and up to the table. Properly so, in the thirteen years since that near catastrophe at the VA Hospital, the pump had become an absurdly simple device. The section given over to oxygenating the blood was made of clear plastic sheeting, suspended from a rack on the side of a four-foot square chromium base, containing the machinery and apparatus for pumping. On the top of the box were several sets of finger-like devices protruding into the air, very similar to those used in the VA case in 1959: hence the term heart-lung machine.

Gannon himself made the series of parallel transverse incisions between the groin and knee of the right leg, exposing a good-sized but expendable vein, running the length of this part of the leg. His object was to remove that vein, full length, without injuring it, and then to tie off the branches so that they would not leak. This was the vein graft to be transferred into the chest.

Meanwhile, the mid-line incision exposed the middle of the chest immediately, with its contained, slowly beating heart. As he watch the heart pump he was one more time truly amazed by the evolution of the vascular system and the modification of this part of the vessels into the four-chambered pump.

Casey's first job was to get the patient "on the pump" and then, when the pump had taken over the function of the heart, to stop that organ dead in its tracks. Swiftly he set about to clip off the appendage of tissue at the extreme end of the first chamber, rapidly inserting the end of an empty plastic tube into the circulating venous blood beneath and allowing the tube to fill with blood to a certain level. A similar procedure was carried out on the arterial side, forming a bridge between the body of the patient and the heart-lung machine, then passing the connecting tubing from DeLaney to Stork, and connecting the patient to the circulation of the pump. As soon as the machine was obviously moving the bloodstream around, Casey nodded to the anesthesiologist, who gave a dose of potassium chloride intravenously, stopping the heart almost immediately. Once the patient was on the pump, everyone in the room heaved a sigh of relief. Things were under control now, and the procedure could be carried out in a reasonably timely fashion.

Casey picked up the arterial vessel lying on the front wall of the left side of the heart, and palpated the calcific obstruction lying between his fingers at the upper end. At least the diagnosis is correct, thought Gannon. Then he handed his harvested vein to Casey, "Thanks, Chris. This is a good vein. Are you sure none of these branches will leak?" he asked, smiling at Gannon as he spoke.

"Well, let's hope not," replied Gannon. "Since we're working under heparin, if they bleed a little, I hope you won't complain." Matejus was always annoyed when there was unnecessary conversation at the operating table, and today was no exception. His body movements indicated he was irritated with Gannon for making light of this difficult problem and perhaps not paying enough attention since his part was completed.

"Loops," murmured Casey. The circulating nurse then put the binocular-like lens on his face, and Casey picked up the vein offered by Gannon. He laid it on the still heart and palpated the small artery lying on the heart wall, picking that line in the heart wall, looking for a soft spot. "Let's do the hard end first," he said. "The distal suture lines will probably take a while."

Actually, he completed the anastomosis within fifteen minutes, and Gannon marveled at how his two partners worked together to complete the connections with the open-ended vessels so efficiently. Neither of the two working in the chest exhibited any kind of tremor, to Gannon's amazement. As for himself, he felt free and easy as he was closing the leg wounds, but then he was essentially finished. Then Casey removed the tiny clamps that had closed the system off, letting the graft fill slowly from the bottom to the top to eliminate bubbles. Then he took off the last clamp, and an arterial thrust promptly went through the grafted vessel and into the tiny recipient artery. It was now merely a question of good arterial blood circulating through the heart wall for it to pick up its rhythm again, and slowly it began to do so. At first there were about twenty beats to the minute, and then they stood, transfixed, as it abruptly moved up to the same rate of firm contractions to which it had become accustomed for sixty years.

Suddenly Casey was enlivened. "Well gosh, that's it! We did it! Now let's get him off the pump, which he ought to do without any trouble." Swiftly he removed each of the tubes connecting the patient to the pump over the bridge, ligating the connections into the vessels from which the plastic tubes had been removed. There were a couple of leaks in certain areas because of the "anticoagulating heparin," but these quickly stopped with just a little gentle pressure. Gannon noted, happily, that his graft had not leaked.

They were done. They had actually brought it off, this first open heart operation in the history of Waterford Hospital. There was no way of guessing where this would go, but at least the first one was over, technically. Now, would the patient's mind work properly? Would he develop any of the other kinds of complications sustained by surgical patients? They all knew that they would be watched intently, and if there was the least little bit of a glitch, they would be made accountable before the audit committee.

Maggie DeLaney collected and washed all of her instruments, setting them in a basin off to the side. She quickly passed along wire sutures to Casey and Matejus, and they brought the sternum together with the wire, burying the cut knots in the front wall of the breast bone. Gannon had finished stripping off his gown and gloves. No matter how much they tried, they were not able to suppress their own elation at successfully having gotten through this "first." This was not just another in a series of firsts but was a supreme achievement of a lifetime of work in the setting of the community hospital. It had been accomplished against persistent negativism and lack of support by some prominent staff members. There would be other chapters to this story, not all positive. But the fact was that they could go as a team to the pastor's wife and give her a good report. It would not always be so.

Chapter 23

Helene Gannon handed her husband a set of car keys. "Well," she said, "I've been driving you around now for two weeks, and I for one am fed up. It's time that we turn you loose and let the devil take the hindmost." As she held out the keys in her extended hand, the accompanying smile suggested that she had decided he could handle driving a car.

The problem was not just manipulation of the wheel and the handling of the shifting devices. His left shoulder was still in a sling and required care and attention to such things as door closings in order not to redislocate.

There were certain other sensory frailties which were naggingly persistent and not yet showing evidence of improvement. At the peak of this list was a blind spot in the four o'clock position of his vision. There was an annoying device there, with the appearance of a circumferentially notched wheel constantly revolving and making it impossible to see anything in that part of the field. Consequently, he was still running off the page when signing his name to checks, with legibility inhibited by large lettering in the first word or so, followed by compressed and tiny lettering and scribbling as he reached the margin of the paper. He had observed the same phenomenon in his mother's writing during the last year of her life.

As he took the keys from his spouse's hands, he embraced her with the good right arm and gave her a firm buss on the lips. "You have been terrific throughout this time, Helene. I doubt that I shall ever again be able to perform surgery. You may have noticed a tremor in my right hand, which will make it difficult for me to manipulate a needle holder."

Helene started pushing him toward the door. "Stop thinking about these things! Today is your day to try and get by the driving test. I noticed you bumping into doorways on the right side. You'd better keep track of where the curb is and where parked cars actually are placed. You were late with the auto insurance payment because we had no income this month. We don't need a string of cracked-up cars while you learn again."

Well, thought Gannon to himself, *today is D day*. He looked at the stack of stapled papers on the car seat beside him as he put the automobile in gear. He realized that the one hundred copies of the new constitution were just a security blanket, a denial of the reality of the other more important event about to take place. For the preceding two months he had been engaged in a rigorous corridor campaign in support of a new constitution, making the case that this was a matter which would guarantee freedom to physicians in the indefinite future. It had been the single major plank upon which he had based his campaign to beat

Urbanawicz and Adams by taking the vice-president's seat away from them just as it was within their grasp. He had decided many months before that he could break up the Travel Club and their control of the Waterford Hospital staff by damaging their control of the elections. He had rolled all the dice and put his personal pride at great risk. He might lose.

As he swung out of the Catholic hospital's parking lot onto the street, he had persuaded himself that the noon meeting was an all-or-nothing issue. He was so certain of his own leadership potential that he had concluded the hospital would be stuck on dead center without his election. But if he won, the opposition would be destroyed and the way would be opened for additional progressive moves both by his partners and the hospital.

The lot at Waterford Hospital was absolutely full. He had to park on the street and walk two blocks carrying the very heavy constitution copies. He could not remember any other previous time when there had been so much evidence of meeting attendance by physicians. He had spent several nights calling all those that he felt he could put in his support column, asking them to be certain to be present for this very critical vote. He was uncertain what the reaction would be of those family practitioners from the communities fifteen and twenty miles away. Most of them were men upon whose support he felt he could rely, but they were not good at meeting attendance because of the distance.

As he crossed the lot, he was hailed by a familiar voice. Caesar reached out and gave him the two-handed shake, and then, as was his habit proceeded to knock him flat on his back. "I like you, Chris, but I don't like your friends. I want you to know that today I'm going to vote against you because I think your challenge comes at the wrong time. You have forced the various members of the staff, your friends and enemies alike, to choose up sides. You left us no room for an alternate decision. You want political power for the sole purpose of removing resistance to your programs. I don't believe that the staff split you have produced is worth it."

Caesar peered at Gannon over his half lens, as though to say, "Well what do you think of that?"

Gannon never broke his smile. He answered, "I really am sorry that I don't have your support. Seriously. But I understand. You have to stick with the men with whom you were in the service in World War II and who are your long-standing friends. I hope we both live long enough for me to prove to you that your vote against me today is not correct. But even if l lose by a close vote, I think I shall blow up that damn Travel Club."

Caesar dropped his hands off his hips as they both turned into the building. "Be careful Chris. I have been a part of that group for many years. It's not as bad as you think." He patted Gannon on the shoulder in a patronizing way as they turned away from the doctors' room and toward the assembly hall.

Gannon could feel the electricity in all of the air space surrounding him Doctors were coming and going, picking up and reading their mail hanging up their coats, and so forth, but nobody was saying anything. Silence reigned until he got to the door of the meeting room. There he was greeted with a sight which he would never forget.

The room was packed. There were at least 150 physicians at lunch, and the buzz of conversation only hesitated briefly when he appeared at the door. Standing in the food line and filling their plates were two physicians whom Gannon had thought were retired for some years. Gannon would learn later that they had retained their attending staff privileges and consequently retained their right to vote. One of them had only one leg and was walking on crutches. The other could hardly catch his breath. Both had just gotten off the plane from Florida. If Adams had persuaded retired men to come 1500 miles to cast a negative vote, then evidently it was his perception also that there was a great deal at stake today.

The surprise which hit him hardest was just inside the door. Placed on a table was a small wicker basket, and surrounding it were physicians filling out their ballots and stuffing them in the basket. He realized then that the election was almost over, even though the meeting had not yet started. When Ken Adams strode up, folded his ballot into the form of a pointed airplane, and sent it flying into the ballot box, Gannon felt it going right through his own chest.

The whole matter was out of order, obviously by design. The presiding officer was a friend of Gannon's, and he could not understand how this could happen. He was so honest that probably he trusted everyone and did not realize that his own good will was being suborned by other friends and acquaintances. It all looked innocent enough, but Gannon knew then that he had no chance. The meeting began and droned on. Gannon's plea to repeat the electoral process with a second distribution of ballots was voted down. He was charged with delaying tactics. A special ballot committee was appointed to count the votes, and they retreated to a side room The presiding officer had been careful to include one member known to be a supporter of each opposing group and a third whom he had apparently thought was relatively neutral. While they were counting, Gannon was given the floor to support his constitutional proposal. Throughout the discussion he was on fire inside his body, as he know that he was being counted out in the back room at the same time.

Sure enough, as the last item on the agenda, when the president called for a report from the electoral committee, Gannon found that he had lost by just one vote. That one vote was a ballot that should never have been cast because both the outgoing and incoming presidents had cast a ballot, and the presiding officer should vote only to break a tie. As he looked around the room, he noted the absence of five or six men from the outer communities, any one of whom could have driven the fifteen miles to represent the winning vote. He contrasted that with the two men who had come by air from Florida for the sole purpose of preventing his election. Crestfallen, he moved about the emptying room, shaking hands with supporters, thanking them, and picking up the copies of the document upon which he had worked so diligently for so many months. It would be voted upon finally at a second hearing three months hence. Since everyone benefited, he was certain that it would pass. But he had lost, and he might never be this close again.

As he was passing Ken Adams near the door, an older physician approached Adams and grasped him by the lapels. "Well, Ken, that sure looks like the end of the Travel Club! That vote was too close and these guys will never come back from Florida again."

There was little satisfaction for Gannon in realizing that that was true. He walked out the side door in order to avoid meeting anyone in the cloak room. He was so angry and frustrated he decided to walk to his office in the warm sunshine and get a grip on himself. As he stepped out of the building, a familiar feminine figure approached him. It was Maggie DeLaney. "Oh, Dr. Gannon, we just heard in the cafeteria that you had lost. We're all, all the nurses, really so sorry. Can you take it?"

Once again Maggie was stepping into the breech. She seemed to always be there, always ready to pay a price, always supportive. "Maggie," he replied, "Ben asked me the same thing—could I take it? What other choices are there?" He tried to laugh it off, but his voice broke with the last words.

"Everybody in the hospital knew how much you wanted to win. It has been your obsession for years. You wouldn't do anything stupid to hurt yourself would you?" She was holding his hand in both of hers. There were glimpses of light in the comers of her eyes.

"No, Maggie. I'll get another chance in a few years. Really nice of you to care, though. But I've got to go to work at the office He pulled his hand away and quickly turned the corner. He would have been mortified had she seen the tears in his eyes.

As he walked along the street beneath the new green leaves of summer, a car pulled up at the curb, and the familiar voice of Sam McKee came to him.. "Hey, Chris, how are you taking this? Can I give you a ride to the office? I have some idea of how you feel. This explains all that fuss about the fake letter last winter. These guys were playing for keeps, and you are still the only thing in their way."

"No thanks, Sam I just want to walk off my anger and frustration. I won a whole series of battles this year but lost the war in the last one. Maybe my partner can get elected in a few years, but I will be on ice now for a long time. I'll walk." He turned and headed down the street toward his office, a mile away.

He was exhausted; every muscle hurt, particularly at the base of his neck. He must have been carrying himself stiffly all day long. Why had this meant so much? His ego again. His father had often spoken from the pulpit about the "sin of pride." It was one of the worst, he had said. "Pride goeth before destruction and a haughty spirit before a fall." Gannon's search for recognition in Waterford had been relentless. As much as Penelope Bayard had wished for recognition, with Gannon it had become an obsession. Apparently, Ben Matejus and Maggie DeLaney knew this also, for they were questioning his ability to handle this defeat. Well he could deal with it. He had been thinking about a program for organ transplantation in a community hospital—first kidneys, then hearts. Why not? But not being an officer of the staff was going to make it more difficult.

Then there was the matter of Maggie DeLaney. Why did she care so much?

Chapter 24

Gannon chose to undergo his baptism under fire by driving the old Bonneville to the orthopedist's office. As he approached the top of the neighborhood hill he perceived that he had made a mistake because quick acceleration was missing in this car and was exactly what he would need to get onto the highway. As he waited impatiently for the cross traffic to thin, he realized that he was not going to be able to gun it across into the far lane without having some problems. This was confirmed as he skidded off the macadam onto the gravel and was forced to drive a considerable distance, weaving crazily before he was able to get back up on the roadway. He was aware of his profuse perspiration as he tried to determine when he should swerve back into traffic.

The right side of the roadway was elusive, and he found himself recurrently sliding off the edge onto the gravel, constantly overestimating the amount of roadway left. It reminded him of his problems with the checkbook and his difficulty in definition of the extreme right of his vision. The blind spot in the four o'clock position of the eye coincided exactly with the right edge of the roadway. He realized that he was going to have to compensate by driving further inside than his perception believed correct.

Arriving at that portion of the community where the streets were lined by parked traffic, he knew he would have to stay well off the perceived edge of the parked automobiles or he was going to have a big insurance loss. His depth perception and its relationship to traffic lanes was still not accurate.

In addition his shoulder hurt like hell. He had cranked open the driver's side with his disabled arm. It only increased the pain. The goal on this trip was the parking lot of the orthopedic surgeon. He drove slowly, hugging the edge of the roadway and then with a sigh of relief, swerved around the corner and into the parking lot and into an empty space. He cursed mightily under his breath, caressing his left shoulder with his right hand, then leaning forward on the steering wheel closing his eyes. *Now*, he thought, *if I can just find my way home.*

Brian Casey placed his hands on the end of the desk and leaned across between Matejus and Gannon . "I tell you, it will never work. It has been difficult enough up to this point. Combinations of general surgery and cardiac surgery have never worked anywhere else, and they are not going to work here."

Matejus was looking at the floor. "Chris, Brian and I should tell you that we have been debating these issues on the tennis court all summer. The two young guys want out. They want to go on their own."

Gannon straightened up in his chair, looking grim "So, Brian, we get to lead everybody to the land of milk and honey but are not allowed to go in ourselves. Is that how it is?"

"C'mon, Chris, you've tried everything else this summer. Don't you see that we are upset?" This latter came from Ho Kim. He had been with the group just two years and was at least as aware as Gannon of the disagreements between the other two men.

Five years had passed since the 1972 election. Matejus had spent three years on the executive committee and had now been elected to the vice-presidency, to ascend automatically to the presiding chair in one year. Gannon had been frozen out throughout this time, relegated to the role of peacemaker between the two older partners. He had indeed tried every possible avenue. This had included new letterheads and stationery so that the practice was literally divided onto the two sides of the paper—general surgery and cardiac surgery. He had written in Matejus and Casey as chiefs of service. He had made progressively incremental increases in income to the two cardiac surgeons, including the most junior in the group, in order to compensate them for their greater earning power. Neither he nor Matejus could equal the dollar volume of work from the two cardiac surgeons because their fees were simply so much larger for the same volume of time expended. The large-fee surgical cases were left to tumors, especially of the colon and vicious tumors of the pancreas and bile ducts. Gannon and Matejus simply could not produce the same volume of gross income as Casey and Kim. It was evident during the discussion that Casey had some sense of guilt as he went to significant lengths to rationalize this enormous change in the direction of their lives.

"In a year or so none of us will feel this parting. We should separate on as good terms as possible. Who knows—maybe we can help one another politically in two separate services, just as well as we helped one another working together. In the arena of staff leadership, I have no ambitions. I just want to run my own service and divide our income as we are able to earn it. I helped you deliver on your commitment to the administration and board in the area of cardiac surgery, and we have a growing caseload, as you know, and we have nearly one case per week this year. Our combined paper, reporting the results in cardiac surgery in a community hospital is ready for publication in the AMA Journal. Nobody else has done anything like that, anywhere. We have added two more films to the College library, so I feel that we have delivered our obligations."

He lifted his hands from the desk and leaned back against the wall with folded arms. "No matter what, we are going to leave, guys. I think we should have a meeting shortly to formalize it all. Wednesday afternoon here at the office."

Chris looked doubtfully at Matejus. The latter nodded his head. "Okay, one week from tomorrow. We'll give the girls the afternoon off and thrash it out. We cannot make you work with us if you don't want to. There have been many right fielders who have chosen to lose the ball in the sun or the night lights when they didn't like the setting that they were working in. And I don't want us to end up with protracted hard feelings. "

Eight days later Gannon met the office girls leaving at noon. "Dr. Matejus said we could have the afternoon off. He said you were going to have a meeting or something." Gannon waved to them as they walked down the hall and out the back door.

Matejus was setting up the waiting room as he came around the corner. The room had been divided into two halves, clearly drawing the lines between the two younger men and the two older. Gannon and Matejus were to occupy the seats against the far wall Gannon smiled to himself. The arrangement was so like that of a certain real life desperado, Wild Bill Hickcock, whose credo was never to turn his back to the people in any room. So it was that the four men arranged themselves for their last meeting together.

Matejus had the same habits present when he and Gannon had had their first conversations twenty-five years earlier. He had added other intimidating patterns. He was still a heavy smoker, and during such times as this, he became a chain smoker. He had developed a way of folding his hands beneath his chin and letting the cigarette smoke drift slowly upward into his own eyes, producing a heavy-lidded stare toward anyone opposite him. This was the position he adopted this afternoon, leaving Gannon rather out of the picture to the right side.

He had also developed a habit of carrying a briefcase. Gannon secretly thought it was another mode of intimidation. He had observed that sometimes this briefcase was absolutely empty. However, when he snapped the latches open, one could usually see his opponents jump a little in their chairs. Sometimes there was highly organized material in the briefcase, with quotations and statements and analysis of old minutes that, taken together, could be damning for any opposition. Watching Matejus carry out this performance on this day, even Casey jumped a little in his chair. Gannon smiled to himself.

The conversation that followed was low-pitched and with short statements from both sides. Gannon offered little. It seemed as though Matejus and Casey had already been through this conversation, probably on those tennis courts during the summer. Perhaps the meeting had been designed by the two of them, although Gannon was certain that Matejus had been as surprised as he by the declaration of the younger men the preceding week. Matejus always kept attorneys and accountants at his beck and call. He also kept the records, particularly the financial records, so he walked the young doctors through the separation procedure. The exchange of words was too cold to be climactic.

Sitting silently Gannon thought of his metaphor or not being allowed to cross into the land of milk and honey. He was not ashamed of feeling that he had led the group through the wilderness and to the top of the mountain. It was true. How did Stonewall Jackson put it? He would never be allowed to cross over the river and lie in the cool shade of the trees.

Casey closed out the conversation with, "We're not prepared to move into other working quarters yet. Do you think we could stay on here the next, sixty days and then open elsewhere January 2?"

Matejus let the cigarette smoke spiral upward into his eyes. He did not blink, and he did not cough.

He said "no."

In the winter of 1978 Gannon became a runner. He thought of himself as a runner in a variety of ways. On his birthdate in February of that year, on the way home from the office early one evening, he abruptly turned his car into the lighted parking lot of the high school, got out, and ran around the periphery of the lot in street shoes and a flapping, black raincoat, shouting hysterically to a nonexistent audience, "I can do it! I can do it!" Of course, he had little idea of what it was he could do and no idea t he had run only one quarter of a mile.

In August of the preceding summer, about a year after the dissolution of the four-man partnership, he had concluded that there might be a future for him in the continuing education of doctors. So he returned to a local university graduate school as an enrollee in a master's degree program. By the time he began to run, he had successfully demonstrated to himself and his professors that he could still learn effectively and fire back answers to their exam questions. For the next three years he traveled every Wednesday evening to sit in cramped armchairs in barren tan classrooms with classmates whose average age approximated 30. He was becoming everybody's "grandpa."

In the years since the election loss, professional matters had gone well for Gannon and Matejus, in spite of the partnership breakup. They were able to put together land-holding units for the purchase of small farms in an area of projected growth. In addition Gannon had ventured into a side business, rehabilitating a huge Victorian mansion into a restaurant. Further, he was taking non-credit evening courses in creative writing at the local junior college. Still there was something missing. He had utterly no sex drive. More and more he had become certain that making love had become a duty for Helene, and he simply cared less and less himself.

One of the reasons for thinking about becoming an amateur athlete late in life was a developing relationship between himself and Maggie DeLaney. Since the training period for the first open heart surgery, they had been thrown together almost daily in the operating room. For six years they had scrupulously maintained a hands-off relationship, addressing each other as "sir" and "Mrs. DeLaney" in the course of their conversations. Never once had their knees touched beneath the operating room table, and their physical contact was limited strictly to the passing and exchange of instruments. Conversation remained on the highest plane, either regarding the procedure taking place or in discussion of some abstract idea during closure. This attested most to their mutual realization that there was a developing attraction and respect, as each went far beyond the necessary in order not to offend the other.

But something was stirring in Gannon's heart during this time, even through he did not recognize its nature. The winter of 1978 was characterized by snowfall of excessive frequency and depth as, week by week, the streets became tunnels with snow packed eight-and ten-feet high on the edges. The more the snow fell the faster and farther Gannon ran. In the spring he went to the sports stores and bought running outfits. He purchased a new style of running shoe, which was light and had turned-up toes, allegedly to deter wear. He bought shorts and athletic socks and ran with a bare upper body on warm sunny days.

One Saturday morning on a buying venture, he found Maggie DeLaney shopping for running clothes. Yes, she informed him she had been a runner for ten years. He looked down at the floor as she shoved hangers filled with jogging blazers, tight biking shorts, halter tops, and the like into her cart. Would she like to teach him how to run better? Maybe they could enter some races together? She slammed a couple of hangers together as though she were giving up on something. She turned and faced him frontally. Her eyes said, why not?

Running became an obsession. Periodically they appeared in competitions together. DeLaney always finished in the top ten, Gannon in the bottom ten. But he improved. In June he ran a ten kilometer race in competition with hospital employees. He was dead last, but DeLaney lagged behind to see that he crossed the finish line on his feet. The observation ambulance from the emergency room lapped him four times before cruising across the line, the three hundred pound driver waving as he went by. Then they ran a celebrity race sponsored by a hotel in Chicago, again ten kilometers. Once more, DeLaney held back, probably because she could see he was laboring. But he finished in the upper two-thirds and best for people in their fifties. In the last kilometer, he felt something snap in his left calf, and he limped across at the line.

Two Sundays later in a neighboring community, they ran another ten-kilometer race of the "up-hill" type. This was a country race, and when going up Gannon noticed pain distributed throughout the entire left calf. For two days prior to the race, he had also noticed some slight swelling of the left foot and difficulty putting on his left shoe in the mornings. He had shrugged it off. But after the turn at the halfway mark, he could no longer deny what was happening in his calf and he had to slow to a walk and waved DeLaney on. She did not leave him. Instead, she hung back and walked along, with concern on her face. They had come to depend on one another for simple things, including company and conversation and an occasional lunch. Gannon had detected in her a responsive warmth when he was around, and he knew he made her laugh. On this morning her concern was genuine and deep.

Gannon went home to bed that afternoon, observing that his left leg was swelling progressively over the next few hours. Still, in spite of his training as a vascular surgeon, the reality of what was taking place was lost upon him. Later he would realize how stupid he had been. He had had the classical case of trauma to the limb two weeks previously, continued to use the limb throughout the interval, and employed it vigorously at the end, and now was developing significant swelling in the entire leg. At midnight he was assailed with a stabbing pain in the right chest, and every breath hurt. He sat on the edge of his bed and thought out the situation. *My gosh, I have thrown a clot from my leg to my lung!* There was no other possible combination diagnostically. In the seated position, he now had pain in the right shoulder also. The combination of a swollen left leg and chest pain, followed by shoulder pain, was only consistent with pulmonary embolism against the diaphragm, a classic set of symptoms which he had observed many times since the onset of the use of the birth control pill two decades previously. He shook his head and walked very slowly to the bathroom holding his chest. He sat down, experienced an explosive stool and fainted.

When he came to, just a few moments later, having passed through that dreaded what am I?, Who am I?, Where am I? level, he found himself lying face down on the tile floor, having smashed his glasses and cut his lip. He called weakly, "Helene, Helene, I'm sick."

When his two remaining sons still living at home came to help him, he gasped, "I'm sure I have thrown a clot to my right lung from my left leg. I have been a fool, but I am sure that I have analyzed this correctly. Don't argue. Call an ambulance! This is a matter of life and death. Another one of those or a big one, and that will be it!"

Chapter 25

Gannon picked up his brand new TYR athletic bag while pushing two quarters across the counter in exchange for a large, dry towel He offered no eye contact with the YMCA employee behind the counter because he was afraid—afraid of doing something stupid in public, afraid of bumping into the door frame, afraid of not being able to figure out the system, and afraid of drowning.

He had thought about aquatics as a method of rehabilitation for the past six weeks, at one time even got close enough to have parked in the lot of the Y until he lost his nerve. He watched the younger men and women coming and going in the dark at 6:30 A.M. and he concluded that it was all too much. He had "screwed his courage to the sticking point" and had gone inside to buy a one-year membership. Now he was in for it, he thought. The humidity in the locker room was cloying and oppressive. Dressing to swim was a painful experience, and it occurred to him that he would have to repeat the process when the swim was over. He stared at the floor and avoided looking at any of the other naked men as he crossed to the shower room. The latter was occupied by men older than he, stooped and cachectic, some gray-haired and some bald, all preoccupied with bathing. Particularly striking was a short, overweight, stubby fellow, who seemed to soap and resoap himself infinitely, as though trying to cleanse himself of eighty years of sinning.

Gannon could not find a faucet with warm water, not being familiar with the plumbing as obviously were the others in the shower stalls. He was forced to stand blanched and shivering under what he thought was the combined gaze of other disapproving males. Across from him was a short, stocky young man with the longest penis he had ever observed. His own organ had shrunk to practically nothing in the cold water, and he turned away toward the wall so that the others in the room would not know.

Then he slipped on a new bikini-style suit, with cap and goggles and strode out into the pool area. He was well enough known in the community to be certain that there would be discussion about this event, on the street and in the restaurants, because this was a small town in every sense of the word, and he wanted to present a brave front.

He had not been afraid of anything related to swimming since the age of six. Now the thought of "the deep end" terrified him. He let himself down the pool ladder with great care, being careful not to overextend either shoulder. Years before he had heard about the predilection for those with chronic dislocating shoulders to have them routinely slip out while swimming the American crawl. Well, obviously, he was not going to do that. So he flattened out to what he later called the Gannon crawl, a modified breast stroke designed to be safe yet still get him to the other end. Turning his face into the water as he stroked along, he watched the bottom receding from his vision and then dropping precipitously out of view as he crossed the halfway mark into the deeper section. He was frightened, and his shoulders hurt terribly. *Only a few strokes more,* he thought, *and I can rest at the other end. Then I have to go back....*

"Here, Dr. Gannon, I have your next dose of heparin for you." He noticed that the 9:00 P.M. news was just coming on the television as the floor nurse, an old friend, sat down by his bedside and deftly inserted the syringe into the recipient reservoir on the hub of the IV set. The needle from the latter lay in the middle of his left forearm.

Since his admission to the hospital he had been receiving individual bolus doses of IV anticoagulant every six hours. Immediately, this injection was different. He felt a firelike pain running up the forearm holding the IV needle and all the way to the shoulder as the nurse was making the injection. He pulled up his sleeve and noted that the entire arm and shoulder were blue, "cyanotic" would be the term applied by examining physicians. Oddly enough, he had failed to notice the extensive swelling of the entire extremity, which had to have appeared since he had put on his night shirt. *My God!* he thought. *What is going on? This made no sense!* The limb seemed to be doubling in size right in front of his eyes and he shouted to the nurse, "Stop! Stop! Something is really rotten! I've had no pain with any previous injection. Do you think the needle is still in the vein?"

The nurse, a middle-aged professional, jerked the needle out and stood up, exclaiming, "My heavens, Dr. Gannon! What is happening to you? Look at your arm! The whole arm is swollen and blue! I'll go out to the nursing station and double-check the ampule; it's pre-mixed in the pharmacy and sent to us prepared. I'll check the label again!"

She ran out, syringe in hand. When she returned, she handed him the ampule with its taped-on label placed there by the pharmacist at the time of the mixing of the drugs. The label was handwritten and initialed by the pharmacist and clearly said, "Aqueous Heparin. 40,000 units."

"Save the ampule and syringe, Mrs. Minor. God, how much this hurts! There is something funny going on. Call Dr. Matejus and Dr. Casey right away. Tell them something awful is going on and that I want them to come over right now. I know it is late on a Saturday night, but tell them that my arm is killing me and is about to split open."

The pain, which had begun as a narrow strip on the front side of the forearm just above the site of the in-lying heparin catheter, had spread now to involve not only the hand and it was extending over onto the shoulder and chest wall. In that area he could make out distended venous channels against a slate blue background of skin. *My heavens,* he thought, *I'm clotting off the entire venous drainage from the arm, right in front of my eyes. How can this happen, when the very medicine I'm being given is to counteract that?* He feared that the rate at which this was traveling, it would extend to the venous drainage from the head and other arm and that he would develop an occlusion of the superior vena cava! By now his fingers had become so stiff that he could not close them into a fist. The skin of the forearm was so taut and shiny that the likelihood of the skin splitting from the pressure within the muscle compartment was more and more certain. Fasciotomy. *Fasciotomy: that's what I need,* he thought.

He punched the call button to the nurses' station. "Call Dr. Lee also," he shouted into the air of the room. "We have to take care of this tonight! I know he drinks a lot on Saturday night but get him in here anyhow. I'll take him drunk as opposed to any other orthopedist I know sober."

Fewer than thirty minutes later, Casey, Matejus, and Lee stood around his bed, looking in dismay at the left arm and hand. From their faces Gannon could see that they were horror-struck and disbelieving.

Casey looked up from pressing on his patient's fingernails, checking the circulation. "Do we know what his platelet count is today?" His eyes were directed to the floor nurse, who flipped through the chart to the laboratory sheet.

"There's a progress note late Friday afternoon from Dr. Samski, who pointed out that his platelets were down to 36,000. He asked the partners to look this morning at what the platelet count was, and I see it has fallen further to 15,000.

Casey ran his fingers across the back of Gannon's hand. "Do you feel anything there?"

"No, damn it, not a thing As a matter of fact, the skin is stretched so tight over the arm, that I don't think I can feel anything on the arm, either."

"Ben, have you and Bob seen the case reports of something called disseminated intravascular coagulopathy, DIC syndrome, developing in some people who are heparinized ? The platelets change and begin to collect along the wall of the small veins, clotting off the vessels. That must be what is going on here!"

Matejus looked grimly at Lee. "Well, there's no doubt about what we have to do. We can't wait til morning for this. Get anesthesia in here and put him to sleep so you can slice the forearm open. If we don't do that right now the least that will happen will be that he will lose his arm!"

Gannon spat out, "You guys are asking me to give consent for you to cut open the fascia on a surgeon's arm? It's a good thing we're all friends." Lee looked at Gannon. "It may not help, you know. At best it will take five or six debridements and a skin graft to close, but I think you know as well as I what I must do. Honestly, I have never seen this in an upper extremity before."

"DIC syndrome, huh?" said Gannon. He managed a wan smile as he lay back into the pillows. How poetic! It would only be better if my first name were Dick. We've all seen limbs like this before and we all know it's bad news." Then he turned to the floor nurse one last time. "Mrs. Minor, don't forget to set aside that heparin bottle. There is something fishy going on here, I'm certain. Label it and put it in the icebox and tomorrow morning, when this is over, I'll tell the nursing staff what to do with it. As a matter of fact, it may not even be heparin. This episode tonight may not be an accident."

As it turned out, Lee's impression of the daily need for debridement of the extensive wounds on Gannon's left arm was exactly correct. Gannon went to the operating room every two days for the next two weeks, the final effort being a huge skin graft taken from his left thigh and placed in the defect that remained overlying the muscles of the left forearm. On the afternoon of the performance of the skin graft, he had a new visitor.

"Come on in, lieutenant. We have a lot to talk about."

"Good afternoon, Dr. Gannon—and you are right. We do have a lot to talk about." Lieutenant Gorski spoke as he was stepping through the door, uncomfortable in the setting of a hospital sick room. He was short, overweight, and took a position standing by the bedside, shifting from one leg to the other throughout the interview, and spinning his wide-brim felt hat between his fingers. He leaned against the metal frame suspended over the bed, which made it possible for Gannon to move himself by use of a hanging trapeze. He chose to do that now, hoisting himself higher in bed and then swinging his legs over the side to a dangling position. In so doing he was forced to swing the heavy plaster mold which encased the full length of the left arm, banging the dried and flaking plaster on the corners of the metal frame.

"Damn this thing," he said. "It's always in the way. It is beginning to break up, and I get fragments in bed and develop a bad case of the itch in the middle of the night."

The lieutenant looked down at his twisting hat. "But aren't you lucky to still have the arm? And you are alive; the rumble is that the arm was becoming gangrenous."

"Yep, it was. But there are two ways to look at every issue. It's bad luck to have had the original incident at all, and good luck to have been able to overcome it. If I get a good take on the graft, I'll be out of here in five or six days. But back to business; do you have anything at all?"

"Well, I don't have many explanations for anything. But I did receive one fact that is devastating. You remember that pharmacy ampule that you asked the nurses to save, the one being used for the last injection? Well, you guessed right. There was something wrong with it. Instead of it containing 40,000 units of heparin per cc, it was 400,000 units per cc, ten times what it was labeled. Is such an accident possible?"

"Yeah, it's possible but unlikely. Heparin has been measured both in biologic units and in milligrams. This has switched back and forth over the last thirty years, but we're back to the unit scaling now. I would guess that's how the pharmacy measures the actual units of the dosage. It is the job of the pharmacist then to dilute this type of medicine at a ten to one ratio. Of course, on that basis, the mixing pharmacist could have become confused and failed to make the dilution. I have some reason to believe that this was not an accident."

The lieutenant shifted the weight on his feet and stared at the ceiling again. Then he moved his eyes to contact those of Gannon. "You're telling me that you think this was deliberate? Would this be in that category of mystery novel in which there is a subtle but scientifically correct attempt at murder? One of your close friends has said that you are paranoid about this...."

"I have thought about this many times over the last two weeks," said Gannon, leaning back into his pillow. "But if you check some old records with the state police, referencing an auto accident near here in the spring of 1972, you will find an anesthesiologist died in that accident. He worked in this hospital and there was some evidence of tampering with the steering gear on his little sports car. It was a bad end, and I never followed up as I really should have. I don't think the sergeant in charge did either. I suppose I just hoped it would blow away. There was plenty of reason to believe that the doctor was set up by an assassin, and there was a probability I would be in the car with him. Is 'professional jealousy' listed among the common causes for murder?" Hardly seemed worth the trouble to me. Moreover, about the same time I successfully destroyed a private medical club, and maybe someone has been waiting in the wings ever since for an opportunity to nail me up."

Lieutenant Gorski was still spinning his hat in his hands and staring at the ceiling, but he moved backward a few steps and stood spraddle-legged. "Well, yes, professional jealousy is a recognized motive and has been so in many classic crimes. But let us look at this from a different angle. Who had access to the heparin ampules, since the preparation was all in the pharmacy and medicines are sent to the floor already prepared?"

"There are a dozen registered pharmacists who work across the twenty-four hour span, seven days a week. You should be able to get the record of assignments for the week preceding that event and determine who exactly had the responsibility for mixing drugs on that day. I know of only one out of the twelve who might be paid off with money to do this. No one in that department has any such motive, but there are several physicians who have plenty of reason for deep-seated professional jealousies."

For the first time Gorski left the bedside and stepped over to look out the window. He spoke slowly. "You know, of course, that you are suggesting a very complicated and difficult-to-prove scenario? Here is a situation in which we are dealing with apparent limited access to what we have to call the murder weapon. And you are asking me to step back one generation to find a physician from our community here who would hire a paid assassin. In this small town that would be a real shake out."

Gannon reached up and scratched beneath his plaster. "Yes it would." He then rose to a sitting position again, swinging himself around with the trapeze and looking hard at the floor. "I am sure that this will have the same kind of blind ending that the 1972 killing of Owen Bird had.

Nonetheless, all of the people who were present at that time and definitely involved in some political business here in the hospital are still alive and functioning. Time has shown that I did destroy the medical club, so motivation has, if anything, been reinforced in the intervening ten years. Are you willing to go ahead with some additional investigation based only on the fact of the known overwhelming quantity of heparin given to me? You have to decide whether it is more likely that this was a gross error or deliberate. I think someone is still trying to kill me."

Gorski, obviously uneasy with this idea, started sliding toward the door, intermittently putting his hat on and then taking it off as he looked around the room. He was having great difficulty with direct eye contact with Gannon. He spoke one last time. "Well, Doc, I'm not qualified to certify you as a paranoid schizo. Even though I might think that that is probably the case. There are just enough objective findings at the moment to warrant expenditure of some of my time and that of one or two others in pursuit of an investigation. I can get the pharmacy records to know who was on call. One of the key things will be accessibility by others to the pharmacy. I would bet that no written record is kept, for security reasons, as to who comes and goes there. I would also bet that the location of the key is known not only to the pharmacy but also to many other personnel within the hospital. Frankly, I think that anybody with any kind of medical training and some guts could have gained access to the heparin and done this. It will be very difficult to follow any kind of trail. At worst I can only call this attempted murder. You are still alive and apparently going to be functional again. I don't think you can even claim civil damage because you will still be able to perform surgery."

"Ha, you are not very funny, Lieutenant Gorski. Actually I had accepted the idea of a practice in allergy or dermatology from the very beginning. On the other hand, I looked at my disability insurance policy, and it is very vague as to the definition of physician or surgeon and what differentiates the two, and whether one's source of income is limited because one only has one arm or not. As usual it is all in the fine print. But it looks like I will be saved all that trouble anyhow. I suppose I could have a case against the hospital and against some of the doctors that took care of me for the clot in my lung, but they're all my friends and people whom I recruited to the community. How can I deny that? It is simply not possible!"

Gorski looked at him one last time, "Maybe the thing that makes it impossible is your own pride. You cannot concede that the people that you brought here made a mistake, even though their mistake resulted in harm to yourself. I have met guys like you before, and I would bet that you have such an ego that you could not admit publicly that you made a mistake in the recruitment phase when you brought them here. Am I right about that?"

Gannon did not answer immediately. Instead, he creased and uncreased the bedsheet with his good hand. Then he looked up. "You are exactly right. One more time ego and pride get in the way. But you don't suffer from any of those subjective problems in this case. You can remain objective and conduct an investigation in an objective way. I am asking you to do that."

"Okay, Doc. I will pursue this for a couple of weeks, but I bet that trail is pretty cold now, and I expect to run into nothing more than blind alleys again. I will postpone asking you to sign a complaint. Wish me luck, I will need it.

Chapter 26

"Sit down, Chris. Make yourself comfortable. Like a cup of coffee?" asked Jay Robinson, vice-president in charge of physicians' affairs. Next to him sat Finley Carabino. He also gestured Gannon to take a seat.

Gannon hated the prospects of this meeting. He had demonstrated his abilities to drive around town to keep his appointments for physiotherapy, to see his physicians, and had spoken enough with his friends on the staff for these administrators to know that he could walk and talk. Apparently they wanted him to demonstrate that he was still employable. Mark Silver had indicated on a visit two weeks before that he also was interested in determining for himself whether or not Gannon could think straight. He had said this in a joking fashion, but Gannon was certain that it was no joke. He had wondered for a week whether this interview would be a pressure type of interview, enjoyed so much by MBA's who had themselves been subjected to job interviews of this nature. He wanted and needed the job. He had lost two months of income, and creditors were getting impatient. He simply could not afford to fail this interview.

Jay Robinson had always been on his side and now smiled benignly as he poured the coffee, saying, "Well, let's get this over with. You know, when my dad had his stroke, he was left paralyzed and could not remember anything, and he was severely disabled. It does not seem to me that this is the case with you. But we'll see."

Carabino was an unknown quantity to Gannon. He was to be his immediate superior, having recently been brought in to run some of the peripheral aspects of the hospital He smiled constantly throughout the interview, as though he were enjoying observing without having to participate. Robinson was the speaker, intermittently rotating on the seat of his chair, with his fingers pursed together in front of his face, occasionally running an index digit over and around his nose. Gannon remained painfully uncomfortable throughout the discussion, shifting from side to side and sitting on his right hand to keep it warm. Clearly, a major portion of the embolus had lodged in the artery to his right arm with tiny fragments breaking off and going into his brain at the same time. That hand now remained cold, pulseless, and often painful.

"It looks to me like you have doubts that I can do the job in the occupational health setting," he said. "I know that I have been a little messed up since this episode, and I admit that I am having trouble remembering certain names, people's names."

The two administrators, who were charged with the responsibly for the development of this new health facility, looked at one another. "Frankly, Chris, we all remember that you have to meet and deal with the public. As I said before, my dad could neither walk nor talk after his stroke. In your case it will be important to know whether you can still handle a needle holder or not; what do you think?"

"I'm sure that you have seen the tremor I have in my right hand, which I still cannot control. But I have been sewing on some leather at home. I'm slow, but I can still make a straight line. What else?" Gannon was sure that both Carabino and Robinson detected some edge in his voice. They both leaned forward and looked at him intently, Carabino speaking first, "What psychological effect do you think your physical and mental appearance will have on the patients at the clinic? There has been no secret about your stroke this winter. How do you think the public will feel being taken care of by a man who has had a stroke?"

Gannon stood up and strode over to the window and looked out at the street. "God damn it! You guys are forever worried about how things look rather than how things are. You should see that I could be an example for those who can use rehabilitation programs to return to their way of life. I never missed a beat on the radio program because I had a couple of shows taped ahead in case of an emergency, and I also was ahead on medical writings for the newspapers; I never missed anything there either. In God's name, what do you guys want?"

Gannon spun around as he finished this last line and looked at the two interviewers. Robinson answered, "Now, now, don't get upset. I admit that it does look like you will be all right. But you can't get mad every time somebody twists your tail!"

"This is a hell of a lot more than tail twisting, Jay, and you know it. For years, the only surgeon better than me was my partner, Ben. I wouldn't attempt sewing a simple laceration unless I was sure I could do it. Put me to work. I need the money!"

"Ben, I'd like to do this case. I have to find out whether my left arm will work like it should. As a matter of fact, we both have to know."

Gannon and Matejus were standing with gloved folded hands in operating room eleven, watching the anesthesiologist slip the endotracheal tube into place.

Sure, Chris. Go ahead. It's just a moderate size hernia, anyway. I worked him up in the office last week, but there's no reason you cant do the case. You need to get your feet wet again."

Together the two of them went through the formalities of prepping and draping. Then DeLaney handed the knife to Gannon, and he looked at it as though it were a stranger, chuckling, "Well, we have done this every day for years and not given it any thought. Although my arm is healed, my head is uncertain as to what to do. Maybe l should just begin."

He reached across the groin of the patient with his left hand, tensing the skin between his index and long fingers, quickly drawing the knife crosswise in the skin line above the scrotum for a distance of not more than two inches. The large venous channel that rose vertically from the groin was exposed by this incision, which then he picked up with mosquito clamps, tying the two ends separately because of the size. Then he took his left hand again and slid it through the fat and cut the next layer with scissors, exposing the glistening white outer fascial layer of the external oblique muscle. He divided these fibers in their direction toward the outer ring of the spermatic cord and then elevated the cord on his hand, quickly wrapping a rubber drain around to draw it aside. "Well, I haven't forgotten anything yet, have I? It does seem similar to riding a bicycle. "

Meanwhile, he noted that Matejus was watching him carefully. Gannon sensed this guarded point of view as Ben moved the retractors up and down, following the course of the action. Gannon divided the coverings of the spermatic cord, and in so doing, a nice pear-shaped sac, about five centimeters in length, presented itself. He opened the sac immediately, stuck his index finger inside in the time-honored fashion, then wiping down a fat layer from the contents of the spermatic cord to the neck of the sac, which was now bell-shaped, with a neck at the abdominal wall not more than the size of the tip of his index finger. He closed that neck with a classic type of purse string suture of cotton and then excised the excess peritoneal tissue that represented the expanded sac, letting the neck retract into the abdomen. Then he stuck the same index finger in along the base of the cord next to the sutured neck of the sac, demonstrating the small defect in the fascial floor at the second and third muscle layer beneath. "I think I'll put in two or three cotton stitches to snug up the neck. What do you think?"

"Looks to me likes it's the thing to do," said Matejus. "You showed me that you can tie now, including the bad left hand. I'll take over the tying now and we'll get on more quickly."

During the time of the wound closure, they were able to discuss other issues, since most of the work was automatic. "Do you think this is my year to run again, Ben? You have been president, although you have been here fewer years than I. Still I think the hate is there, and the Travel Club will still do all they can to block me. What do you think?"

"It is certainly now or never," said Ben. "I can ask the president for a special meeting. Someone may make a constitutional issue of the fact that you are the education director and try to freeze you out. You're right. They still will do anything to block you."

Gannon stopped as he was applying the dressing. "Did I tell you that I had a criminal investigation launched after the episode with the heparin?"

"No, but I guessed that you would. I heard a rumor that there were really 400,000 units of heparin in the IV syringe. I guessed that you would think that was not just an accident. Did the investigator come up with anything?"

"No. It was as blind an alley, as the one involving Owen Bird. They learned that the security in the pharmacy was very poor and that almost anyone could have had access to the key and could have made any dilution adjustment. The investigating officer didn't think he could find any way to pin it on one of the pharmacists, as none of them had a motive. On the other hand, a paid assassin would have to be someone skilled in the use of syringes and computation of doses from within ampules, and so forth. He said he'd keep looking but that he doubted that it was going to lead anywhere. I suppose you agree with him that I'm a little nuts about this." Gannon smiled as he untied his face mask and let it drop.

"Yes, I do. But you know that anyhow. I have always said you were a dreamer, and you are one of the few people I know who would think an assassin had been hired to kill him in some way. By the way, there was an incident in Deerfield Hills while you were in the hospital. I never told you about it, because I thought it would lend credence to the thoughts in your head."

Gannon looked at him as he inverted the paper gown and threw it and his gloves into the disposal hamper. "I read all the newspapers, and I know exactly what you're going to describe. And the fact that you noticed it and set the information aside tells me that you have a suspicion also."

"Let's get a coffee, Chris." Matejus actually put his arm around him and patted his shoulder. "There was a home invasion in Deerfield Hills one night, about two months ago. The entire family was wiped out, literally slaughtered by an unknown group of assailants. The rumble was that they were from the south side of the city. The most significant fact to me was that the home was located two houses away from Ken Adams. In any event, I think Adams got the same message that the rest of us got."

"What do you mean? Do you think the killers got into the wrong home?"

"Yep," said Matejus. "You know, about five years ago Adams was in a business on the side from which a large amount of money was embezzled by a smart accountant working with a computer. It was Adams who gave the testimony that put him in prison. Some of us think that this was a failed 'hit' by the south-side killers. Another reason I think that is because Adams immediately put his house up for sale and moved into an apartment several miles away."

"Ha!" said Gannon. "At least somebody got his number. He's old enough to retire, and maybe he will do that now. Meanwhile, you have to decide what you can do about getting me nominated to run for office. Do you think you can manage that?"

"The president is an honest man," said Ben. "I will appeal to his integrity. There's nothing else that he can say other than that you should have the chance. it would really be wrong if you did not have a shot at being staff president. I'm going upstairs to see tomorrow's patients."

A few weeks later Gannon was sitting in the back of the assembly hall, surveying the staff members who had come to this special meeting. The president had called an official meeting so that he could get support for Gannon's election as an officer, even though he had been education director, which was a salaried position for the hospital. No doubt this was setting a precedent. No pathologist or radiologist, who traditionally had been regarded as company men, had ever been elected to the chairs.

Gannon sensed some tension in the room, but nothing like the meeting from 1972, when staff appointments for two aged men had deliberately been prolonged to permit them to travel 1000 miles to vote against him. There were empty seats in the room, and the conversation around the tables was of general matters only. There was some evidence of agitation at the table with Penelope Bayard, her young associate, and Ken Adams.

They sure look down in the mouth, he thought to himself. It was just possible that they had not been able to generate much interest in defeating him this time. In the intervening thirteen years since he had last run for office, he had been elected and served at St. Benedict's. The influence of the Travel Club was no longer palpable. All of these thoughts were passing through his head as he sat, picking at his lunch. While the degree of tension was nothing like it had been previously, it was that this was his last chance. If someone tried to beat him on a constitutional element, that he was a hospital employee, he would be defeated. Of the two positions, education director versus staff officer, the former was a must, because he still had two sons in college.

The matter of eligibility was placed on the table at the beginning. As expected, both Penny Bayard and Ken Adams ripped him. They cited the precedents of radiology and pathology people, pointing out an alleged conflict of interest for those who could be called company men. Bayard pointed out specifically the absence of appointment for hospital-based people to any significant committees or hearings. Adams made the point that hospital based physicians could always be counted upon to vote the administration and board line. Oddly enough, no one else spoke to the issue. It was not without apprehension that he listened to the putting of the motion, to some quarreling about how to phrase it, with various amendments, and then he was thunder-struck when the president asked for a voice vote.

For heaven's sake, Gannon thought, of all the times that would require a secret ballot, this was certainly one of them! So he was amazed when there were only four votes against his candidacy. There were smiles all around the room and an obvious wish to bring the whole thing to an end.

The chairs scraped and squeaked back as everyone rose and moved across the room to shake his hand. But in the middle of the room stood Penelope Bayard. Gannon could hear her in a stage whisper saying, "This is only one small defeat. There are three other ways we can get him. If we just stick together, we can get him. Why won't you listen to me?" Her voice rose to a crescendo of sound and pitch, and as Gannon left the room letting the doors swing closed behind he could still hear her shouting in the distance, "We can still get him, we can still keep him out of there. We still have a chance, if we only stick together!"

Gannon went to the cloak room. Standing at the working counter was Ken Adams, sliding his arms into his coat sleeves. Gannon's face flushed hot; he wondered what Adams might be thinking. "Let's talk," said Adams. His usually abrupt manner had somehow softened.

Gannon was cautious. "What about?" asked Gannon.

"Everything, Doc, covering a lifetime. You have been a stiff-necked, son-of-a-bitch thorn in my flesh for thirty years. I tried to like you at the beginning, but you kept switching me off. You despise people that you think are 'born to privilege.' Well, I despise people who are too weak to take advantage of their inherited opportunities. You are one of those; you could have had it all!"

He began buttoning his coat and drawing on his gloves. "Now, there's been some Waterford dick hanging around my telephone the past month or so, asking questions about where I was when you were so sick. He pressed me hard about my knowledge of heparin, asked what access I had to the pharmacy, and so on. If you or somebody else sicced him on to me, then call him off. I am retiring this week, moving south to Arizona. Wife has multiple sclerosis—totally dependent upon me."

"I'm truly sorry, Ken. Nobody deserves that, either patient or caregiver."

"No, we don't deserve it," replied Adams. "It is a living death for both of us. I am depleted, burned out. But here's my last parting shot before I leave town. Whenever you can't get it up anymore, don't bother taking testosterone by mouth; take it straight, by injection. Remember, I'm a urologist. It will work. I promise you!" Then he pulled his expensive camel-hair coat collar up around his ears and slammed the door shut. Gannon could hear him laughing in the parking lot. He never saw him again.

Chapter 27

Gannon sat in his kitchen, staring out the south window, as he had done on so many different occasions over the preceding thirty years. This room had seen many reviews of incidents in which his sons had been involved, such as victorious basketball games, depressing and tearful discussions with his sons at various times when they appeared to be failing, and scenes of excitement in preparation for holiday dinners. And then there were other times, like the present, when he had to unload some bad news on his wife.

She was at her usual position, bent over the sink. "I'm sorry, Helene, but neither hospital is offering me anything in an administrative field. I always thought that one of them, for sure, would gave me some kind of salaried position in hospital planning. But they are not offering me much."

She slammed down a sponge and turned to face him. "You always expected to be medical director for one of the two hospitals. Did that idea just evaporate?"

"Even if they made me such an offer, I would have to advise them against it. They're already top-heavy in administrative personnel, paying good-sized salaries to people who can't produce much in terms of income for the institutions. Furthermore, I think they hold physicians in such low esteem that they do not think being a doctor would have anything to offer in an administrative capacity. The worst thing for them would be to have a physician take such a position and succeed at it."

Helene's face was set with the lips in a thin line at she turned again to face him. She seemed to spit out the question, "Well, get on with it! What did they offer you?"

"They are developing a new approach to industrial medicine by contracting with factories and companies to take care of job injuries and to do pre-employment examinations. It is what Mark Silver has been doing the last three years. What a waste of his experience! But that is what they have offered me, and we need the money."

"Well, we do need the money. We've poured out your retirement into six post graduate educations and went all out for the kids. You wasted a lot on that silly restaurant! I'm sorry that I was never a wage earner, but we agreed that my position was to be the best possible mother. You were never one to enjoy taking trips, and I have lost out along with you. And now you have to work, even though you have tried to retire. I think it is disgusting. You have been selfish by doing things which you enjoy for the community and for the hospitals, and for offspring, but you have forgotten me. It is my turn!"

The peculiar thing was that when Gannon was finally elected to the presidency of the staff, he had run out of ideas. Oh, he went through the motions all right. He wrote out "goals and objectives" and presented them at the first meeting of the year, reviewed them at the end of the term, and tried to show what had been accomplished. Everybody in the room knew that his time passed. His era of concepts and ideas and vigorous and strong leadership was over when he was put in the top job. The staff elected him president more as a reward than as an incentive. He became a caretaker of the Constitution, defending attacks upon it placed there by other young competing surgeons. He could not protect his friends, particularly Casey, from competition in the field by lesser men. He had fought for physicians' rights, and he had to back that up by giving equal freedom to all applicants. He learned, too late, that the staff president merely became a figurehead and protector of the process.

Toward the end of his term, he began to suspect that there were simply no more medical horizons left for him. There was doubt in this, and uncertainty, because it occurred to him that perhaps he had just become reactionary and negative about change. Perhaps he had not kept up with the technical variations taking place and had let himself become outdated. Young surgeons were removing hemorrhoids by employing the first generation of lasering devices. He thought the procedure ridiculously expensive, using high-tech instrumentation, that cost thousands of dollars instead of employing a twenty-five cent cold scalpel blade. He could not prove it, he suspected that the same younger colleagues were charging their patients as though the use of the laser was some kind of magic. But the fact remained that he was truly falling behind. He did not want to take the new risks of changing procedures and changing techniques, and he rationalized it by saying that it was too expensive and part of modern medicine that was going to hurt the field as a whole.

Seen from an economic point of view, he had sustained a series of failures. Instead of just plugging away at the thing he knew best, surgery, he had ventured into side businesses which he had hoped would produce income in his retirement years. This had been a mistake. He was successful in persuading associates into the land partnerships, but he made money for everybody else but himself. He helped develop a private tennis club for the community that was a failure. His purchase of a Victorian mansion for opening a restaurant was a colossal defeat. He had lost money every year for fourteen years: he was constantly distracted by the needs of this failing business. Ultimately, the tax people decided he was losing too much money too often and scheduled him for an audit. It was at this time that Ben Matejus decided to retire.

Both men had talked about this event for some years. Each had agreed that it was the responsibility of each to tell the other when it was time to quit. Gannon had never come to that conclusion about Ben. One day he simply said, "I just spent the weekend thinking about this. My wife and son have reminded me that my insurance coverage is up at midnight on June 30. I'm going to quit on that day. Medicine is no longer any fun, and I know that I'm not the operator I used to be."

Gannon knew that they had had their run and had brought many years of present medicine to Waterford. He also knew that with Ben on the sidelines, his own work would decrease. He would be forced to use a referring doctor as a first assistant in all cases and could not look to rely upon Ben for good judgment or great hands. So it was on the succeeding June 30th, they did indeed stand in the operating room, hands folded, while the draping was put on for repair of a hernia through the abdominal wall. For inexplicable reasons, he did the procedures himself. He had done the work up in the office, and usually the operator was the man who had done the history and physical exam. So Gannon set to work.

Rapidly he excised the old scar. This is a type of dissection which they had done together for many years. There are several loops of small intestine matted against one another and three loops making up the content the hernia. Matejus picked up each loop of intestine and put it on tension so that careful dissection could take down the adhesion. Once the edges of the defect had been defined, it was possible to incise the fascia up and down and to make out the edges of the hole. Matejus and Gannon put heavy clamps on the peritoneal and fascial edges and pulled the defect together. Gannon placed the heavy synthetic suture material continuously through the full-length of the defect, lapping the left side over the right side to make the classic double-thickness repair.

During the closure Gannon suddenly realized that this was the last scheduled case for their practice with the two of them still working together. How stupid, he thought. This has been Matejus's last case, and I did it. How dumb and how thoughtless!

As he lay the last dressing in place he noticed that Matejus had turned away and started for the operating room door. He was turning his gloves and gown inside out; the last consignment of his operating room were to the hamper. "Delaney was cleaning up," said Gannon, right behind there were tears in his eyes, and he knew he was through if he said anything to Ben. The first love of Ben's entire life had been working in the operating room, and now this was gone forever. Gannon had not had the common sense to see that Matejus's last case should have been operated on by himself. *Such is life,* thought Gannon. *I wonder how I will feel when I have done my last case?*

With Ben Matejus gone, the practice of surgery was no longer a pleasure for Gannon. Certain physicians who had trusted Matejus to do good work, better than Gannon could do, no longer referred to the practice. He was back where he had started: alone. Malpractice insurance had risen to forty thousand dollars a year, and that, added to office help salaries and business expenses, set his costs at one hundred thousand dollars annually. He had to gross this income just to open the door. He began to think of trying to find a job at one hundred thousand dollars a year, with no expenses. For the next two years he kept his eyes open and discussed the option with certain colleagues and hospital administrators. Perhaps he could find such a position.

In the meantime, liability insurance at his restaurant suddenly skyrocketed to thirteen thousand dollars a year. This was the last nail in the coffin. Because of the failure to withhold income tax on part-time employees, he found himself with the significant federal tax liability. The payment of this was taking every extra cent he had, and suddenly there were cash flow problems. When the present owner of his own office building, a building which he and a few of his friends had conceived and built twenty years earlier, suddenly doubled his rent, he decided to cut his losses. Having closed the restaurant, he moved his office into the Victorian mansion, realizing that patients might have some loss of confidence coming into an old building occupied by an old, gray-haired surgeon. Slowly but inevitably, month by month, his practice decreased. Physicians who had referred work to him for years were rather suddenly sending patients to his younger competitors. Even personal friends chose other surgeons. Whatever was wrong was only perception, not reality, he thought, but he was unable to stem the tide. It was only a question of time until the line of expense crossed the line of income, and his practice of surgery inevitably was to become a losing proposition.

He considered letting one of his employees go, but he could not bring himself to do that to one but not the other. So he found himself looking at turning the key in the lock a few months hence, providing he could find jobs for the two people who had been with him for so many years. In the late afternoons, when nothing was happening in the office and the girls were trying to look busy, he thought back to the time when there were five surgeons working out of that practice, employing four young women just to keep it all straight. It was a time when, routinely, this practice started three operating rooms at 8:00 A.M. on separate cases, five days a week. The annual deposits had been in excess of a million dollars for several years, with salaries for five surgeons consistent with that same range, also supporting several families of the office employees. He was determined not to let things trickle away. One day, abruptly, he would decide to close up shop and simply walk out.

Then two events took place, the sum of which slammed the door on any ideas of possibly going on. One morning while working at a St. Benedict's he received a call from a friend with whom he had done surgery four days previously. A registered nurse at Waterford Hospital had removed an elastic drain tube from the bile duct system of a young woman who had a stone in that duct, the removal taking place on the fourth post operative day. This was about one week too soon. Gannon had no luck in this matter because bile accumulated in the abdominal cavity and secondary surgery was required. The nurse who had made the mistake was young, and Gannon had never been in the habit of dumping career-ending episodes on young people who had paid the price of years of work and effort and money to gain training in their fields. She just had been given too much responsibility, too soon, with inadequate experience in surgical care. So Gannon knew that somewhere in the future would be depositions to endure, and perhaps a trial and that, when under oath and faced with the new wrinkle of the National Data Bank, a computerized summary of physicians' losses and lawsuits, he would have to demonstrate the fault of the young woman.

Her employer hospital had downsized its nursing staff one year previously, making fewer nurses available for patient care and employing younger people with less experience in order to save expenses. If there was blame to be placed, it would have to be on the Board of Trustees and their employed representatives, the administrators. But these were all people with whom Gannon had shared a lifetime of planning for progressive medicine, and he was sickened by the thought of having to turn against them at the end of his career in order to save his own reputation and possibly his own estate.

The second event was even more vague and ill defined. He had operated upon an older man for gallbladder disease, and the patient developed a wound infection requiring secondary surgery. Being an older person and having other associated diseases, he did poorly and spent three weeks in the intensive care unit before going home. He developed a hernia through the abdominal wall; this required a third operation some months later. He suspected then that this too would result in a lawsuit. The thing that made it different was that although the patient's wife had been understanding, there were two offspring who were terribly angry with Gannon. It was the first case in his life in which he had simply been fired as the attending surgeon. Furthermore, his physical well-being was threatened in a family waiting room one night by the patient's son. Putting all of these events together, Gannon decided that it was time to quit.

Soon he found a job for each of his office girls and gave the balance of the practice to the only surgical colleagues he really trusted. He sent out the final bills, gave the girls their last bonus check, and sent them home for the last time. Then he conducted his own ceremony by driving, on two separate days, to the operating room at each of the two hospitals after sunset. It was a cold and bitter part of the year, and the mission in each instance was a miserable one.

For some years the only content of his surgical locker had been operating room shoes. Government and professional regulations had vacillated for some time about disposable shoe covers, but inevitably the leather had become stained with old blood and dried pus. It seemed as though there was a force of pride that on each day, the various surgeons pulled these filthy and foul-smelling items onto their feet, as though they saw themselves as warriors slugging it out on a muddy battlefield.

Gannon visited Waterford Hospital first. Coming out of the locker room, he was startled to see Penelope Bayard pouring a cup of coffee. Instead of being the highly visible and frank enemy that she had been for all of their careers, she had simply melted away after the shouting match at the election. Shortly after, she had retired and moved out of town. Gannon had not seen her for some time.

"Well, Chris, we meet again," she said, smiling sweetly. "Shall I pour you a cup?"

"It would be a first, Penny. What are you doing here tonight?"

"I have some of the same legal problems, as have you and everybody else. I'm on for a deposition tomorrow in Chicago, so I'm here to review the chart. So, that's life."

"At one time, Penny, I would have said that you richly deserved a lawsuit, but in my dotage I have become much more mellow. I have forgiven all of you in the Travel Club for having done things to us that I never saw as forgivable at all. Probably all of you believe that you were doing the right thing also."

"Absolutely, Chris. We saw you as the last of the fee-splitters, someone to be put out of business."

Gannon resumed his side of the conversation. "So you were sincere when you tried to keep Ben from getting his boards and equally sincere when you fought the open heart program?"

"Certainly. Without the thoracic board, you had no business working in the

157

chest; you just kept barging ahead."

"But tell me, Penny. Was it Adams who set me up in the Owen Bird matter? Was I supposed to be with him in the little car? Did Adams pay somebody to give me ten times the usual heparin dose after my lung embolized?"

"Whoa, hold up, Doctor Gannon. Ken Adams never tried to kill you, so far as I know. Nor did I. Both of us would have been far more direct."

"Well, thanks, Penny. But I don't believe you for one minute. Your method of operation was always to have someone out in front of you carrying the spear. Furthermore, I think my potential killer will try again. But it's his style to hire someone, also yours."

"Enough, Chris," Gannon. "We should be smoking the peace pipe, not having a final scrap! See you around!" She swept through the door, heels clicking down the corridor, disappearing from Gannon's life for the last time.

The next night he pulled his office door closed for the last time. It was after dusk, and the profile of the frozen zinnias were barely visible as he slipped the key into the car lock. A new moon cradled the evening star in its points and outlined the bare branches of the Ginkgo tree against the last pink of the western sky. The practice was finished.

Gannon reviewed matters to himself He had done the requisite other things: notified the American College of Surgeons that he would not be paying their dues this year; canceled his liability insurance payments; tried to cancel the phone line; discussed chart disposition with attorneys; written off uncollectible fees; even shared a glass of champagne with the office staff. There remained yet one ceremony to be carried out.

He made all of the green lights at the bridges, crossed town to a parking lot labeled "Doctors," which he had sought out for thirty-five years on a daily basis. He entered the emergency room door and hung his London Fog in a place where it was unlikely that Irving Wren would exchange coats. He had mailed his request for transfer to the "honorary staff," recognizing the implicit fact that no longer would he be able to pick up the phone, call the admitting office, and request a bed for a patient. He wondered if there was "honor" in that?

He looked down a corridor to an area labeled Cancer Care Center, recognizing the 1970 battles to distribute the programs between the hospitals rather than duplicating them. Peering out a window, he observed heavy construction machinery, looming in the dark among half-built cement wall forms. The center was enlarging.

The halls were silent behind him, at this hour empty of the myriad of support personnel deemed necessary in this era of so-called cost-cutting and economic pressures. He perceived that his ideas of cost containment were obsolete.

He passed the elevators because he didn't want a chance meeting with a friend who might ask him why he was weeping. He took the backstairs. He passed the door behind which forty years previously, older colleagues had reviewed his work and behind which, for many recent years, he had sat similarly in judgment on the work of the younger.

Behind another door were the desks at which he had helped plan the direction of the institution. Beyond that were entrances to nursing administrators, with whom he had held an occasion shouting, table-pounding exchange. Stepping onto the second floor, he observed young, capable women busying themselves with devices and machinery and units that were only a dream twenty years previously. He passed by a room which had alternately been occupied by his successes and his failures, some producing within his memories pride and others regret.

All in all, it was a scene with which he had become increasingly unfamiliar and uncomfortable, and yes, even afraid. He had been aware of a certain paranoia, the feeling of having been under surveillance by nursing staff as he had gone about his daily duties. Communication with floor personnel had deteriorated, and rarely were there any verbal exchanges. What would they talk about, anyway? They did not know his name or who he was. He did not know them. Neither had knowledge of where the other had been, nor what hopes and aspirations lay buried in their respective hearts. He had known for some months that it was time, time for him to leave.

He slipped down the corridor to the surgeons' lounge. He flicked on the lights and noted the stale coffee. He looked across to the OR door, realizing that he had given up the privilege of entering. He would no longer be permitted to pick up the knife and enter into that world of the interior of the human body, a universe into which only a few, himself included, had been admitted. But he was relieved because also he no longer had the responsibility. He had done his last case.

He entered the locker room and opened the door to his shoe storage. This last pair had endured thirteen years, the third of three sets. They were covered in paper, a symbol of the present generation's idea that there was purity in paper and the sacrifice of trees. He stripped off the shoe covers and dropped them in a waste can. The shoes were worn at the heels and split at the counter. The smell of his feet mingled with that of patient detritus. They were old, as was he. They had to be retired, as did he.

He held on to them as he left the building, stepping out into the dark. The moon was lower now, but the star was brighter. A light breeze stirred the snow about his feet. He walked over to the garbage can and dropped in the shoes. "Merry Christmas, everybody, wherever you are," he whispered into the night.

Chapter 28

He was seated at his mother's bedside at Waterford Hospital at 3:00 A.M. She and he had agreed some weeks before that when death appeared imminent, he would request the nursing staff to make no heroic efforts at resuscitation. When the call had come in at midnight, he selected a small overnight bag for personal effects in her favorite color of blue, and then drove slowly, hoping that it would all be over when he arrived. It was not.

Her body was slowly drowning in its own fluids, her heart no longer able to drive her blood, and her kidneys no longer able to empty the body of its wastes. Liquid accumulation in her lungs had decreased her air space until she was breathing in very short and barely detectable gasps. Unconsciously, her neck had progressively extended like that of a singing robin, and her mouth had taken on the pointed configuration of a panting sparrow. Gannon sat in the dark shadows of the room and waited.

He remembered waiting with her at dawn on a train platform in May 1943. She was pacing slowly, clutching for black patent leather purse, occasionally speaking with other walking passengers. She was wearing her Sunday best coat, the one with the fake fur collar. Spit curls peeked out from beneath a small, pert hat. She was wearing black pumps, a mistake, he thought, for a trip to Chicago. She was lovely in the early light.

The Rock Island Rocket, always on time, even in wartime, was wailing its horn from the west on its daily round trip to Chicago from Peoria. His father had already been in England over a year, serving as an Army chaplain. His younger sister was asleep at home, so the situation involved just two of them.

His mother had been secretive and mysterious about this trip to the city, offering no explanation for something she had not done since her husband had gone overseas. She said she trusted him with the car, and he was to meet her at the 4:30 return. She gave him a good bye kiss and slipped up the steps into standing room only space among soldiers and sailors. Then she was gone.

Eight hours later she stepped off the same train, looking as though she had had a difficult day. She was carrying a huge, orange, split-skin leather suitcase.

"It's for your graduation," she laughed, "And to take to college in the fall. It didn't cost much, only fifteen dollars, but was almost impossible to find."

"Well, it's beautiful," he replied, holding the door for her. "Okay if I drive?"

"Certainly, but take it slowly."

Actually, in Gannon's view, that bag was hideous and heavy. The surface was studded with pits, producing an imitation pigskin appearance. It was bound by two heavy straps and couples and latched by three locks. It was enormous.

Letting the clutch out, he turned toward home. "Where did you find it?" He asked.

"Fields had nothing, she replied. "Carson's had nothing. The clerk said it was the war, that there were no leather goods at all. I kept on going. I even tried the store on Wabash.

"Finally, I took the "L" around the loop, to north Chicago Avenue, and then the street car out to Monkey Wards of all places, and that's where I found it. Good old Monkey Ward's, just like in South Dakota," she laughed Gannon never forgot her pilgrimage for him. He carried that bag for fifteen years, teased about it as a college freshmen, razzed by medical students, and laughed at by fellow officers in the Sea of Japan. Each time he was tempted to give it the heave, he was restrained by the memory of her struggling around Chicago in high heels, trying, alone, to find a suitable gift for her son's graduation.

For most of his early life, that was how it had been: just the two of them. His father always seemed to be elsewhere, first as a late bloomer in college, and as the divinity student, then in the service. But there was his mother, usually alone, making the best of things. He and she tended the garden together. They climbed the school hill in the snows of '36, ate mashed potatoes with butter with Mrs. Zellers and her daughters, played matching card games on Saturday night, printed the church bulletin. They were a team on the golf course, sang in the choir, cued one another in church programs, and waited alongside one another for their man's train from Chicago. And now, finally they were alone together again. He peered out at the unlighted snow, pacing a little, taking a sip of water now and then. Then he was aware of silence in the room. Her breathing had stopped. He looked at her frozen position, so unlike the tall, straight woman who, even at the age of eighty, had properly wrapped her blue cloth coat around herself and driven her big Buick like a race car.

He opened the little blue overnight bag and placed in it those very personal effects which each person leaves behind: the toothbrush, comb, mirror, and a pad of rouge. As he picked it up and kissed her good-bye, he thought once more of the orange bag and her love for him.

He tried to slip out quietly, but his heels squeaked on the waxed tile. In the nursing station the attendants were openly trying not to make him feel any worse than he did. He pushed the elevator button down.

About one month later, ironically, on the day after Thanksgiving, Gannon met with his younger sister on the floor before the fireplace in the living room of their parent's home. This was a space which for many years had been the site of family celebrations: graduation dinners, Thanksgiving, Christmas and all of that myriad of events which marked the American family history in the middle half of the twentieth century. The heat had been turned down after the mother went to the hospital, so there was a penetrating chill surrounding the kneeling figures. The empty rooms echoed with the laugh of their mother basting a turkey in the kitchen and both heard the voice of their past: her father creating a prayer just prior to sitting down to a festive table.

Lying between them on the carpet was the purpose of their visit together. All of the used and tired furniture had been given away, all of the closets emptied of their dinner dresses, officers' uniforms, pastoral gowns, letters, records, books, tax receipts, and unfulfilled hopes and aspirations, there remained a collection of disorganized debris too small in size individually to make disposition by mass disposal. The bulk of the pile made before them was a group of small boxes filled with pennies. During the cleansing of a house, they had repeatedly come across each of these containers in widely scattered areas; the far corner of the desk, beneath heaps of scented underclothing, behind an ancient Underwood typewriter, possibly representing some dream of their mothers during the course of her last illness; there was no accompanying explanation. These boxes were covered by letters and photographs, many of them black and white snapshots obviously taken with a black box in the twenties. Looking at the old photographs was interesting but not revealing.

His sister was forced to question him about films dated from the thirties. She was ten years younger, and they seemed to have been raised in two different families. She was still an infant in the Great Depression and had no memories of the storms, place of grasshoppers, or cattle heard crying out for thirst. Gannon's childhood was marred by the need to work, and sister's childhood was deeply affected by her father's sojourn with the military in Europe at a very formative time in her life. The episode on this day was simply another effort to bridge the wide gaps between them, which had been brought about by events outside their control. New sisters seem to want to save everything, while Gannon wanted essentially to save nothing.

Ultimately they turned together to the remaining pile of all letters and correspondence. In the end there was just one envelope which piqued Gannon's fancy. Its return address was Dakota Wesleyan University. The formal letter within was dated February 1946, two months after their father's separation from the Army, and signed by the comptroller of the university. As he read through the body of the communication, Gannon was taken back to a childhood history dating from summer of 1933.

The setting was the graduation of his father from college, at a time and place when many tuitions were paid with a wagon load of small grain or a few pigs. A boiling-hot sun beat down on the small collection of relatives and friends milling about immediately after graduation ceremony. Gannon tugged at his father's trousers leg, asking to see the diploma. There was hesitation in his father's motion as he gave him the box, the child rapidly pulling the tissue for the container and pulling out the blue leather package, exhibiting that same kind of eagerness that went with opening Christmas gifts.

"But, Poppa, where's the diploma?" Tears were beginning to glisten at the corners of his eyes.

Quickly his father had replied, "The diplomas were all mixed up on the platform. The president told us he would give us blank containers and we could pick up the real thing later."

For forty years, an element of doubt had remained in Gannon's childhood mind regarding the episode on the burnt-out lawn of the small college. His father had gone on to receive a divinity degree from Garrett Seminary in Northwestern University and had been granted to honorary doctoral degrees from other universities. The letter in his hand now explained the history.

The comptroller was notifying the student that his tuition debt of $112, dating from 1933, had now been cleared in the winter of 1946. He had not been granted

162

his diploma because he owed the university some money! And where had he gotten the money to pay the debt? By his mother and father saving through the war years, his father spending essentially nothing in Europe and sending home every extra bit for their common account to pay the old college. He handed the letter to his sister, saying, "Here is a small mystery about which you never knew anything. Our folks were wonderful people!"

Gannon turned his head away toward the cold and empty fireplace. He did not want his sister to see the tears in his eyes as she read this mysterious letter. How like his father! Gannon was certain that letter had been left for him: his father, now dead these past ten years, being the wise man that he was, knowing that one day in this setting, he would open the letter and solve the one and only lie that his father had ever told.

Chapter 29

The three young men arranged themselves in a semicircle around the couch occupied by Gannon. Gannon motioned them to take a seat and opened the discussion. "I asked the three of you younger boys to come and see me in order to discuss how a couple of my health problems might affect you in the future. Hypertension and diabetes are definitely familial."

Michael, in his early thirties and the oldest of the second group of three offspring, responded first. "This last business remains a mystery, right? If you guys don't know the source, how can we project to ourselves?" Michael, always the logical goal oriented, and the only one to inherit his grandfather's curly hair: how like him to ask the reasonable question.

"You can't," replied Gannon, "Unless we relate this stroke to hypertension, which would be a different story. All of you are at risk for high blood pressure."

Jerry was a couple of years behind Mike and usually deferred to his leadership. He was a coach and a high school teacher. "What can we do about that? We're your sons, all with driving personalities."

"I suppose that we could say that we have more chiefs than indians. For one thing, Jerry, you and Mike could easily shed twenty pounds each and never miss it. You got your chunky and more stocky builds from your mother's side. Just give up the beer, and you'll get rid of the belly."

"Well, you know you don't have to worry about me," said Martin, the youngest. "I don't drink any more than you. But what about the diabetes? Nobody else in your family had that.

"Right," was Gannon's rejoinder. "You'll just have to keep checking your blood sugar. I'm bushed, guys. Let me take a nap."

DeLaney kicked the snow off her boots before getting into Gannon's car. After fluffing out her hair, she ventured, "Well, doctor, I am indeed honored by your unusual request to meet me after work. What's up?"

Gannon hesitated. "Maggie, we've been running regularly now for two years, and we haven't touched one another. It occurred to me that perhaps you might be wondering why I've not been more aggressive."

Maggie answered, "Honestly, I have wondered why you haven't said something before. Do you like boys better than girls?"

Gannon flushed a bit as he put the car in gear. "No, that's not the problem. Let's go for a short ride. We need to talk. And no, it's not that I'm not attracted to you. When we run together, you are always ahead. I suppose it could be said that I have been chasing you for two years and still have failed to catch you."

She laughed lightly, "Good joke, Doc. So what's the mystery? You just don't want to go to bed with me?"

"I've never had an affair, although I've thought about it sometimes," Gannon replied. "I don't really know where to begin. "Night was falling, so he pulled on the automobile lights, continuing to cruise the back streets in the hospital neighborhood slowly. A thick, quiet snow was on the streets, already packed high with the winter's heavy accumulation.

"Turn up the heat, Doc," she said. "My fingers are freezing." She pulled off her gloves and rubbed her fingers together briskly. "So, come on, out with it. What's the story?"

Gannon pulled the car to the curb and studied her silently. She wore her hair short, above the ears, a style probably related to her profession. Possibly she tinted it; he had thought so before. Her greatest asset was her smile, deep and broad, punctuated at the comers of her eyes by early crows' feet, giving her lean face its distinctive appearance. Her long legs and tall body were always well in front when they ran together "1 hated my height," she said. "1 was always chosen to play center on the basketball court!"

Tonight she wore a classic camel-colored coat, with shining brown boots. Her neckline displayed a multi-colored silk kerchief, the outfit completed with brown kidskin gloves. "You are one beautiful woman, Maggie. If I could, I would take you to bed with me in a minute, as often as possible. But the fact is, I am not potent; it is a problem I have had for several years." His eyes dropped, as he looked at the steering wheel.

Seemingly undismayed Maggie DeLaney opened her purse and took out a lipstick, speaking as she expertly applied the color without benefit of a mirror. "I don't believe you," she said, firmly and abruptly. "No man is dead from the waist down at sixty-five. You just need a better partner!"

"No, really, Maggie. It's related to all these illnesses and medicine. I'm sure, especially the antihypertensives. l just cannot do it anymore! Believe me, nobody wants to more than 1!"

"Then let me help you and, incidentally, it takes two to tango. I've been a widow for ten years now, but I think I can remember some of the tricks!"

"Well…when, and how?" said Gannon, hesitantly.

"The ball's in your court, doctor. You make the arrangements!

New Year's Eve came just a few days later. As usual there were no plans in the Gannon household for any celebration other than a few shrimp and a little champagne at midnight. This was still the week of Gannon !s retirement, and he did not feel very good about it. Helene had sent him out to the local grocery store after the ten o'clock news to buy some additional cold meats and cheese. Their kids were all involved with their own agendas. He smiled to himself as he drove through the snow. At least his kids had learned how to entertain themselves and have a good time, although this was somehow something that had escaped his own interest. He wondered if there were still time to learn how to play.

While walking up and down the aisles of the store, he became aware of vague rumblings in his own abdomen. These were the kinds of cramps which he had experienced before and which he knew and understood He also knew that this store had no toilet set aside for customers. He was going to have to do something and soon or there was going to be an embarrassing incident. His now-closed office building was less than a mile away, and with it could come relief. He hurried through the checkout line and ran to the car and drove faster than he really should. A heavy snow was falling again, along with significant wind, and the streets were busy with people on their way to New Year's Eve social events.

My gosh, he thought, *I wonder if I can make it?* By now his gut was audibly rumbling and bearing down, and it was all he could do to keep from soiling himself. He jerked to a halt beneath the portico of the old house, ran up through the side door and onto the landing leading to the basement where the toilet was located. His eyes were just adjusting to the darkened stairwell when he had a violent cramp and made the decision to run. As he reached for the top step, he felt a cutting sensation on his ankle and then found himself lurching over and flying out into the darkened stairwell. He grasped a rail to deflect the fall and tried to roll his body into a ball as he was going through the air. All of these events were instinctive, and then everything went black.

When he regained consciousness, he found the stairwell was still dark. Again there was the familiar question of, "What am I?," as opposed to, "Where am I?" His memory was of falling into the darkness in the stairwell of the basement of his office. With the memory came terrible pain. He ran his fingers through his hair and found no blood. He surely had bumped his head as he had gone down headfirst. He had severe pain in the left shoulder, and presumably that had taken the brunt of the fall. Worse than that, his bowel had let loose and filled the lower half of his trousers. The smell of the latter was intolerable.

He remembered that there was a shower in the toilet room, so if he could just get down the balance of the steps, he could disrobe and clean himself up. Very slowly he inched his way into a standing position by using his feet to push his back against the wall and up into an erect stance. Dangling his left arm, he struggled down the rest of the steps in the dark, feces running down his pants. With great relief he struggled out of his clothing and stepped into the hot shower. He stood in the running water a long time, letting the heat penetrate the shoulder while he soaked and resoaked the lower half of his body. Drying off was difficult, and he was certain that he had either broken or dislocated his left shoulder.

No one knew where he had gone because he had set out to buy some last-minute food at the store. Surely someone would start looking for him before long. He wondered what time it was. It might even be after midnight. There was a clean maitre d's uniform in the basement closet, left over from the old restaurant days, so he dressed in this with great difficulty. Still he felt much more comfortable as he ascended the stairs to locate a telephone. At the top step, he hesitated, then turned around, bent over, and felt along the edge of the step. He had been wondering what it was that his ankle had struck just before the fall. He soon found the problem; broken ends of a heavy wire lay coiled up against the stair banister on either side, where obviously the separated pieces had retracted when struck by his ankle. Fingering the wire, he thought, this was no accident. This was a trap that had been set.

As he was feeling around the wall for a light switch, it occurred to him that perhaps the same person who had set the trap might still be around, waiting to check out the results. Perhaps it would be better if he did not turn on the light, he thought, he used a penlight for dialing his home, and happily Helene's voice picked up the line.

"Hello?" came a faraway voice.

"Now listen, carefully, Helene. I'm at the office building in the dark. I had an attack of the Gls at the store, and I came here to take a crap. But I fell over a wire on the landing and had a bad fall in the stairwell. I may have broken my shoulder. But I'm alive. What time is it anyway?

"It's after one o'clock. Good heavens, are you sure you're all right? I had about decided to send the police to find you in some ditch! Is this another one of your ideas about someone out there trying to kill you? You're as nuts as you were ten years ago. You've got to get over that!"

"No, I'm not nuts! I found a broken trip wire on the top step of the main floor landing. I pooped all over myself and had to shower and cleanup.
I just wanted you to know where I was. You must not come in here; it would be dangerous. I will sit down and think it out and try to come with a plan. Please stay away. I will call you in about half hour."

"I still think you're nuts," she said as the telephone clicked.

Exhausted by his physical and mental efforts, Gannon stood in the dim light coming through the office window from the street. He surveyed the yard on all four sides of the building. Parked on the other side of Division Street was a van. There was a reddish glow, easily visible from the window, consistent with a burning cigarette. As he watched, the window was lowered, and a cigarette was thrown into the snow on. the street. He knew then that he was being watched. Probably this potential assassin would stay there all night if necessary, to check out the results of his efforts.

His heart pounding and his shoulder throbbing, Gannon sat down again to think out the problem. Then he picked up the dictaphone. He dictated a long letter for his wife, describing the events of the night and trying to fit them into the principal happenings of the last twenty years.

In addition he described to her a plan which he had developed for dealing with the present situation. The police would regard any phone call as a crank call as they had had many from this address in the years when it was a restaurant. It was unusual that they would come for any reason. His only hope was simply to get out of town. A cab called to this address would be answering a call to a place which had been answered by cab companies for fifteen years, both during the restaurant and office years. A cab company would respond, although the police almost certainly would not.

Having put the phone down after calling the taxi, he then picked it up again and dialed his own home. Again, Helene answered promptly.

This time, Helene seemed to be more accepting of the validity of his reasoning.

"Somebody is definitely across the street, in a van. I have called a Yellow Cab to come to the west portico and to take me to O'Hare. I have dictated a tape at my desk which you can just play back in the light of day when it's safe. Briefly, I will take six A.M. flight on American directly to Hayden. The tape will tell you what I intend to do after that. If all goes as I have planned, I will call you from Steamboat Springs tomorrow afternoon. Don't bother the police. They are not going to listen to anybody's complaint on New Year's Day. Trust me."

"Fearless leader, I always have," she said. "Good night and good luck."

The pain in his shoulder was down to a steady throb. He was familiar with the physical findings of dislocation, and he could not feel the knob of the humerus hanging in front of the shoulder. Probably it was only broken, and if he kept it suspended vertically it would hurt less.

Intermittently he looked out the window to see what the occupant of the van across the street was doing. What was he waiting for? Presumably, the fuss of getting into the building through heavy doors would make such a disturbance that he would attract attention from the neighbors. The trickiest part of Gannon's plan was the early part, getting out of the building and getting out of town. At the latest, he must be at the O'Hare ticket desk by five o'clock in order to catch the six o'clock flight to Hayden in Colorado. Surely by going to the ski area at Steamboat, he could shake his pursuer. When he called the cab company, he specified a pick up at 4:30 at the door beneath the portico. Promptly at that time, the driver pulled up. The lights in the portico and over the steps off the west porch had been burnt-out for months, so it was simply a matter of Gannon pressing gently on the panic bar of the steel door, sliding out onto the landing in the dark and slipping into the rear door of the cab, held ajar by the driver. The driver was an old patient, and Gannon was immensely relieved to know that this was a man who would take him to the airport without a debate first.

Dragging his painful arm behind he crept in on the floor of the rear seat and whispered, "Good morning, Harry. It's me—Dr. Gannon. I must get out of town, and I cannot explain why. Please, quietly put the cab in gear and take me to the toll road and then to O'Hare as fast as you can. We may be followed by a van, but the New Year's traffic is just beginning going into the city, so we won't know for sure. I'll tell you which airline when we get to O'Hare. I'm going to keep my head down, just in case."

"Okay, Doc. Whatever you say. I'll keep my eyes open and try to keep you filled in."

Gannon knew the streets of Waterford sufficiently well to know almost the moment they passed through the toll gate onto the road, and it turned out that his estimate of the quantity of the traffic was correct. His driver mentioned a time or two that possibly there was a van weaving in and out behind them at some distance, but he was uncertain about that. For his part, Gannon was certain that once they reached the lighted overhangs at the curb adjacent to the ticketing area, nothing directly could happen to him. There were too many people coming and going at this early hour for a drive-by shooting. His pursuer would prefer a different setting, and most likely would follow him until he was in an area in which he could be picked off with a heavy handgun, without witnesses. If the assassin were a professional from out of town, he would regard escaping by commercial airline as just another routine step.

As he pushed his American Express card across the counter, he spoke. "I need a one-way seat to Hayden, Colorado. Then get me a seat coming home on the seven o'clock plane from Denver tomorrow evening. I don't think I can make the three o'clock returning flight from Hayden. I'll need a ticket on the Continental Express from Steamboat Springs on down to Denver. Holding his injured arm. close to his waistline, he signed the various papers. Taking a final look around, he noticed nothing out of the ordinary and no one standing alone watching him. It was probably a vain hope that they had lost the pursuer on the toll road, he thought.

When he arrived in the waiting area for the 6 A.M. departure, there were several adult males sitting a few feet away, one or two wearing dark glasses, with their heads buried in the morning *Tribune.* The plane was a full load, as over two hundred people got aboard at this early hour. Good gosh, he thought, are all these people simply going to ski at Steamboat on New Year's Day? He noted that one of the men wearing dark glasses took a seat ten rows behind on the aisle, and promptly lit a cigarette. There was no way he could get off at this point, so he put his arm in the most comfortable position he could find and leaned back to take a nap.

Of course, he could not sleep. His heart was pounding, and no doubt his blood pressure had skyrocketed. His shoulder throbbed unendingly, almost in time with the hum of the engines. He thought about what he would do when he reached Hayden. He could mix with the crowd and take a multi-passenger ground vehicle to Steamboat. With the time change, he could be in the Sports Stalker Shop getting his rental ski equipment fitted by 9:30 A.M.

The plane landed in a blinding snowstorm. It was bad for air travel but good for skiers. Good for me also, he thought. If I can get him up high in bad weather, I have a good chance of getting him in a tough spot on Storm Peak. So Gannon followed his plan, noting that the man he presumed to be his pursuer was not part of the crowd in his vehicle. It was just 9:30 when he stood at the counter of the ski rental agency, again placing his American Express Card on the carpeted surface. "I need the works; boots that fit well, skis that are not too long, and only one pole. Minor adjustments were made on the bindings, taking a little longer than he really had planned, but still his pursuer was not in sight. He could ski in his maitre'd's pants, but he really needed a heavier jacket to get through the day.

Crossing to the ski shop, he had noticed the wind picking up and swirling the heavy snow around his legs. He bought a hooded jacket; so his face would be hidden and headed toward the gondola line. He was almost ready to slip into a car on the lift when he noticed the familiar figure earlier in the morning standing behind him in line with skis and poles, waiting to follow him onto the slopes. He was dismayed, and once again his pulse began to race. He could call security, but they might regard it as a crank call. In the end he knew he would be on his own, as he had been so many times before.

He hunkered down in the gondola. He had been unable to get his disabled arm into the parka sleeve, so he had simply slipped it up high onto the neck. He had skied with one pole before, following a previous injury, and he knew he could manage. He knew the Steamboat layout, the runs and lifts, like his home town, and he began to design his movements, thinking that perhaps he could maneuver his pursuer into a position of vulnerability. If he could just get him in the right place…With his left shoulder still throbbing, he carried his equipment off the gondola and out into the open area south of the restaurant. Fortunately, his bindings were of the modem type, so he slipped in with just a hard step down. He deliberately stabbed his one pole into the snow and took off down Rudi's Run. He was not sufficiently skilled to be able to constantly look over his shoulder and also to watch where he was going. While he made good progress to the bottom of the Storm Peak lift, he still did not know whether his pursuer was behind There were only a few people in line, so he slipped quickly onto a seat with two others. His arm was still throbbing, and he was not acclimated to the altitude. He was panting, even on the lift, and as it approached the ten thousand-foot shelter for leaving the chair, he was quite breathless and uncertain as to how well he could maneuver at the top.

If he turned left, he would end up on Buddy's Run, which was a medium-level ski run, but which was wide open and would be highly visible. If his pursuer were still with him, a few chairs behind, Gannon would be an easy target and there would be few witnesses. Better to turn to the right, and maybe I can take him along the High Line, he thought, and then become obscured by dropping down into the trees. There is an overhang there, and maybe, just maybe....

He took the turn to the right, noting that nobody else was going this direction. He wondered why. Perhaps it was because everything was a Black Diamond run in this area and that the visibility was too low to be safe. At this height, with the wind and the heavy snowfall, visibility as reduced to about ten feet. Perhaps that would help him. He began finding his way with the tip of his skis, trying to locate the drop-off that would take him further into the trees and hide him. Then, there it was. The edge of the traverse was made up of a series of flat rocks hanging over, creating a cliff. Snow had accumulated all winter, and now fresh, wet snow was rapidly building the weight on the overhang. Just before reaching the rocks, he slipped down over the edge and entered the trees.

He skidded behind one of them and waited. Wet snow stung his cheeks, obscuring his vision. Within moments, a solitary skier wearing the same pair of sunglasses that Gannon had seen following at O'Hare and getting off with him at Hayden came sliding along the cat track, somewhat hesitantly. He peered ahead, and apparently seeing no one, stopped. Gannon smiled to himself. Now, if he'll drop off the cat trick, if he'll just notice my ski tracks going over the edge....

That was exactly the sequence. His pursuer gingerly pointed his ski tips over the snow-covered lip of the cat track and then side-slipped a few feet down in Gannon's direction. Abruptly, Gannon shoved off from his position behind the tree, traversing parallel to the snowy overhang and stopping at the far edge of the run. He turned and shouted toward the barely visible figure. "Over here, asshole! I can't go any farther. I'm beat down to nothing. Just shoot me and get it over with!"

Gannon could see that his would-be-assailant was carrying a heavy handgun. His ski poles were dangling from his wrists, as were his gloves, and he was fingering the trigger with both hands. Slowly, ever so slowly, he crossed the space between them, narrowing the distance until he was only thirty feet away.

"Hold it right there, doc. I know you're hurt. I'll just come a little closer." He side-slipped few feet then stopped again. If he'll just stop right there, thought Gannon.

"Before I close you out, I think you deserve some understanding of what's been happening the past twenty years. You were always looking in the wrong place. Yes, I was the guy who cut the axle on Owen Bird's car; you were supposed to be in it with him. I grabbed the stuff in the envelope but never understood any of it. I changed the dosage in the heparin bottle. I set the trip wire in your office building yesterday. But you have led a charmed life—until now. You have a lot of enemies, all right, most of whom you deserve. That made it easy to cover my tracks all these years. Just call me Javert."

"I'm not going to beg," Gannon shouted against the wind. "I'm finished anyhow. But you haven't yet told me who hired you."

"A doctor named Sparacino! You witnessed him killing a man thirty-five years ago. Each time he was up for appointment or something he sent me after you. He works in Gary. He has done pretty well. Paid me $50,000 for your neck."

Abruptly, Gannon shoved off with his single pole, flying between the trees at an angle, well below the assassin. *Shoot now!* thought Gannon. Sure enough with the noise muffled by the high wind, several shots rang out behind him, one bullet shattering a spruce tree just at his head. And then came the lovely sound of the overhang buckling and crashing down through the trees. By now Gannon was on the far side of the run, but if he had planned well, the assassin should be just under a major avalanche, set off by his own gun shots from the large caliber handgun, and the snow should be knocking him flat and carrying him down the slope. Gannon himself was blinded by the flying snow and had not seen the disappearing hit man. The avalanche carried everything in its path for a quarter of a mile: trees, rocks, and the buried Javert. Gannon was sweating from exertion and fear. There had been very little time to think this out and to expect it to work. His arm was terribly painful, and he still had a long way to go.

Now if he could just find one of the caterpillar tracks, such as See Me, he could get down by standing in the snowplow for two or three miles. No one had witnessed the events on the mountain. His would-be assassin would lie frozen on the slope until the snow melted. He could stay buried until spring, and no one would know or care.

Chapter 30

Gannon was right—this time. The would-be assassin was not found until April, when the snows melted. A fourth-page article was present in The Steamboat Pilot, describing an occurrence that week in which a ski patrolman had pulled an exposed ski pole out of the melting snow and had found a frozen arm attached to it. There was no identification on the body. By crossmatching fingerprints, officials had traced him to Cleveland. He had a long criminal record.

"Well, Helene, that's that," he said. "The Pilot says the guy has been identified by his fingerprints. I don't think anyone can hook me into that episode. I heard that Adams now lives in Arizona, and Penny Bayard has retired and gone to Florida, so I think that is all over. Besides, who would want to rub me out now?"

"Oh, come off it. Stop your everlasting complaining," his wife answered. "I think that that whole affair was in your head anyhow. You were back here in bed twenty-four hours after the fall in your office. I think it was all just a bad dream, a confabulation to cover something else." She folded the Tribune, which she had been reading, and left the room.

So be it, thought Gannon. *Maybe the business on the mountain top was just a nightmare.*

Fatigue and exhaustion were a daily fact of life. His broken shoulder had been managed by a hanging cast, but only six weeks had elapsed between that incident in the stairwell and the episode of his stroke. He complained every day through the rehabilitation time, most particularly because of pain in his shoulders. But he was alive, and even the additional factors of sleeplessness due to prostatism and diabetes could not repress his gratitude for being among the living.

Now where am I? He seated himself at the dining room table and looked at the array of correspondence, most of which was unpaid bills. Again he thought, *what a mess!* He had been out of work for three months now, and he realized it would take him a year or two to catch up. There was the mortgage on the old Victorian mansion and a mortgage on the ranch in Colorado. There were two final payments yet to be made on a land investment in Steamboat Springs. There was just no doubt he was going to have to get to work, starting this afternoon at 2:00 P.M. Certainly there was no other way he could disentangle the complex economic factors lying in front of him. He realized, now, that his greatest mistake had been in structuring his future inheritance around real estate and not having it paid for by the time of his illness. He was certainly going to pay through the nose now. There would be $15,000 in outstanding real estate taxes to be paid in a few months, and he was sure that there would be times when there would be holes in his shoes and an empty icebox. Also these surface matters would be accompanied by deeper problems, such as returned checks, bounced because of insufficient funds. He hated that, and it had been many years since such financial straits had bound up his family and himself. Yet, with patience and planning, he was sure he could get through the year.

He had four hours before he was due for his first day on the new job, so he lay down for a short nap. "Wake me at one o'clock, please, Helene," he called. He fell asleep immediately.

He dreamed of frail Owen Bird and his death alone in the dark. From that, his dream passed to himself watching his arm turning black. And then he saw himself pitching into the darkness of the stairwell, followed by the pursuit to the mountain top and the death of the hit man.

Then, as happens so often in dreams, a kaleidoscope of events and faces floated together, the center occupied by the face of Ken Adams, laughing. He was laughing as he had laughed one day when Gannon had driven a golf ball off the first tee into a crowd of nearby hecklers.

Gannon woke with a start. There was something there, a memory, a piece of information, but he could not grasp it. He was covered in a cold sweat; his pulse was racing. He snapped his fingers, jumped off the couch limped to the bathroom, jerking open the medicine chest. Rapidly, he pawed around among the myriad of toilet articles and found a piece of printed paper, a fold-out from a medicine package labeled "Testosterone Propionate, injectable." His eyes flew to a section with the heading Side Effects and Contraindications. As he read, Adams's face and voice returned, repeating, "When you need it one day, when you can't get it up anymore, use injectable testosterone, not that synthetic crap, and don't take it by mouth."

He read rapidly from the fold-out; "injectable testosterone" is contraindicated in patients using antihypertensve medications. The combination produces cardiac failure." *That's it*, he thought, *the source of my stroke!* Obviously, he had been in failure, developed a clot on his left atrium, which then broke off and embolized to his brain!

How well Adams knew me, he thought. With the onset of impotence a couple of years before, he had secretly begun injecting himself with testosterone, as Adams had suggested. So Adams had had one last shot at him! Gannon had done it to himself, as Adams was sure he would.

He was stunned at his own stupidity. Slowly his rapid pulse subsided. He smiled at the face in the mirror. Somehow this closed things out. The testosterone had never worked anyhow. He had always placed too much value on sex. He deserved every bit of what had been dished out to him. He sighed and put on his jacket. He had to go to work.

He called through the door, "I'm on my way, Helene. I feel like I'm back in 1957, doing industrial medicine. But it is a job, and Lord knows we need the money." He gave her a peck on the cheek and stepped out into the spring sunshine. She handed him a brown lunch bag, as she had when he was still a medical student.

He walked first to the mailbox at the street, thumbing through the pieces. He came upon one with the return address Department of Registration and Education, State of Illinois. Huh, probably somebody wanting to take his license away! Since he was going to be early to work, he, chose to drive by his old office building. The tulips were up, and all the beds were in blossom, this representing years of work in the outdoor when his shoulders didn't hurt and he didn't get so short of breath. He knew it would be a long time before he could work the flowers again. He looked at the odometer on the old Pontiac and noted 108,000 miles. *The car's about as old as I am, functionally,* he said to himself. The one-hundred year old Victorian mansion with all the tulips was in better shape than he was. Still, he could walk he could talk and somebody would pay him for being a doctor again.

He crossed the river and turned north on the state highway toward the outlying building that was his work place. The traffic was horrendous, suggesting that Waterford was coming to life economically again. There was road construction everywhere because of major modem industrial movements into the community. Even though his own personal situation was not the best, he felt that his offspring could do well during their lifetimes in the valley. Then he saw the sign for Burger King and the flashing lights of a newly built bank. He turned between the structures and parked.

He stepped out of the Pontiac and crossed the parking lot toward a low, brown, uninspired looking building. As he approached the door, he noticed a small white envelope tucked into a corner of the window pane, addressed to Chris. Positioned in the corner for the return address was the name, M. DeLaney. He smiled and tucked the envelope into his pocket. Painted on the door were the words Waterford Occupational Health Division. This was it. He put his hand out and turned the doorknob.